THE FOREIGN —STUDENT—

Cover design by Bill Toth
Book design by Iris Bass

THE FOREIGN STUDENT

Philippe Labro

Translated by William R. Byron

AVAILABLE
PRESS

BALLANTINE BOOKS • NEW YORK

For my mother and father

"The past is a foreign country; they do things differently there."

L. P. Hartley

CONTENTS

PROLOGUE: PARIS

It was January, and outside, in the gloomy, gray cement courtyard, frost had whitened the branches on the bare trees.

I was sitting in the fifth row of my high school English class. The teacher was correcting a passage we'd translated when the door opened. Two drearily dressed men entered the room, bringing with them a breath of the icy air already seeping in through the old building's poorly insulated windows. I have completely forgotten their names, ages, faces, even their functions, but I know now, thirty years later, that their arrival in our classroom that morning started me toward the first major turning point in my life.

They had come to tell us there was a chance of winning a one-year scholarship to a college in the United States. This was an unusual opportunity, they stressed over the buzzing of inattentive voices. Normally the competition was open only to university students. This year a few of the scholarships had not yet been awarded, and the authorities had decided to open the competition to high school students. It was a unique opportunity. I raised my hand.

Long afterward, a thick envelope came to my parents' home addressed to me. It was made of sturdy, oddly textured blue paper and had a crest in the upper

3

left-hand corner surrounded by a Latin motto. On the right were two large, multicolored postage stamps depicting feathered birds and strange plants. From the mere weight of the envelope, its unusual size and unfamiliar color, I guessed even before I opened it that it contained wonderful news. Then, as in the dream I had dreamed during countless nights, I heard the whistle of the ship I was to board a few months later, and which was to carry me into the unknown.

PART ONE: AUTUMN

1

No one ever really knew why Buck Kuschnick killed himself.

What was the meaning of that eighteen-year-old body, clothed only in a conventionally striped pajama bottom? Why were his ankles tied to the steel bars at either end of his bed . . . in his room in the freshman dorm, west wing, first floor, on the right when you come in from the courtyard? Why had he trussed himself up like that on a Sunday night at the calm, quiet hour when the boys in the fraternities—houses built of pine and red brick set among the hills and valleys— were eating fried chicken and rice and listening to Mitch Miller and his band singing "Barney Google"? What had Buck been trying to do?

His name wasn't really Buck. In the freshman section of the 1954–55 yearbook, *Perianth,* his full name, in all its three-part splendor, was given as Balford Frank Kuschnick. I don't know the first name Balford, but I imagine that early in his childhood he was nick-named Buck, a fairly common name then in the part of the country where he was born. Buck: sounds like a race-car driver, a basketball player, a rambunctious little boy who breaks things and is pursued by distant calls of "Buck! Buck!" at an hour when all good children are already home. "Buck" is the cry of an impa-

tient parent at sunset. His mother must have wanted
to call him Balford at first, for like many Southern
mothers she could not help seeing her son as a rein-
carnation of a nineteenth-century gentleman—especially
if the Kuschnicks did not, in fact, belong to high society. And then the mother must have dropped the idea
and the father settled the matter: it's going to be Buck;
that has the right ring—rhymes with luck. At college,
when we were kidding around with Buck, we'd say
it rhymed with fuck, and he would clown it up and,
with a rush of embarrassed laughter, would quickly
change the subject.

His first, middle, and last names are printed beneath
his picture, the size of a large postage stamp, on page
sixty-eight of the *Perianth,* in the middle of fifty other
faces all as smooth and innocent as his. Fifty remote, unreal glimmers emanating from my past. The
faces are all so similar: short hair, smiles for the photographer, clear brows and perfect teeth—good college boys, still bathed in the glow of adolescence. Of
all the boys on the page, Buck is the only one who
doesn't have a crew cut; he is smiling less forth-
rightly than the others; and his dark eyes seem to stare
with a slight squint that momentarily catches your attention. All are dressed so alike that they might almost be in uniform: button-down shirt, striped tie,
herringbone-tweed jacket or dark blazer.

These are only head-and-shoulders pictures, but I
know what the rest looks like: charcoal-gray or brown
flannel pants in fall and winter, chinos with the coming of warm weather. In winter, heavy black or dark
brown lace-up shoes that the boys laboriously polished to a high luster each night in their double
rooms. In summer the shoes were white bucks with
dark pink rubber soles, or saddle shoes with a piece

of blue leather set in the middle of the white upper. The shoes were solid, meant to last four years, the length of a college career. That was how you dressed, with no exceptions. There wasn't any rule, simply a unanimous insistence on conformity to a single image, a single style. You were almost always spotted immediately, wherever you were, in big cities or on the road, in a restaurant or at a bank window: you were a college boy, and from the South, not the deep South, but a brighter, less muggy South. Not the South of swamps and mosquitoes and bayous, but the South of blue skies and tidy, smiling, green and white valleys.

I opened the yearbook to look up Buck, something I hadn't done in thirty years, and I was struck by a penetrating, haunting scent of starchy, glossy paper that gave me an odd chalky feeling. I did things I don't do: I snatched up the yearbook with its thick, treated-leather cover and thrust my nose into it, inhaling deeply. I closed my eyes and the aroma overwhelmed me; I went pale with it.

I repeated the process once, twice, cut off from the world, drunk with it, my bearings lost.

It comes back to me all at once, like a piece of music, the music of my youth in the heart of Virginia, in the Shenandoah Valley. First there is the throbbing rhythm of those three-part names that seemed so exotic to me, each of them expressing family hopes and dreams as well as traditions dating from before the Civil War, names from the South and West and Southwest. A nostalgic parade of boys with names more imposing than the bearers themselves. One was called Beau Anthony Bedford; giving someone the first name Beau in Louisiana, where he came from, showed such

arrogance, so much confidence in a son's future: And
I can hear the sound, at once drawling and flashy and
affected and haughty, of Page de Ronde Crowther, John
Cameron Hostatter, Daniel Boone Langston, Paxton
Hope Moore, Cotton Munro Hudson, Jr. And Aristides
Christos Lazarides—at least you knew he came of im-
migrant parents.

Then the demisemiquavers of those triple names give
way to other resonances linked by other fragrances.
They come back to me like a piece of music that en-
folds me, catapulting me back in time to where the
present slips away and memory alone calls the tune:
whiffs of green lawns; the bubbles of Pabst Blue Ribbon beer over the metallic taste of the chilled can; the
scent of the bay rum the boys sprinkled on themselves on Saturday nights when an entire male community primped and powdered for the great stampede
to any girls' school within a sixty-mile radius. Like an
overdose streaming into my body the memories come:
the trombones in Stan Kenton's band during the big
spring concerts, with all the young people sitting on
the lawn; the red mud on the long cement footbridge
that crossed a straggling train track and linked the
football field to the gym; comings and goings under
the colonnade on a sparkling fall morning with the
sun sliding across the grass from behind Lee Chapel. I
hear the silence of the campus during classes when,
through open windows, a tardy student's anxious steps
echoed on the flagstones as he ran.

And I remember how my heart beat faster as we
neared the ivy-covered façades of Mary Baldwin or
Hollins College, where the girls waited in sky-blue car-
digans adorned with mother-of-pearl flowers that
molded their breasts. Again and again I smell that same
heavy scent that I somehow associate with milk, and

that opens a secret door onto rooms and corridors and nights I had long since shrunk from exploring.

In February the days were white and magical; a sort of cold halo spread over the snow-covered slope. In October, the red glow of elms and maples permeated the campus. As for the weather—it either rained hardly at all in that region or there were hurricanes, downpours that flooded the streets in the town adjoining the campus and dug gullies through which swept heaps of sycamore leaves and cedar branches.

In spring the dogwoods blossoming around the professors' homes announced evenings of languor and bourbon, of promises and discoveries, the urgency of a meeting or a conversation that would change our week and therefore our whole existence. That summer I went on the road, headed west. And of that, too, I want to speak.

Opaque and squeaky clean, Buck's features come back to me until they blind me, like the blue-green eyes of the big, beveled headlights on the Southern & Allegheny train, the one that dropped me there the first time. But why do I feel I have to start with Buck Kuschnick?

2

IN FACT, TALKING ABOUT IT ISN'T ALL THAT HARD.
At the same time, it's agonizing, because I have to
rid myself of everything extraneous if I want to recover intact the texture of Sue Ann's skin or recon-
stitute the cajoling, ambiguous tone of Harrison Riddle's
voice.

Sue Ann was the first girl I went out with more than
once. That had to mean something. You didn't just
blithely ask a date, "Can I see you again?" That could
get you hung up in a whole, complicated affair.

Harrison Riddle? He was the brightest light on the
campus when I got there. He was a senior, at the
end of the road, and he could bewitch the new boys
one after another, enlisting them in his secret band
of adoring acolytes. He reigned so absolutely over the
little college, and took such pleasure in dominating
and scheming, that for the rest of his very short life
he would try to recapture those golden days when
his slight edge of depravity and experience gave him
the illusion of being the master of a great game. Harrison: thick lips, eyes lurking behind horn-rimmed
glasses given him by a teacher who was probably
smitten with him; nimble fingers nervously drumming
on the aluminum counter at the diner where he held
court on weeknights before the fascinated younger boys.

Poor Harrison, who disappeared ten years later in the great whirlwind of the Sixties.

If I want to get across why Sue Ann Creston's skin, under the fine veil of pink powder she dabbed on her face, made me sick with desire, I really have to strip away all the superimposed images that have piled up since then. I have to scrap the standard essay structure with a beginning, a middle, and an end. Wash everything away. Be clear, tell it like it was.

I must recapture that velvety, springy, downy sensation, the feel of it, the dampness misting the curl of her lips, the sensuality she wasn't aware of and maybe didn't even have. Perhaps I was merely the victim of a minute chemical reaction caused by the touch of her skin against mine. I don't really think so. I think that to me Sue Ann was supremely exotic because she was so typical of her region; she was so unequivocally Sue Ann Creston of Wallatoona, South Carolina, that I was violently stirred and attracted by her. My friends just smiled. To them she was a dog, a pig—ordinary, insipid, and boring. They'd been going out with girls like that since they were thirteen. To me, Sue Ann Creston was strange fruit, the first I'd ever been allowed to taste. I nibbled and nibbled, and we got nowhere, neither to love nor pleasure nor possession. I remember the Sue Ann period as a long chorus of frustration, of whole hours spent working up to something, a kiss here and there, a hand barring my way at mid-breast, at mid-thigh, her denial of the body and that drawling, muffled voice saying, "Come on, please, stop it, no, no, stop, don't . . ." over Burt Lancaster's voice coming from the individual speaker, the square black box hooked to the front window of the green Buick convertible in the State Drive-in north of Route 250.

In the front seat, Cal Cate was trying with equal fu-
tility to make his own date, a girl named Ashlyn.
She was just as unwilling as Sue Ann: good girls didn't
do it. On the way back, after we'd dropped the girls
off in front of their school, and, with a sound like
shredding silk, the Buick took off to massacre moths,
we'd have a hard time remembering what the movie
was about. (The beers we were drinking didn't help
our memories.) Must have been a western. *Sure, that's
what it was,* Cal would say, holding the big, imita-
tion onyx steering wheel with one hand and finishing
a can of Schlitz with the other.

I was thrilled to be with him. Cal was one of the
football team's three returning quarterbacks. He had
a rugged frame and the round, jovial, slightly crazy
face of a guy who could run headfirst into a steel
locker in the Stevens Gym locker room to show the
coach he had a tougher skull than any other asshole of
his generation, and that no matter how hard the hulking linesmen hit him, he would still get up first. Cal
Cate's skin was dull and pale, which made his inso-
lent, gap-toothed little smile shine even whiter—a
Bugs Bunny head on an iron pumper's body. Girls
found him irresistible. So did I.

He loved to horse around; he'd nonchalantly toss his
empty beer can over his shoulder into the darkness
of the highway vanishing behind us. He could bend a
can double between the thumb and fingers of one
hand. It's an act of sheer strength, something you have
to get the hang of, like whistling through your fingers, but it also takes an iron fist and immensely powerful hands. It was a trick performed during evenings
spent drinking in the fraternity houses. It made you
stand out from other boys on campus; there were
those who could and those who couldn't. I quickly

spotted this and was to spend months mastering this particular part of the game. The coolest thing was to hold the beer can with your right hand while driving the car with your left, the way Cal did, in a single, smooth flow, no strain. You had to be rugged and smooth, like Cal. I was thrilled to be with him.

He told me to watch out ahead, behind, and on both sides of the road—anywhere a state highway patrol car might be lurking.

"I'm telling you," he said. "This time of night, on a Saturday, they're hungry. They're drooling for a chance to grab a college boy. They've beefed up the patrols—at least four units in the area. I can practically hear them talking to each other from car to car. They know what time we come back from the girls' schools, and they try to trap us by hiding behind billboards. That's what you have to look out for—billboards, clumps of trees, that big bush up ahead at the turn. Keep your eyes open. Yaahooo!"

He let out an Indian war whoop that meant *danger* and stamped down on the wide brake pedal of his wonderful, gleaming Roadmaster convertible. I felt the Variable Pitch Dynaflow automatic shift down instantly and silently with the purr of a relaxing panther as the car slipped under the speed limit without missing a beat; the phosphorescent needle on the big, round speedometer now registered thirty miles an hour. We were law-abiding again, and when we passed the inevitable patrol car with its lights flashing, we knew it wouldn't U-turn after us, but we still felt we'd had a brush with some great danger.

We looked at each other wordlessly, with the complicity of desperadoes who have crossed the border and could now breathe easy. That's how friendships are born. Cal was twenty; I had just turned eigh-

teen. Autumn was ending, the days and nights trembling
with beauty. I was starting my second month in America, and, although I still knew little about the unknown and astonishing world I had plunged into, the
notion dawned faintly on me that maybe I'd weath-
ered the first stage of a very long, very intricate initia-
tion.

I see myself again.
I am a young man with unfurrowed cheeks and
brow, a virgin thrown like some extraterrestrial onto
a planet with an undeciphered language and mysterious symbols. I thank Cal, whose Buick makes a
U-turn and pulls away. (Cal belongs to a fraternity and
he is going to sleep in the house over yonder.) The
young man returns to the freshman dorm and runs into
one, two, then several boys also returning from their
Saturday-night dates.
We call to one another across the courtyard, then
from window to window: "Did you do it? Did you
get to do it? How'd you do?" The questions echo off
each other, unanswered, then the concert of voices
dwindles and, one by one, the windows go dark like
the lights on a switchboard after the afternoon rush.
Your roommate is back and already asleep, forcing you
to be quiet, or perhaps it's the other way around. A
last look into the empty courtyard: one window is still
lighted—Buck Kuschnick's. The orange shade on his
desk lamp bobbles behind the thick windowpane.
Maybe that's why Buck killed himself, because he
was the only one of us who lived alone, in a room
of his own.

We all shared a room with someone. Someone we
hadn't chosen. Sometimes it worked out well, and the

other person might become your friend for life.
Sometimes it was a disaster, but at least there were two
of you, and that helped. Through some peculiarity
of the dormitory's architecture or some quirk of fate
in the assignment of space, Buck had ended up with
a single room in a little alcove on the ground floor.

I often went to see Buck because I hated my own
roommate. I was furious with fate for having assigned an Austrian to share my life for the whole school
year.

I thought then it was fate. Now I see that we were
paired because we were the two foreign students, only
there for one year, recipients of exchange scholarships
with no hope or possibility of locking into the social
system that college life created. We had no place in the
blueprint for fashioning an American citizen. In hind-
sight, I now understand the concern for efficiency that
guided the person in charge of room assignments. At
the time, though, it horrified me. I saw pretty soon,
really very soon and with crystal clarity, that living
with the other foreigner on campus was going to turn
me into an outsider, second class, a little misfit in
that community that was so closed and so hard to
penetrate.

I couldn't stand that. I wanted to fit in. I wanted to
be American, like any ordinary student, because I figured that was my only chance to survive the immense
loneliness ahead of me. I was elated to be there, in
that remote Virginia valley, on that campus that was
so beautiful and so immaculate that my first sight of
it was like a kick in the heart. I was elated because back
there, far away in France, my brothers would never
experience this. And the high school friends I had left
behind after the last big final exam—they, too, were
missing out on this tremendous adventure. I thought

about them often then, at least in the beginning, and that excited me, awoke in me all that had driven me to keep trying despite my morbid shyness and protective modesty.

What had always goaded me to do things I didn't think I could do was my consciousness of The Others —my peers in the society I was a part of. *I'll show 'em what I'm made of.* But there were no Others here in the dorm, or on campus. I had left them behind. I liked to imagine them thinking of me and aching with envy. Pretty soon I'd forget them.

Of course I was elated to be in America. I never thought: look how lucky you are; you're living out an adventure that few French kids will ever have a chance to match. At eighteen, I was incapable of that kind of analysis. Still, my thoughts ran vaguely like this: James Fenimore Cooper, Jack London; Gary Cooper and Rita Hayworth movies; the prairie, the unknown, the challenge of America. I was brought up on all that, and now here I was, and even if it's not exactly like that, somehow it *is* like that. This is the distant planet I longed for and wrote page after fulsome page about in my secret schoolboy diaries. Now after diving into that mysterious river, I wanted to be just like the Americans I was in contact with. I wanted to change my stripes.

I didn't understand much at first—what was said around me, the words, the locutions, the terms; what was done, the mannerisms, the poses; what was worn, the clothes, the colors. Everything was new and had to be absorbed. It was scary, yet it made my heart soar with happiness and longing. I hadn't the courage or the honesty to come right out and say to people, "Please explain this to me." I didn't want them to despise me or ignore me or make fun of me. So I had

to learn while pretending I already understood everything. That meant putting on my own act within the
larger social play taking place among the students on
campus, in the little town, and in silent, heartland
America—the quiet America of those quiet years when
its president was a fatherly man with white hair, a
bald forehead, and gold-rimmed glasses.

This pretense wasn't hard for me. It was like learning a new way to swim or suddenly having to write
left-handed. I trod stealthily through a shimmer of
green, a different green, perhaps, from the one I'd
known since childhood. I lived every moment of every day in a land of marvels where fear gave way to
wonder, and wonder to fear.

3

THE AUSTRIAN HAD A FRINGE OF WAVY HAIR THAT
came down over his forehead. He smoked a long-
stemmed pipe and wore a diarrhea-colored felt hat.
His name was Hans. I didn't like him at all. I didn't
like his retiring manner or his looks, which reminded
me of the Old World. And I didn't like his not coming from Texas or Tennessee. In a whole year of co-
existence, we were never to confide in one another.
No current of feeling flashed between us. He wasn't
interested in the same things I was.

He settled quickly and soberly into a routine, going

from his classes to the dorm and from the dorm to the fraternity where he was a temporary guest and where he watched Victor Borge piano recitals and the Arthur Godfrey show on television. He relished the daily reading of a comic strip by a guy named Schulz about a bunch of kids and a dog named Snoopy that was catching on then with East Coast college students.

Undergraduates that year were also wild about a book entitled *Catcher in the Rye,* by one J. D. Salinger; it was the first paperback I bought at the co-op, the minimarket next door to the Cyrus McCormick Library that was the only place authorized to do business on the campus itself. That was where I first learned I could live on greasy, sugar-coated doughnuts; pancakes with maple syrup; Coca-Cola, which I learned to call just Coke; and two concoctions above all others: a blend of chilled milk and vanilla ice cream that worked on me like a tranquilizer—and chopped beef fried in round patties and served on a kind of soft round roll called a bun. Milkshakes and hamburgers were unknown to Europeans then.

One word made its appearance on my horizon very early on: *date,* as both a verb and a noun, rich in variations. If you dated a date more than once, it seemed, she became your *steady date.* If you were a newcomer and didn't know any girls, you could be set up on a *blind date.* To me, coming from socially starchy France, this was truly another world; it wasn't just that the French never dated blind—they'd have been horrified by the very idea.

Blind dates could lead to the worst disasters as well as to the most enchanting surprises. You might wind up with a dim-witted, unbearable hag or land an exquisite beauty, though this was much rarer, since exquisite beauties seldom ventured on blind dates. And because beauties were very much in demand, they often insisted on knowing in advance what sort of boy they were going out with and what his pedigree was. So you submitted to this law and went exploring at mixers in the girls' schools to undergo a sort of pre-date inspection.

It was a rite. I soon realized, without formulating it so clearly, that everything here was a rite, a ceremony, a symbol, a stage in a vastly complex apprenticeship. It was one game among many games within the great game called the American Way. I yearned with all my soul to play all the games.

The girls lived and studied in six or seven colleges located in our area. In that part of the United States, the schools were distinctive for their strict adherence to a particular way of life: they were all non-coeducational. Our college, one of the country's oldest, founded by Scotch-Irish pioneers in 1749, had clung prudently to this tradition. We had boys only—all white, of course. Set in the green jewel box of the Shenandoah Valley, our college was really a hot-house nurturing fifteen hundred gentlemen, mostly from the finest families in the South, although some were from the West, the Midwest, and even the East. And the neighboring girls' schools were like so many pools of honey to us boys from the beehive. Over the years, a dense and sophisticated network of exchanges had developed between the girls' colleges and ours. The most intensive activity began on Friday as soon as classes ended, and lasted through the weekend. Outings, dinners, frat parties, movies.

Another thing I had seen clearly—something concrete, cruel, and inevitable—was that if you didn't have a car, you were out, you were a nonperson. Either you had a car of your own or you worked out

an arrangement with someone who drove a Ford,
Chevrolet, Chrysler, or any of the other automo-
biles whose names rang so satisfyingly in my ears.
There were no girls for a boy who walked. The Austrian walked. He would never have any dates. I wanted
them. I knew Cal, and Cal drove a green Buick convertible, the lucky devil!

With him I made my first trip to Sweet Briar—the
name alone set me dreaming—to check out girls and
be checked out in turn. Cal told me he refused to go
steady. He liked to change his dates. In his freshman
year his heart had been broken by a girl whose name
he wouldn't disclose. In his sophomore year he had
broken up several times with another girl, a steady.
Now, as a junior, he was on the make again, looking, as he put it, for "the one and only." His eyes lit
up when he intoned this phrase. He believed in it.
He spoke in a hushed voice, as if confessing a secret.

"She's out there. I'll find her someday, so I'd rather
start from scratch every time, as if I were a frosh like
you."

Cal added that he had gone out with more than one
hundred thirty-five girls since he'd entered college.
How many of them had he *done it* with? He laughed.

"Hah! Good question."

He looked at me impishly.

"Rule Number One: good girls don't *do it*," he said.
"The trouble is, there's Rule Number Two: it only
counts if you *do it* with a good girl. A real college boy
doesn't *do it* with dogs or pigs."

Not daring to look directly at Cal, I risked a few
carefully worded questions. They were easier to ask
in the moving car. I had discovered that when I was
in Cal's Buick and the V-8 was humming its music
into my ears I could speak in a way I couldn't when

on terra firma. It was a strange sensation, a sort of intoxication. The Buick was making me drunk.

"And . . . mmm . . . when you want it too badly," I asked, "when you can't take it anymore?"

Cal wasn't looking at me, either; his eyes were riveted on the road to Sweet Briar.

"You do like everybody else," he said. "You make out with your right hand in the shower. Ivory's the best soap for that. Nice and white, smells good, it's cheap, lathers up fast, and you can find it everywhere."

I kept on looking away from Cal while we talked profile to profile.

"What about . . . whores?"

Cal answered fast—in Indian style, one of his favorite tricks.

"Danger. Disease. Gossip. Disgrace. Thrown out of frat. Bad reputation. Money gone. Disease! Heap big danger, no touch 'em, me know nothing, me Southern gentleman. White whore no exist. Black whore off limits. And besides—"

"Besides what?" I asked.

Cal turned sentimentious, but I couldn't tell if he was kidding or serious. I still hadn't mastered all of the inflections of my adopted language.

"Rule Number Three: there are no whores in the Shenandoah Valley."

And that was that. We drove on in silence, deep silence. Why had I mentioned whores? Why use words that were still just words to me then? I had never in my life gone near a hooker. Why was I playing the man-about-town, the Frenchie who knows everything about love?

The truth was I knew nothing. I was as uninitiated as the most naïve freshman, but I wore a mask. From the day I got there, it seemed to me that in the eyes of most young Southerners my being a foreigner meant I'd had plenty of experience with women and sex. When they talked about deep kissing, they called it a *French* kiss, and when, toward the close of a weekend, some girl with a buzz on began showing her legs and running wild on the dance floor, she'd say "Let's get French" as a signal that caution was being thrown to the winds. I thought that in this arena I was expected to be very French, very sophisticated. And foolishly, to gain some sort of advantage over those boys whose apparent ease paralyzed me at first, I went and played the part of the guy who has been around, who got laid, who knows what it's all about. This didn't last very long, a few weeks at most. But maybe, while it did, it explained why Cal Cate took me along to the girls' schools. He was carrying a Frenchie, a new and rare thing that might arouse interest. Offering to bring a French student could make things easier for him on a double date, get him girls who were especially popular, standoffish, or jaded.

I could imagine the conversation.

The girl, playing hard to get: "I never go out without my friend Priscilla. Find a double date for her. She's awfully fussy."

Cal: "No problem. Tell Priscilla I've got a Frenchman as a blind for her."

Girl: "A Frenchman?"

Cal: "Yeah, he's great, you'll see. He's funny and everything."

Girl: "Everything?"

Cal: "Priscilla's gonna be thrilled."

Girl: "Really? Well, I don't know . . . maybe."

So Cal would use me, and I would use his Buick.

My run in the role of the experienced, seductive Frenchie wasn't long. Three dates with three differ-

ent girls quickly relegated me to the ranks of my freshman friends: inexperienced, stammering, hesitant,
sometimes daring, more often bashful, and, above all,
obedient to the rules of decorum in an organized,
closely watched, puritanical society. Permissiveness was
a term that hadn't been coined yet; nobody in the
green and white valley knew what it was. Still, at ir-
regular intervals, but very violently, I would feel the
same promise well up in me, the same hope that had
surged in me when, from the deck of the liner bringing me from the Old World, I first saw the fog-veiled
skyscrapers of New York. It was the same hope, the
same thought that ran through my mind when suddenly, at first sight, I embraced all Virginia and the
whole campus—its columns and its lawn, its tranquil-
lity and its look of another day, another age. I thought
then, with the lofty wisdom of a boy just turned eighteen, that here, in this valley, I was finally going to
learn what love is, that I would love and be loved. My
life as a man would begin here. The day I leave this
valley, I will no longer be the boy virgin I am now,
the innocent I was hiding from the world.

4

THE BUICK TURNED OFF THE LOCAL ROAD AND WE
entered enemy territory—Zulu country, Cal called it,
where the girls were. The buildings looked like those
at our school, except that they lacked those white col-

umns everyone associates with the South and which,
on our campus, adorned the Neoclassical redbrick buildings perched atop the sacred hill that, gradually, each
of us came to think of as home. Status, security, and
pride, too; it wasn't everyone who could attend our
school.

We moved on among the Zulus. There were girls
everywhere. They paralyzed and attracted me. They
fascinated me as much as the boys on our campus did—
the boys, as I've said, for their apparent ease, the girls
for their unblemished pink skins, the look they had of
being repositories of certainties. Like that one hurrying across the lawn. Her faintly reddish hair danced
on shoulders sheathed in a pomegranate-red blazer.
An off-white sweater was knotted around her waist.
In her pleated plaid skirt and flat-heeled moccasins,
she moved musically through the dust-flecked morning air. Everything about her breathed smiling resolu-
tion. She winked at girls going by, her eyes like blinkers
signaling recognition. This girl had set her goals for
the day; her march toward each of the tasks she was
to accomplish gave her a shock-resistant air, a hint
of toughness. At the same time, her lithe body and
shapely legs, the wavy hair fluttering on her neck,
suggested sweetness and frailty, making me want to
know her immediately and—why not?—to love her.
She was probably a star on her own campus, since
heads turned to look at her, hands and arms waggled to attract her attention, people called to her,
courted her. She walked on, regally. I heard her answer another girl's call. Her accent wasn't Southern; it
was more distant, perkier. It didn't quite blend with
the music of those local voices that I was beginning to
recognize.

The girl stopped when she reached us and, hugging

a strapped bundle of books to her chest, confronted
Cal Cate. She flashed a smile at him.

"Hi, Cal," she said firmly.

He didn't say a word. I looked at him, bewildered.
He seemed to hunker down inside himself.

"Can't you even say hello?" the girl asked.

"Hello," he said reluctantly. "How're things?"

She spun toward me. I had hung back a yard or so.
I got the feeling she was looking right through me,
not allowing her eyes to meet mine.

"Aren't you going to introduce me to your friend?"

"Sure," Cal said, his voice surly. And he launched
into the ritual formula: "Elizabeth, I'd like you to
meet—"

She cut him off in a crisp, commanding voice, talking to him without looking at him, still acting as if I
were the only thing on her mind.

"You don't sound happy this morning, Cal," she
said. "What's happened to Calvin Parnell Cate, the
great football hero?"

Teeth clenched, voice low, as though he didn't want
her to hear, Cal replied, "Shut up, Liz. Just shut up.
Go away."

She laughed, a small, tinkling sound in the tense
silence.

"Well well, Calvin Parnell Cate," she said, staring
at Cal, "losing your legendary cool?"

He laughed and straightened up.

"Sorry, Liz, that just slipped out."

I couldn't recognize my friend. He seemed dull, awkward. His pale face was flushed.

"You've got a good memory, Cal," the girl went
on. "What was the name of that song everybody was
singing a couple of years ago? Funny, I couldn't get it
out of my head this morning, but I can't remember
the title or the lyrics. I'll bet you remember it."

Cal didn't answer. He was hunching down more
and more inside himself, as if he were in pain and
didn't want to show it.

"I'll bet you remember," Liz insisted. She turned to
me.

"I guess your friend doesn't know the song. I don't
suppose they played it in Europe. Or maybe it did
get overseas . . . it's possible, after all . . . sure, why
not?" she said, as if she were thinking out loud.

I didn't know what to say, so I shut up, but I realized Liz was using me as a tool to demolish Cal. She
moved closer to me, all warmth, all grace; the honey
in her voice lost the acid edge it had had when she'd
addressed Cal. This time her eyes seemed to try to cap-
ture mine.

"Isn't this just the most beautiful day? There's something in the air that brings back old songs. Don't you
feel it?"

"I don't know," I said.

She burst out laughing again, as though meeting these
two stiff, tongue-tied young idiots filled her with
boundless delight. She jumped up and down with her
feet together, a little bounce of happiness.

"Of course, now I remember! You wouldn't know,
but it was called 'Your Cheatin' Heart.' Just an ordinary tune, maybe even a little common, but everybody was singing it then. We all loved it."

She hummed the song, still standing close to me,
her eyes dancing, taunting me. I was so close to her
I could see how her tongue curved between her teeth
to trip through the notes, each tone distinct, like Li-
onel Hampton's beats on his xylophone: *dong, ding, do,
di, dong-dong, dang, dong day*.

I felt Cal move behind me, then I saw him grab Liz
hard by the forearm. She shook herself free just as

hard, her hair whipping her shoulders. Cal stepped
back.

Liz's voice was dry, steely, cold, an ageless voice,
as hard and quick as a killer's. "Don't you touch me,
Calvin Cate. You don't belong here. I could even call
the cops if I wanted. So scram! Out!"

Cal wagged his head to me to come on, and I followed him, brushing by Liz.

"You could apologize," she spat out tonelessly. "I
thought you went to a school that trained gentleman."

I stammered something incoherent and raced after
Cal Cate, who was striding toward the Buick. The
car tore off. We were off the campus, headed home.
For a while Cal didn't open his mouth. He drove with
his hands clenching the wheel, without his usual
smoothness. After a few miles, he muttered something,
probably to himself, that I didn't quite catch. Then he
turned to me.

"What was that I told you on the way out? Oh yes:
there are no whores in the Shenandoah Valley. That's
what I said, right?"

"Yes," I replied, "I think so."

We drove back to the campus, slowly, not saying
another word about Liz, or in fact about anything.
But that evening in my room I reviewed the whole
scene. It left me with mixed feelings. I didn't know
whether to be disappointed in Cal, who'd seemed helpless and vulnerable, or to like him even more for having suffered so, to envy him a past fraught with sorrow,
with breakups, with thwarted love. Nor did I understand if Liz had simply been using me as a wall to
hammer back a ball at an opponent, or if the way
she'd cozied up to me to hum "Your Cheatin' Heart"
had really been a signal, an invitation. I wanted to
think so, and I kept telling myself I'd clicked with her,

as they said then. At the same time something told
me I was just a supporting player in that scene. She'd
shown me her pretty little pink tongue curling to push
the notes out between her perfect teeth and those lips
barely filmed with lipstick. I remembered that she
had exuded a fragrance of apples or peaches or cherries
—I wasn't sure which—that had enticed me. But the
bitterness of the scene submerged my fond illusions.

I fell asleep feeling confused, and the feeling was still
with me when I was awakened the next morning by
the noise my friends made in the hall, and by the
Austrian's persistent coughing. Later, between eco-
nomics and world history, the confusion dissolved, leaving only that fragrance of fruit. I forgot the bitterness and remembered only the charm and sweetness.
They thrummed in me all day long as I moved on
to other things with a single thought lingering in my
mind: there's a lovely, dangerous girl at Sweet Briar
College; maybe you've got a chance with her and
maybe you don't.

5

WHEN YOU WALKED THROUGH THE COLONNADE
to change classes, or from one building (journalism)
to another (science and geography), a jam-up always
materialized. Students coagulated in the narrow walk,
each hurrying to his next class. And since everyone

observed the Speaking Rule, there was always a point in all the jostling when you had the impression that everyone was talking to everyone else at the same time. This impression was heightened by an echo bouncing off the vaulted ceiling so that it sounded like a full choir swinging into its climactic coda.

The Speaking Rule was one of the college's two indestructible traditions, the other being that every student had to wear a jacket and tie. Under the Speaking Rule you had to greet ("Hi!") everyone you met and to respond if they greeted you first. I'd been surprised at first, not so much by the idea of saying hello to someone I'd never met just because he happened to be crossing the campus near me, as by having to say it and say it and resay it all day long, whatever my mood and however the other person struck me. But I had obeyed the Rule. It wasn't a law inscribed on the college walls, but since everybody did it, you were quickly marked down as a lone wolf or an oaf if you didn't—or as someone who wouldn't play the game, which came to the same thing. Besides, if you happened to overlook the Rule, there was always someone, at some point in the day, who called you on it. Either by ironically stressing his "Hi!" while looking you straight in the eye and forcing you to respond or by reporting you to the Assimilation Committee.

There were lots of committees, societies, fraternities, associations, clubs, and leagues on that small campus. It took me a while to sort them out and understand what they were for. But I very quickly learned what the Assimilation Committee did. Its name was self-explanatory: it was there to assimilate you, to make sure you knew the rules. You said hello, you responded, you dressed correctly, you were a gentleman. The committee, like all those on campus, was

made up of students, part of an annually elected student government that worked in tandem with the
school's administration and faculty.

Chairing the committee was a senior, a big guy from
Texas named Gordon Nichols. He was swarthy,
thick-nosed, and thin-lipped when he wanted to look
stern; but his face could light up like the summer sun
when he chose to smile. Gordon had big hands with
strong fingers, a ballplayer's hands. He had gone in
for every sport and he starred in basketball, but he was
also a brilliant student. He had been elected to every
office he'd ever run for, and his commanding figure
always stood out at those rare times when the entire
student population converged—when the fifteen hundred boys gathered for a big football game, or for
one of the three annual dances, or the college president's address opening the school year, or for graduation ceremonies.

In the quasi-uniform mass of young men in blazers,
striped ties, and crew cuts, with red blotches of acne
on some of the faces that were turned toward the
speaker, the playing field, or the bandleader, you
could always spot Gordon's huge frame, like a sort of
control tower—broad-shouldered, thick-necked, flat-
eared. Gordon had everything going for him; a distin-
guished career was expected for him in banking or
politics or the law. I had noticed him on the campus,
but we'd never met, and my first conversation with
him took place in the Assimilation Committee's office, where I'd been summoned to appear at six
o'clock one evening, heaven only knew why. This happened in the first few weeks of my life at the college.

Gordon was seated behind a gleaming cherrywood
table; his huge hands lay clasped on the bare table
like the hands of a priest receiving the faithful. He wore

a brown herringbone-tweed jacket, a blue Oxford
shirt, and a tie the same color as the jacket with a pat-
tern of ovals and sky-blue streaks; it was the smart
tie that fall, all the rage at Neal W. Lowitz's, the men's
store across the street from the post office.

Beside Gordon sat two other boys whose names I
didn't know. They introduced themselves to me and
motioned to me to sit down facing Gordon in a chair
made of the same wood as the table. We were in a
room off the library. Gordon cleared his throat before
speaking. His voice was a soft, deep, grave instrument he seemed to enjoy playing. It was a voice that
held no room for doubt.

"How's it going?" he asked me.

"Just fine," I said.

"Not too many problems in class?"

"I don't think so, no," I said. "When I fall behind,
I go and see my adviser. That helps me a lot."

"That's a fact," Gordon said, looking at his two assistants. "The advisers have always been a big help
to foreign students."

I thought he had come down a little hard on the
word *foreign,* but maybe that was just his Texas accent; he had a way of drawling the ends of his sentences. He spoke slowly, keeping his big brown eyes
trained on me. I began to feel uncomfortable. I wasn't
sure if I should keep on looking at him or glance over
at the other two. One of them was a redhead. The
other had ash-blond hair. And they looked puny beside Gordon's mass of meat and bone. So far they
hadn't opened their mouths except to greet me.

"Of course, this is a purely informal get-together,"
Gordon told me.

"Purely informal," the redhead echoed.

The blond didn't say anything. For a moment, nobody moved. I waited.

"We entirely understand," Gordon said at last, "that it takes a foreign student a little longer than the others to get used to our customs. We understand that."

The blond boy still wasn't saying anything; an angelic smile began to bloom on his unblemished face, a smile etched with a trace of pity. I felt more and more uneasy. *What do they want from me?* I wondered, and this was immediately followed by another question: *what have I done?* I didn't realize that they'd already succeeded in arousing an obscure sense of guilt in me. As I looked at them and listened to them, I felt my whole body going weak; I was like a kid facing his judges. Yet they were my age—two of them were, at any rate—and I hadn't done anything wrong, anything I could blame myself for, so what did they want with me, anyway?

Gordon chuckled and his voice took on a still more confidential tone. "I remember—I think it was two years ago—when another scholarship boy like you arrived on campus wearing a mustache. Can you believe it? A mustache! He was Portuguese, I think. A mustache!"

The notion of that Portuguese mustache sent a sudden ripple of hilarity through the three boys. I watched it swell to a cascade of laughter, the blond watching the redhead to detect exactly when he'd stop. A moment later Gordon's big hand, held palm down, sliced the air over the table to signal that was enough. They stifled another giggle or two, then quieted down.

"Naturally," Gordon went on, "he shaved it off. He was the only one on campus who had a mustache, just him among fifteen hundred students. You see how it was."

Until Gordon brought it up that day, I had never thought there was anything so shocking about a mus-

tache, that it might strike a single false note in a har-
monious landscape of college gentlemen's faces. But
hearing them howl with laughter, and knowing the
unanimous if unexpressed consensus that our campus be kept clean, immaculate, I could easily imagine
the effect the poor boy must have made among all
those beardless youths. In those days no one wore a
beard or a mustache or long sideburns, and certainly
not long hair. Among the faculty members, only a few
teachers, and then only the oldest, the department
heads, permitted themselves that luxury, that touch of
singularity. But they had age on their side, and the
power and prestige of their positions. Some of them
had been living in Virginia for over thirty years. They
were the Brahmins, the masters.

The back of Gordon's hand swept the air and he
turned his voice a notch more familiar, giving it a
note of connivance.

"Your Austrian has a mustache, too, doesn't he?"

"Uh . . . no," I said, "not that I've noticed."

"Well, it's not really a mustache, just some down
on his lip. It doesn't bother anybody because you can't
see it, it's not obtrusive. That other one was bushy and
pointed at the ends and *black*."

No comment from the blond or the redhead. Gordon dismissed the absurd and frightful memory of
the black mustache. He leaned toward me.

"Everything's fine," he said. "Everyone's very pleased
with your behavior on campus, but there is one thing.
The Speaking Rule—we've had reports that you're not
going along with it. Not really."

"That's a lie!" I said. "It's not true."

Gordon smiled. He sat back in his chair, certain of
his facts.

"Hold on, please. The Assimilation Committee isn't

in the habit of making such charges lightly. We always double-check."

"Always," confirmed the redhead.

The blond nodded silently.

"But I do say hello," I protested. "I'm sorry, but I
greet everybody and I reply when they greet me."

For the first time since the interview began, Gordon
looked a bit strained. He searched for the right words,
his bushy brown eyebrows puckered with the effort.

"You say hello, that's true enough, but—" He groped,
hanging his heavy head as if to avoid my outraged stare.

"But what?" I demanded. "What?"

Gordon went on in a tone of embarrassed regret.

"It's not that you don't say hello, or that you don't
return greetings. That's not it. We checked. So that's
not the problem." Then, as though reticent to voice
so horrendous a notion, he blurted out: "It's that you
don't smile when you do it."

He repeated this accusation more forcefully, this time
preempting any repetition of the key words by either of his assistants.

The blond and the redhead both looked at me the
same way, as if to say: *You see? It's really pretty simple.*

Things went very fast after that. I didn't know what
to reply, but the Assimilation Committee seemed to
feel it had done its duty. Gordon stood up and shook
my hand. I felt a tremendous surge of relief. Night
was falling as the four of us walked out onto the library's front steps, which were spattered with red and
black leaves from a giant sugar maple. There was something soothing in the air, something vaguely sad, too.
I wanted to sit on the steps and chat with these boys
while the night fell softly around us, but they were
in a hurry, and I watched each of them go off about
his business. Gordon walked faster than the other two.

I began to hate him fiercely, and to envy him just as intensely.

This was a small college, and we formed a tiny student body. I quickly got to know every face in this little community, and it grew much easier for me to say hello to people after I'd run into them at least once before. I even wound up enjoying saying hello and good morning and good evening, the way people do in country towns. At times I was genuinely moved to hear all those greetings and responses reverberating along the colonnade like a chorale rich in colors and accents and timbres, the sound amplified by the echo from the vaults above us.

When I began to make a few real friends, I told them about my session with the Assimilation Committee and about the dreadful black mustache, and it became an imperishable private joke; there was always someone among the people I liked who would throw Gordon Nichols's faltering, solemn verdict at me: "It's not that you don't say hello; it's that you don't smile when you do it."

6

I DON'T KNOW IF BUCK KUSCHNICK BECAME MY friend, but I saw him frequently, mostly in his small single room in the dorm.

He often spoke to me of his girlfriend, the one to whom he'd given a diamond-studded brooch that she'd pinned to her cardigan at the end of the school year, an accepted sign that they were on their way to becoming engaged. She was the reigning beauty in the small town Buck came from: Genoa, West Virginia. The girl's name was Abigail and he, of course, called her Abby. A photo of her, behind glass in a silver frame, lorded it over the night table in Buck's room. Abby had languorous eyes and long, heavy, curly hair; a kind of invitation to delight emanated from the picture, as it did from Buck's stories of his fun and games with Abby. She was warm, melting, a joy to kiss, though she hadn't yet gone all the way with him. He talked about her as if she were a cream puff. He received long letters from her that he assiduously answered.

He showed me another photo, of him and Abby together with two other couples their age. I was struck by that snapshot. They were on a street in downtown Genoa. Buck was wearing a leather-trimmed jacket with woolen sleeves and a big letter G sewn to it above the heart. He was holding Abby's arm and radiating health and happiness. All the boys and girls, then in their last year of high school, were carrying textbooks.

Buck was the school hotshot, the star of the basketball team, the town beauty's steady date. They owned the world. The six of them were walking down the middle of the street, and the picture gave you the optical illusion that all the cars around them had stopped to make way for them.

Abby was sexier in this shot than in the photo on the night table. You saw her full length, her figure shapely and beautifully built—the thighs, hips, and breasts well developed. She displaced real space, palpable, enticing space. In fact, she embodied the beauty typical of the period, the Miss Rheingold pin-ups elected by beer drinkers who dropped their ballots into small boxes on hundreds of thousands of bars across the country. Miss Rheingold's election had become a sort of national event and, as the admen had planned, linked the name of Rheingold beer to a certain kind of woman. For from one election to the next, beer drinkers invariably chose the same type of beauty—a sexy blonde or redhead. Even now I remember the 1954 Miss Rheingold's teasing little face, and I can still hear the jingle that carried the message in the radio and TV commercials:

> *My beer is Rheingold,*
> *The dry beer. . . .*

It used to be sung by a slick-voiced crooner named Mel Tormé. We heard Perry Como a lot then, too, the same smooth, honeyed sound. Later I discovered the country singers like Lefty Frizzell, whom I worshiped, and Hank Williams, but that was after I'd hit the open road, and if I get into all that now I'll mix everything up. I haven't come to that yet. We've got to get back to Buck and his fiancée, Abby, who looked so much like a Rheingold girl in the photo taken on the main street in Genoa, West Virginia.

That snapshot probably represented the most wonderful period in Buck's life, but he didn't know that when he showed it to me. He had been a young local hero, tops in his class. His parents were proud of him and he had even been accepted by the college in the neighboring state that trained gentlemen. So he had left his hometown nimbused in all that glory. Here, now, in his small room in the dorm, Buck at eighteen was just another anonymous freshman who talked about Abby the way a soldier at the front talks about the girl he left behind. When I thought about Abby, I had the same reaction beer drinkers had to Miss Rheingold; she aroused the same ideas in me, the same desire.

To tell the truth, I desired all American girls. Sue Ann had turned my head on our first date. And I dreamed of Elizabeth, the strange and dangerous girl at Sweet Briar College. Each encounter with a new date was a source of exaltation, of hope, a blaze of excitement no sooner lit than extinguished; each weekend brought its quota of discoveries of that unknown and unsettling cosmos, the American girl.

Like all boys my age, I grabbed up a new monthly magazine as soon as it hit the newsstands; it had been started by somebody in the Midwest and was called *Playboy*. In it I found the same feminine curves, the same velvety skin, the same come-hither looks, and I spent a lot of time under the shower with my Ivory

soap, as Cal had counseled. I didn't know if Buck and
the other frosh took the same recourse so frequently
because we never talked about such private matters,
but I wondered quite a bit about Buck and Abby. I
wondered why, when he had access to a peach so pleasing and ripe—one he had the right to touch, to bite
into—he didn't rush home every weekend to sample
it. After all, Genoa wasn't so far from the college; if
Buck languished to see that succulent girl, what kept
him from rushing to her? You drove all night, reached
there in the morning, started back on Sunday night in
time to be in class on Monday morning. Lots of students lucky enough to have a girl within striking distance made these frantic trips, a thousand miles through
the dark, with radios blaring, in pursuit of flesh to
touch, a mouth to kiss.

Apparently Buck had settled comfortably into college life. He joined Sigma Alpha, a fraternity that had
invited me over repeatedly, and I saw him there at
mealtimes. He was on the second string of the basketball team and knew how to cheer at football games,
where we all sang that famous Southern anthem,
"Battle Hymn of the Republic." Apparently he was just
a freshman like any other, more melancholy, perhaps, more taciturn. To be fair, I didn't think of him
as melancholy and taciturn until afterward, after they'd
found his body. Until then he had always seemed to
me to be like the rest of us—laughing, boastful and
shy, exuberant, and withdrawn. Normal, in other
words. That's why I said that no one ever really knew
why he killed himself.

One of the dorm counselors found him, late one Sunday afternoon, at an hour when the building was always three-fourths empty. The counselor was doing

his regular rounds and had stopped to drink from a
water fountain at the intersection of two corridors on
the ground floor. He later said that what had alerted
him had been the silence in that section of the dorm.
Not that he was expecting noise, since the place was
usually very quiet on Sundays. It was, he confessed,
another kind of silence that stopped him.

The door to Buck's room was shut, which wasn't
uncommon; but it was locked from the inside. None
of us had keys that could open doors from the outside. Only the counselors had passkeys to all the
rooms. Protocol prescribed that a counselor knock several times before using his key. This one listened at
the door first, and heard nothing—nothing but the silence that bothered him, for some reason he'll never
understand.

The counselor's name was Dave. He was a tall,
shrewd guy, close-mouthed, hook-nosed, with hair
cut short that stuck out every which way. He opened
the door, figuring it didn't make sense that no one
answered a knock when the door was locked from the
inside. And he found Buck Kuschnick, wearing only
his pajama pants, his eyes popping and his tongue half
out of his mouth, his legs stretched and tied with belts
to the bars at the ends of his bed. There was a third
belt around Buck's neck, but it wasn't attached to
anything, which led one of us later on to describe it as
"a hanging that wasn't one." The belt around his neck
was buckled at the third hole, and Dave opened that
one first, probably to try and get Buck breathing again,
but it was far too late. Buck was long gone. Then Dave
called the sheriff's office.

I got there at the same time as the police. I had been
to the movies with two junior-year students who had
left me to return to their fraternity houses. I saw the

patrol car with its revolving roof light park in front
of the porch to the dorm. A big, imposing-looking man
wearing a peaked cowboy hat and rigged out with
handcuffs, a police whistle, a bunch of keys, and a Colt
.45 got out of the car. He accosted me in a loud voice
that dripped with the local accent.

"Sheriff McLain," he told me. "Take me to the dead
boy's room."

"What dead boy?" I said, astonished.

"Take me to young Kuschnick." He grabbed my
shoulder and deftly spun me around to face the dorm,
as if I'd been a top, and as if he'd done that hundreds
of times.

"Has something happened to Buck?" I asked.

"Take me to him," insisted the sheriff, who now
realized that I didn't know a thing. He was still grip-
ping my shoulder, and it hurt.

"Let go of me," I told him.

"Oh, sorry."

He released me. That was my first encounter with a
representative of the law in the United States.

Dave was waiting for us in the hall. The sheriff
looked at us and pointed at the wall. Obviously we
were supposed to stand against it.

"Let me look it over alone," he told Dave. "Then
we can talk. You haven't touched anything, I hope."

Without waiting for an answer, he stalked into the
room. Dave looked at me.

"What were you doing with the sheriff?"

"Nothing," I said. "He just asked me to take him
to Buck's room. I ran into him when I got back from
the movies."

"Buck's dead," Dave said. "He hanged himself . . .
strangled himself."

I slumped against the wall, incredulous, feeling suddenly hollow. "How?" I asked.

"I don't know," Dave said. He told me what he'd found. Then he shut up.

I couldn't take it all in. It seemed unreal. But reality was visible across the corridor. Sheriff McLain had left the door to Buck's room ajar and, by inching along the wall—still leaning on it, though, because I was afraid I'd faint and collapse on the floor—I could see Buck's naked ankles and his two bare feet, the toes spread, looking grotesque.

We heard footsteps, then a knot of uniformed police burst into the ground-floor alcove along with two men in plain clothes, one of whom carried a small black doctor's bag. Sheriff McLain came out of Buck's room, took Dave aside to ask him some questions, and motioned to me to skedaddle. Other adults were arriving, some of them school officials. The cluster of students gradually grew denser, but they were not allowed into the corridor.

The commotion went on all evening and far into the night, because the boys who had known Buck couldn't sleep. There was endless coming and going in the hall, surreptitious powwows, and abundant speculation. Someone would stammer out something stupid; someone else would burst out laughing to exorcise the presence of death floating through the ground floor, even though the body had been whisked rapidly away to the morgue.

Finally Dave, the counselor who had found Buck's body, opened the door of his big room. "All right, knock it off!" he yelled, loudly and firmly. "No more talking about all that."

The next day, and this was the strangest thing of all, no one did talk about it. It was a radiant, sunny Indian summer day in early November, and the leaves on the oak trees, the sycamores, and the tulip trees dazzled us when we looked up on our way to class. No one talked about it. On campus, everyone went about his business; at lunchtime in Buck's fraternity, not a word about him was uttered; not a line in the local newspaper. Nor was there, in the twice-weekly school paper we put out and distributed free all around the campus, the slightest mention of Buck Kuschnick and his improbable death.

"We don't talk about it because it was no surprise," Harrison Riddle said.

It was ten o'clock in the morning and we were having coffee at the co-op.

"What you don't know," Harry said, "is that it happens every year at about the same time, always in the first semester."

"What do you mean?" I asked.

Harry pursed his lips with pleasure at the chance to distill the vast fund of knowledge he had accumulated in four years at college. I'd seen him come into the co-op. His arrival anywhere always caused a stir, a murmur. He fascinated the first-year students; to them he was the acme of elegance, intelligence, and a kind of dissipation. He wore a yellow cashmere scarf tossed back artfully over his shoulder. Behind his horn-rimmed glasses, his eyes sparkled with irony.

"Ah," he exclaimed in his nasal twang, coming toward me, "a young man who's curious about things. Buy me a cup of coffee."

He sat down, and I questioned him.

"Yessir, it's an old story," he explained. "There's always a sharp curve during the first semester, and there's always a freshman or two who skids in that curve. They can't adjust, or they're lonely, or they can't live up to the school's standards, or they're confused. That's the way it is. It happens, and that's why nobody talks about it. The college closes ranks and shuts its eyes and life goes on. Five days from now we'll forget Buck ever existed."

Harry finished his coffee and coughed noisily. He took his time, playing on my curiosity.

"Now, you have every right to wonder if there was a specific reason, some special event that triggered his suicide, but don't waste your time. You won't find one."

"Maybe so," I said, "but it's a funny way to kill yourself."

Harry looked at me. A perverse light flickered in his eyes. He leaned over to me. His voice dropped and his lips suddenly puckered judiciously. "So it was," he said, "so it was."

"Listen," I said, "do you mean there won't even be a police investigation? Hasn't anybody even wondered why he tied his legs to that bed before he put the belt around his neck?"

Still leaning toward me, Harry screwed up his eyes, still talking confidentially, still clowning.

"Do you mean to suggest, doctor, that some unknown hand assisted him? Was there an audience for an experiment in pleasure that went wrong?"

"I don't know what you mean."

Harry's smile was thin and ugly. "Surely, doctor," he pursued, "a Frenchman wise in all the expedients of vice and every depravity of human nature must know that strangulation is a highly complicated way to stimulate an erection and an orgasm."

"Uh, no," I said, "I didn't know that."

Harry laughed derisively. I thought back over the things Buck had confided to me, I thought of his innocence. I saw again the boy on whom the whole world had smiled, walking down a street in Genoa, West Virginia, in his wool-and-leather schoolboy jacket.

"Buck?" I protested. "Buck? That's impossible."

Harry stopped laughing. His face went white.

"Who knows? What do you know about anybody?" He suddenly began declaiming like a tragedian. "What do you know about me? Who am I?"

Heads turned in the small co-op snack bar. A lot of freshman were sitting at the tables and at the narrow, unpolished aluminum counter. Harry pushed his chair back, swept the air with his yellow scarf, and uttered an oddly shrill laugh that contrasted with his Shakespearean voice, a slightly crazy laugh. He stood up.

"Who am I and who are you?" he yelled, pointing at me while he scanned the ranks of wide-eyed new boys. "You're all sheep lost in the woods!"

With that he left the table, threw open the door, and marched off in a great swirl of cashmere, hips swaying outrageously, while a hush fell over the astonished assembly.

7

IT WAS A COLD MORNING. COMING FROM SCHOOL, MY friends and I had driven across the Alleghenies to Genoa. I remember that the mountains were orange and dark blue, and that we had passed through dirty, compact little towns with empty, badly lit streets huddling under the smokestacks of brick buildings. This

was mining country. And I remember a deer that ran
a few yards through the ferns alongside us. We slowed
down to stay with him, but he veered off into the tall,
black pines. We kept the car radio tuned to the country music that, with its indefinable, nostalgic twang,
was to haunt me for years; I always associated it with
those long, unfurling ribbons of road and a never-
ending plunge into the unknown, the night, adventure, night.

There were three of us in Dominic Rosa's Chevrolet
Bel Air two-door hardtop. We'd been chosen to rep-
resent the student body at Buck's funeral in his hometown.

Genoa is a humdrum place, population two thousand at most. To reach it we had to turn off U.S.
64 and climb to the top of a hill overlooking the Ohio
River, not far from the Kentucky line. Genoa was
an out-of-the-way little hole crushed by its proximity
to a real city, Huntington. Seeing it helped me understand the deprecating remarks I'd heard about Buck
being a "small-town boy." The graveyard was pretty
and unpretentious, a carpet of grass stretching along a
hilltop from which you could see the big river curling toward the limitless horizon of distant flatlands. We
had driven straight through the cold night to arrive
in time for the funeral.

Buck's parents had greeted us with a few polite mur-
murs. They looked as if they still didn't quite understand what had happened. Abigail was beside them,
with an older woman who looked like her and must
have been her mother. I recognized her at once, but
she didn't really resemble the girl in the pictures in
Buck's room. Shivering, she wore a tan coat cut narrow over the hips and little lined ankle boots like slip-
pers. Over her stockings she wore thick socks. A long,
cream-white scarf was tied around her head. She was

pale, doll-faced, wore no makeup; she cried a bit during the ceremony, as we all did.

Afterward, Buck's parents invited us for hot coffee
and a bite to eat, because we couldn't leave without
a little food under our belts and we had a long drive
ahead of us. We ate scrambled eggs with thinly sliced
potatoes swimming in bacon grease; Buck's mother also
served us sausages and carrot cake. We swallowed
all that, I remember, and washed it down with milk
to cut the taste of the bacon fat. We didn't talk much;
I didn't say a word, at any rate. The food was delicious, a bit heavy. After we finished eating, the
townspeople said their goodbyes. We heard car doors
slam in the yard in front of the porch of the Kuschnicks'
unassuming house. I looked through the window for
Abigail, and I got the feeling that there were two very
distinct groups: we, the three students, the gentlemen
in collars and ties, and the folks from Genoa, more
natural country people. I saw that Abigail was about
to leave with her mother. I hadn't driven all that way
to let her escape like that. When they had asked for a
volunteer in the freshman dorm to accompany Buck's
two older friends to the funeral, I had immediately
raised my hand, and I knew it was because I wanted
to meet Abigail. So I got up and walked out of the
Kuschnicks' house and asked her if we could talk pri-
vately for a few minutes.

"Sure," she said, not looking at all surprised. "Mom,
wait for me." To me she added, "But I'm late, you
know."

We sat in the back of what must have been her mother's car. That didn't surprise me; I already knew that
people around here did everything in their cars, and,
after all, why not? It was warm, restful, and quiet in
the car after that icy morning that had saddened us all.

Abigail looked at me. I searched for something in her round hazel eyes, and found nothing but curiosity: *what do you want?*

"I'd like to talk to you," I said. "Buck—"

She interrupted me. "I'm running late. I have to be at work at the five-and-dime in half an hour."

"You mean you're not going back to school?"

She shook her head. "I don't go to college. I dropped out after high school. Now I'm working. Gotta earn a living, you know."

That stopped me. I wasn't dealing with a college girl. Abby didn't belong to the establishment, the world of ivy-covered walls. She talked in a monotone, doling out her meager store of information with a polite smile. We were sitting close together.

"Buck talked to me a lot about you," I told her.

That seemed to perk her up. She blinked her big, round eyes and smiled, a little flirtatiously.

"What'd he say about me?" she asked.

I didn't dare repeat the voluptuous terms Buck used to describe her and the way she kissed and how cute she was. For a moment I said nothing. Then, since she had nothing more to say, either, she began with neat, precise gestures to execute what seemed to be an essential, urgent operation. She removed her scarf, revealing pink curlers in her hair. Then she leaned forward, reached across the front seat, and adjusted the rearview mirror so that she could see herself in it. She rapidly removed the curlers, dropping them into the scarf, which she now held wide open on her knees; each of the metal cylinders released a dark chestnut curl that contributed its touch to the skillful modeling of her hair, an arrangement she completed by shaking her head vigorously, three times in each direction, with grave concentration. I wanted to talk.

"Abigail," I said.

"Nobody calls me Abigail, you know. They always call me Abby."

"Abby—"

"Yes?"

She wrapped the curlers in her scarf and tucked it into her big handbag, from which she then, almost in the same sweep, plucked a compact and lipstick. *Click-clack,* the compact opened and she peered into its mirror; *click-clack,* she pulled the cap off the lipstick to reveal a gleaming, pointed, scarlet rod that she proceeded to apply to her lips. I was silenced again by this terribly intimate exercise, by this girl making up only inches away from me and apparently attaching no importance to the proximity of my body. Our breath had gradually fogged the car window so that we couldn't see out and no one outside could see in. I didn't know how to interpret what was happening in the car; I felt humiliated by Abby's seeming indifference to me, yet excited because she treated me as if I were a part of her private life.

"Abby," I asked, "what are you doing?"

"Making up, of course," she said. "I have to look nice at work, you know."

She closed her boxes, her tubes, and her bag, then turned and presented a different face from the one I'd seen earlier that morning, the pale baby face partly hidden by her scarf, with her head bowed over Buck's grave. She was smiling brightly, looking not at all like the girl Buck told me about. Something was missing, I didn't know what. She was very crisp and poised.

"That's it," she said. "Am I okay?"

"Yes," I told her, "you're very beautiful."

"Thanks," she said. "You're sweet."

The breakfast Buck's mother had given us suddenly

lay heavy on my stomach. I had nothing to say to this stranger, and she had nothing to offer me, nothing. Now she launched on a new undertaking. She removed her booties and stripped off her socks. I could see her toes through the nylon stockings. She fished around under the front seat and brought out a pair of high-heeled shoes, slipped them on, and stashed the booties where the pumps had been. She partly opened her coat, her round knees touching mine.

"You're sweet, you know?" she said, showing me her legs.

I gestured toward her knees. "Abby, do you know why Buck killed himself?" I asked.

Her empty eyes peered at me, and she gently pushed away my hand, which had barely brushed her leg. "No."

"But you were engaged to him. You wrote to each other all the time. You knew him better than anyone did."

She smiled an embarrassed half smile. Her voice became brittle, at last losing its neutrality and that almost professional timbre I would later hear in the voices of waitresses in the all-night diners along the big interstate freeways.

"You're so refined," she said. "Too bad we don't have time to get better acquainted. I'm gonna be late for work, you know."

"Why won't you answer me, Abby?"

She threw up her hands, then dropped them in her lap. "You know, it was a lie, all that." She was talking more rapidly. "We were engaged, but it was a lie. We were making believe, lying to everybody. All that business about diamond brooches was just a gag. It wouldn't have come to anything, you know. We were kids. You lie all the time at that age, you know. It

wasn't a real love story, all that—we were just playacting."

"Maybe, but that doesn't explain why Buck . . ."

She took my hand and put it on her knee, freezing
me with that simple, unmistakable movement.

"That had nothing to do with me, you know, nothing at all," she said. "It happened up there in Virginia. That's where it happened. It was there, not here.
It was none of Genoa's doing."

We didn't move. She had said her town's name with
pride and confidence. Genoa wasn't to blame; if Buck
hadn't left his small town, maybe he would still be
alive. I could feel her skin under the stocking and I
should have been sick with wanting it, but inside me
nothing was happening. I just wondered how long
this conversation was going to last. Abby released my
hand and it retreated from her knee. She heaved a
wheedling little sigh.

"You know, if things'd been different, we could've
got along real well." Then, hurriedly, her voice im-
personal again, she added, "I have to go now. I'll be
late. I'm pleased to have met you."

She cast a last glance at herself in the rearview mirror to check that her lipstick was on right and her
curls were in place. The carrot cake was repeating on
me, with an aftertaste of bacon grease that ascended
to my temples, and I was relieved when the door
opened and a blast of cold air slashed at my face.

We left Genoa around noon. As we passed the traffic light on the town's single real street, actually called
Main Street, I looked through the window of the five-
and-dime store and saw a woman sitting behind a cash
register. Her back was to me, but I thought I recognized Abigail's wavy hair and her square shoulders un-

der the pink smock. Then we left the small town
behind. A few minutes later, still trying to forget that
breakfast that refused to go down, and the sight of
Abigail rolling her socks down over her nylons in the
stifling car, I fell asleep.

We maintained a good speed, with Dominic and his
friend taking turns at the wheel, and we didn't stop
except to buy gas or a BLT or a hamburger that we
ate as we drove.

We got back to the campus at dawn the next morning. A bluish light shafted through the red and gold
masses of elms and oaks. The car slowed down as we
rode through the streets, empty at that time of day—
Jefferson Street, Letcher, Madison—that automatically
led us to the still more familiar lanes of the campus. I
had a new feeling I was to recognize several times
later that year, the feeling of coming home.

November! Winter would be on us soon, but there
was still no bite to the air to herald it. On the other
side of the mountains, past the mining country, at the
top of the small cemetery in Genoa, the air had been
raw and harsh. We'd felt naked and frozen beside that
freshly dug hole in the ground into which a few flowers had been thrown. But here, back at college, it was
still mild, and we knew we were going to see our
teachers and friends again, and the thought comforted
us.

We drove past the still curtained fraternity houses,
the lifeless college buildings, the white Doric columns, the gray slate roofs, the ochre brick walls, General Lee's historic old clapboard house and the chapel,
where the Notables, the student choir, met once a week
to sing "I talk to the trees, but they don't listen to
me . . ."

In silence we drove twice around the circular outer

driveway before making up our minds to separate. The only person we passed was Sam, one of the three black groundskeepers, in his lilac-colored coveralls, peacefully pushing a cart bristling with long-handled brooms. Then we parted, and we forgot about Buck.

And then winter came.

8

NOT LONG AFTERWARD I HAD A CHANCE, WITH DAN Notts's help, to visit the football team's locker room at halftime—during a game we were losing by several touchdowns. Dan was on the team. He was a huge boy with crew-cut blond hair, a turned-up nose, and skin as pink white as a porker's. He had broken his collarbone in the previous game and was sitting with us that day on one of the wood and steel benches in the stands of our small stadium, Wilson Field. We were hosts to a team from the northern part of the state, traditional rivals to be beaten at all costs. The kind of team you didn't feel too bad about losing to on its home grounds, but never here, on our own field. Dan hated being sidelined by his injury. He'd rather have been in uniform on the team bench, even if he couldn't play, than hanging around in civvies with nobodies like us while his teammates were getting their faces ground into the muddy grass a few yards below us. So at halftime, he couldn't wait to rejoin the team, and he suggested that I accompany him to the locker room.

"You're disgraceful! I'm ashamed for you."

There were more than twenty of them sitting on unpainted wooden benches in the big, tiled room that smelled strongly of sweat, liniment, and animal heat. Only two of them still wore their blue-striped helmets, maybe because they were too tired to take them off. The others held their helmets in their laps. Their heads were bowed, making their padded shoulders look even more artificial. Their legs, too, enormous in their padded pants covering leg pads, knee pads, and shin guards, didn't seem to belong to those young faces. The antiglare grease streaks under their eyes accomplished their secondary purpose of making the players look more warlike.

The first time I saw a football game I grasped that American football is war—without death, perhaps, but war all the same. Armored men plotting offensive and defensive strategies would smash into the soldiers facing them to conquer marked territory sectioned like a general-staff map. It entranced me. Even if I couldn't understand the subtleties of the battle formations, the overall spectacle grabbed me hard.

"You're lucky there's no mirror in here so you can't see what you look like!"

With his fists rammed into his pockets, Coach Mallard bellowed at the silent players. He barely opened his mouth as he spat out a stream of curt insults punctuated by brief pauses. Between each comment his jaws clamped down like a dog's on a piece of meat; you could almost hear the jawbones crack.

"I thought you were men. You're girls! Daddy's little girls!"

The coach's two assistants, with their fists also rammed into their pockets, followed Mallard's every word, every movement. Mallard—small, piercing black eyes deep-set in a taut, wizened face—looked at no one and everyone at once.

"I see I'm going to have to tell you again what you're supposed to know already. This is not a game for sissies. This is not a game for schoolgirls. Football is for men. Get that into whatever you use for brains: football is played by men. It's a man's game."

He began pacing up and down, without taking his eyes off the players, his footsteps keeping time with the words he repeated like a drumroll.

"Besides, it's not a game. It's life. And in life there are winners and losers. Only dimwits and apes and weaklings like to lose."

He stopped and spun around. "Does anybody here like to lose?" he yelled.

Silence. The lowered heads rose to look at him. I spotted my friend Cal Cate among the players, his forehead bulging and arrogant, a crazy gleam in his gray eyes.

"Does anybody here like that?"

The voice bounced off the bare walls and ricocheted back toward the shower room.

"Personally, I couldn't care less if you come off this field bloody or broken or on a stretcher, as long as you come off winners. I don't give a damn, because I'm a man. It's for you, so that you're not ashamed of yourselves tonight or tomorrow. So that you're not ashamed to be alive. To be men. Winners. Win! Win!"

The voice had dropped, the words again coming in staccato bursts, but the boys didn't take their eyes off Mallard. He barked a brusque, strained laugh.

"What? You dare to look at me? Not bowing your
heads anymore? Not ashamed anymore? Something
you want to say? Well, if you feel like talking, I want
you to answer me. With just one word. All together. I want you to answer just one question. What
do you have to do? What's your aim? All right, yell
it at me, and loud!"

Together, their voices low, almost muffled as if by
a kind of shyness, the knot of players replied. "Win!"

Mallard took his fists out of his pockets and raised
them chest high, waving them like a boxer dropping his guard to move in and finish off a helpless
opponent.

"Louder!"

"Win!"

"Louder, goddamn it!"

"Win!" the players bellowed. "Win! Win!" Some of
them pounded the tile floor with their spikes. Others drummed on their helmets with the palms of their
hands, and this time there was no reticence. There
was jubilation in those voices—and something else, too.
Fear, perhaps. The fear that destroys itself by screaming yourself into a frenzy. I strained to stay out of sight
behind Dan's broad back, certain that if Coach Mallard discovered that I was witnessing this exorcism he
would make mincemeat out of me. But Dan was my
rampart, his body a wall between the room and the
doorway behind us. I felt his hulking frame moving
in time with the others and I heard him yelling, too,
and I saw that his legs were quivering.

"That's enough!"

Mallard's command silenced them at once, but the
reverberation of that "Win! Win! Win!" wafted in the
air for a few seconds more on the fumes of rubbing
alcohol.

"That's enough. I see you can still use your vocal cords. Now I'm going to ask you something. I'm going to ask that in the next half you use your guts, your legs, your arms, your hands, your shoulders, your fists, your eyes, your heads, your balls. I'm asking you to kick the sonuvabitchin' fucking shit out of them!"

He spat out this invective with a kind of disgust that communicated itself instantly to the bunch in front of him. I saw some boys bow under the insult while others scowled like children being forced to swallow bitter medicine.

There were things I was aware of and others that partly escaped me. I knew that Buck Kuschnick should have been sitting with those players and that he had probably heard that sort of exhortation before. What I didn't know as I listened to Coach Mallard vociferate was that on that Saturday afternoon in November scores of coaches in hundreds of locker rooms across the country were making the same cruel and brutal speeches to thousands of boys and young men. I wasn't aware of it because I was still too green to have learned how to transform an experience, a personal observation, into a generality that could be applied to a whole culture, a society, to all men and women. You acquire this skill as you progress through life, when you have encountered death and violence and beauty and coarseness, or all of them at once, often enough; then you gradually establish a range of values, of forms of behavior. You can then define what once seemed impromptu and unexpected, things you observed but couldn't comprehend. The Sphinx can then solve its own riddle. If each man is the sum of all history, then we should be able to explain everything through each man's individual experience, a nation and its history as well as the people of that nation who made its history. I had read that in Emerson, but it took a long time for this notion of the multiplication of human actions to sink in. It has stayed with me ever since, sometimes in a simplistic sort of way. The same things are happening at this very moment thousands of miles apart, yet they are not at all the same things, and yet they are.

Coach Mallard seemed satisfied. He knew how far he could go. He recognized that he had to stop short of telling the boys, "Do anything you want. Cheat the referee. Poke their eyes out, but win!" He knew perfectly well that the honor system was the college's basic principle (you don't cheat; you take your exams without supervision; you can leave your books or clothes anywhere on the campus and find them there later, untouched). A college that teaches its students to behave like gentlemen cannot allow its coach to incite them to win at any price. Coach Mallard therefore had to steer between an obsession with results, winning as the only rule in life, and an overall framework of fair play and uprightness. So he had resorted to something just as shocking as cheating: he had been obscene, vile, vulgar; he had whipped up the team's pride with thugs' language, with truck drivers' expletives. The exhortation had brought a pitiless chill of reality into the room, of mean streets and back alleys, of the other side of the tracks, of slums and bums and drunks. Mallard had talked to them like men. Football is a man's game.

Now he relaxed. He resumed his former stance, fists rammed into his pockets, legs wide apart, gazing over the boys' heads, his face absolutely blank. He spoke calmly, his tone flat, almost indifferent, almost bored.

"You're the best. You're better than those guys. You're gonna win. You're gonna do what you know how to do. You're gonna beat 'em. You're gonna walk right over them and win. You're the best. You're terrific guys. Now go to it!"

He smiled briefly, took his hands out of his pockets, smacked his fist into his palm, and turned his back to the players, who bounced up feverishly and pounded their fists into their palms. Mallard's assistants moved through their ranks, encouraging them, smacking them on the ass, distributing lemons, salt tablets, and water. A tumult of hope and enthusiasm replaced the silence that had prevailed while Mallard spoke. The boys' voices mingled with the clatter of their spikes on the tile floor and the din of the fans' chanting filtering through an open door into the narrow, steamy corridor to the now empty locker room.

PART TWO: WINTER

9

AND THEN WINTER CAME.

Overnight the campus was covered by a thick, immaculate cushion of snow that deadened the atmosphere and muffled all sound. Teachers and students went to classes bundled in wool, fur, and ski caps, but the buildings were overheated and we worked in shirtsleeves. Then you had to bundle up again to go outside, so that you were perpetually switching from piercing cold to suffocating heat. The dorms and fraternity houses also maintained the same subtropical temperature.

You were thirsty all the time, and on Saturday-night dates, you drank more beer and booze than you did in the fall; the girls drank, too, drowning their bourbon in glasses brimming with ice. Meetings and conversations took on an extra effervescence. Kisses were edgier, more electric. You flirted harder and more boldly, as if the new season and the approach of the Christmas holidays brought a new intensity, a determination to bring to the boiling point the romances that filled our weekends.

That feverishness overcame me, too. I was tormented by the need to love and to be loved; winter's sudden onslaught had made me more aware of my loneliness. Evenings, in the dormitory halls, I heard the guys conjuring up the Christmas vacations, ripe with warmth and happiness, that they were going to spend back home. But where could I go? With whom would I experience Christmas, my first American Christmas? My family was across the Atlantic, and I didn't have the price of a round trip.

France was a long, long way away. There were no jet planes then; I'd have had to take a twenty-hour flight aboard a Constellation that stopped in Iceland to refuel, or go by ship, but the big liners didn't make winter crossings. Besides, all that was expensive, too expensive for my budget. Most important of all, I'd have interpreted returning home as proof that I couldn't live abroad alone, that I'd failed in this unique expedition that The Others hadn't been lucky enough to undertake. I missed those Others, but, at the same time, I already felt detached from them.

This, then, was to be my first Christmas away from my parents and my brothers. Until now, that hadn't seemed very important, but with the bunches of mistletoe already dangling from chandeliers in the frat houses, with "Jingle Bells" forever tinkling from car radios, with the Christmas holly branches and decorated trees already standing all over town, I began to grasp the meaning of this ceremony that a whole nation spent so much time and money preparing for. I felt shut out of it, and this awakened a kind of sadness in me. It put a lump in my throat. One evening in Bob Kendall's room across the hall from mine, I probably talked a little too much about this. Bob looked at me with his laughing eyes and, in the most natural way in the world, said, "Come home with me. Come celebrate Christmas with the Kendall family."

I hesitated before answering. Bob was a rich boy. We'd talked now and then, been casually friendly, but we were far from bosom buddies.

"Sure, come on," he insisted. "I'll call my mother tonight. She won't object. We'd be delighted to have you."

The next morning, with the same simplicity, with that spontaneous sense of hospitality that only Americans possess, Bob confirmed my invitation for two weeks to the Kendall home in Dallas, where he'd been born. Dallas! It was so magical, so American, so mysterious. I was beside myself with joy and pride. From then on I could do what all my friends were doing: cross off the days on the wall calendar. Before long, I would leave on a new adventure. I had a future appointment, a new goal. Meanwhile, sometime before Christmas, something even more amazing happened to me that was to transform my life at college. I met April.

10

IT HAPPENED ON ONE OF MY TRIPS TO THE BARRACKS.

These were tiny prefabricated houses—two rooms –kitchen–bath—perched like children's blocks on wood-and-concrete stilts on the other flank of the hill overlooking the east side of town, well away from the college grounds. They really looked like barracks, and they had been put up to house the few Korean War vets who had come to the college, fresh from the horrors of war, on the G.I. bill. These men were married, had one, sometimes two, children. They lived among the young, still untenured beginners on the faculty whose salaries were too small to pay for the lordly homes occupied by the deans, the department heads, and the full professors.

So the barracks sheltered an intermediate society, not yet fully adult, but certainly no longer the kids we were. People in the barracks did not appear on the glittering circuit of fraternity parties or journey to the girls' schools. They didn't put on white monkey jackets and sing in the choirs; they didn't worry about who they'd take to the big February dance; their faces did not reflect the same dazzled confidence that ours did in an untroubled and successful future. They knew the problems they faced in making their way in a community in which they formed a kind of subproletariat. Some of those we passed seemed to look at us with bitterness, or was it merely condescension?

The barracks residents had pregnant wives and squalling babies. They could hear their neighbors' radios and their quarrels through the thin walls of their flimsy houses. They did not inhabit the Virginia dream we represented. The barracks contrasted oddly with the romantic atmosphere of the campus. We students did not generally frequent the barracks.

Yet I liked to go there. One of my favorite teachers, Rex Jennings, lived there with his wife and their three-year-old daughter. Jennings corrected my papers in comparative lit, gave me coffee and chocolate pecan cookies baked by his wife, Doris, and introduced me to what he called "the minor writers," including one named Raymond Chandler, whose paperback novels I devoured. Doris wanted to learn French, so I gave her hour-long lessons twice a week. I went on foot, walking down the wrong side of the hill and taking a shortcut across a vacant lot, then along the monotonous row of stilts overhung by those cramped barracks where the sound of radios filtered through some of the walls. The Jenningses' shack was the last on the line, and the coldest, since the last prefab wall gave on nothing but the wind and the steep slopes of an abutting ravine. You clambered across a narrow footbridge, up three steps, over three planks, and into their home.

It was cold that day, and I had been walking through snow. Doris wasn't there. I found a note on the door: "Had to take my daughter to the hospital. Keys are under the mat. Have some hot coffee, excuse me, and see you next week. Doris."

I went inside, made some coffee, and sat down to drink it, pulling my chair up close to the coal stove that heated one of the two rooms. This room served as a combination office, dining room, and playroom for the little girl. The rickety black stovepipe added to the makeshift shabbiness of the place. I sipped my steaming coffee, and when I began to thaw out I took off my duffel coat and began looking over the bookshelves that lined the narrow walls.

I had often done this when Rex Jennings was there; I'd take down a paperback whose title and author I didn't know, and he would say, "That one, yes" or "That one, no . . . you wouldn't like it." In that case I'd replace the book and pick another one and leaf through it, awaiting my teacher's verdict or advice. I seldom left there without a borrowed book or two. But today I was alone, and that changed everything. I felt like poking around further, beyond the rows of books. I felt like searching the place. Something beat inside me, like a dull sound.

This was a feeling that went back to my childhood.

For a long time, beginning as far back as I can remember—probably because I had always shared rooms with my brothers—I had been uneasy when I was alone in an empty room or house that shouldn't have been empty, or that I shouldn't have entered. As if I were stealing something I'd been forbidden to touch, I used to love to open drawers and closets, to run my hand over the shelves and furniture, pick up piles of linens and folders. I was obsessed with the unknown, alive with curiosity, the will to know, to penetrate others' territory. To search, search, perhaps because there was a secret, or maybe because I wanted to get past a dark wall into an area I didn't understand: other people's lives, especially grown-ups'. Over and over I wandered at odd hours through my family's house when everyone else was away, examining their beds, their possessions, their intimate, inaccessible world of clothes and objects, things soft and palpable. Later, as a teenager, the pull was weaker, but I hadn't lost the quirk entirely, and that day in the barracks, with the November wind whining through the footbridges and the pilings, the old yen welled in me again, heightened by the strangeness to me of American things—smells, colors, and fabrics I didn't know.

So, that day in the Jennings home, I went into the bedroom, opened the plywood door to the closet, and slowly inspected the jackets on the hangers, then the dresses. I stroked a pile of blouses, then the sweaters, the underwear; I was enveloped in that long-dormant feeling that I was doing something wrong, and loving it.

Doris was a short, slight blonde with straight hair, utterly without sex appeal, an ordinary woman. But touching her clothing disturbed me, and I brought one of her skirts to my lips, as if to bite it; desire swept

over me, and I plunged my face into it. I don't know
how long I'd been doing this when I heard a sound
behind me that wasn't the wind or the crackling stove.
I turned around. Standing there was someone I'd
never seen before, a young black woman with yellow
eyes, wearing a coat that buttoned down the front.
She was standing quite still, looking at me, with a
slight, indefinable smile.

"Who are you?" she asked. "What're you doing
here?"

Momentarily paralyzed by the feeling of being caught
red-handed, I hurriedly dropped the skirt and shut
the closet door behind me. My heart was pounding
in panic.

"I . . . I'm one of Mr. Jennings's students. I was looking for a book."

The young woman was still smiling. I stood rigid.
A handbag hung from her arm; she looked as if she
had just entered the house. Her voice was low and
even, and when I walked toward her, I had the impression that maybe she was scared, too, at finding a
stranger in the house.

"You were looking for a book?" she said.

"Yes," I said, moving away from the closet.

I walked firmly past her to the shelves in the other
room, keeping up my act.

"Yes, I must have got the wrong room. They must
be in here."

The woman followed me into the other room.

"You can bet your book's in here," she said calmly,
flatly. "Hard to imagine it among a woman's clothes
and underwear."

I turned to face her. I knew nothing about blacks. In
those days the Virginia I'd found was completely seg-
regationist. The only blacks I'd had occasion to talk to

were the college's three groundskeepers and, occasionally, some waiters from restaurants in town. Even in town we had no reason to talk to blacks; their neighborhood was off limits to us and we just didn't enter it. This was the South.

Devoid of experience, I had no idea how to talk to a black. But from the way this woman spoke, and the irony that seemed to tinge her voice, I realized that she wasn't in the same category as the others, the ones I'd met so far. I had the feeling that she was making fun of me. She had, after all, caught me with my face buried in Doris's skirt, and I could see that she was taking advantage of that, that she was exploiting my shame and embarrassment. I defended myself as best I could.

"Mr. Jennings often invites me here to borrow books. And besides, I give his wife French lessons."

She smiled with that expression I couldn't interpret: kindness, indulgence, or mockery?

"Sure, I get it now, you're a foreigner," she said. "I thought you had a funny accent. You're not an ordinary student, then."

"No, not entirely."

My answer seemed to erase the sarcasm that, because I felt so deeply guilty, I had thought I detected in her voice.

"My name's April," she said. "I come here regularly, too. To clean the place." Her chin went up and, as if to forestall any contempt on my part, she quickly added, "I'm not a cleaning woman. I work by the hour to earn a little extra money. It pays well. But it's not my profession."

"Sure," I said.

"I teach school on the other side of town—the side you never go to."

I didn't comment. She was still smiling, her eyes holding mine.

"I should have seen you weren't like the others," she said. "Just by the fact that you don't avoid my eyes. Americans have trouble looking a Negro in the eye, especially if she's beautiful. Haven't you noticed that?"

"No, I've never had occasion to."

She laughed. "You won't often have. I haven't myself. What does it do to you? Is that how it is where you come from?"

"I've never thought about it," I said.

She laughed again, but this time it sounded harsher, more bitter. Then she took off her coat, dropped her bag on a table, and flailed the air with her hand as if to disperse a cloud hovering around her.

"Forget it," she said. "I have to get to work. I've got things to do. You planning on sticking around here?"

"No," I said, "I'm leaving."

But I couldn't stop looking at those strange yellow eyes, at that smile that sent so many messages at once: irony, bitterness, superiority, then inferiority—followed by a recapture of lost ground. It was a subtle game she had set up between us, a power game. She had an advantage: she'd found me in a situation that left me defenseless. I had the advantage of my race, and of my status as a gentleman from the college, and even if I didn't belong to this country, to this South and its customs, I had imperceptibly acquired its habits and mannerisms, so that the difference between me and the other students was marginal. April was trying to put us on a par, and that was impossible. A current of pride and belligerence flashed through this beautiful young woman—who declared frankly that she was beautiful—that drove her to try to dominate me, to make me bend under the power of those eyes and to envelop me in the apparent maturity of her judgment.

"Aren't you taking the book you came for?" Her voice had quickly regained its barb of sarcasm, of treachery.

When I didn't answer, she held her hand out to me and switched in a split second to a disconcerting kindliness.

"Don't worry, I won't tell a soul about this."

"Tell them if you like," I said. "I wasn't doing anything wrong."

She blinked and moved closer to me. Her hand came to rest on my forearm, a common mannerism in this part of the country, but one that the situation rendered uncommonly intimate. My heart was pounding again, but not for the same reason as before. Did she notice how disturbed I was?

Her voice, that voice I was so drawn to, went rough. "You're right," she said, slowly and deliberately, "there's no harm done in trying to ease your loneliness by stroking a woman's skirt. But, come to think of it, wouldn't you rather do it when there's somebody in the skirt?"

She took my hand and put it on her hip. The sensation under my palm was round and warm, and I slowly slid my hand a few inches down the small of her back, my eyes never leaving hers, holding my breath. Outside the silent shack, the wind was still moaning. April's eyes held mine, too, not resisting my hand as it caressed the cloth over her stomach, then dropped down to her groin. With both hands I pulled her to me and tried to kiss her, but she pushed me away.

"No," she said in a clipped tone.

We looked at each other. She was breathing as hard

as I was. In her eyes I saw that slightly mad gleam, that golden glitter swelling the brown pupils that had struck me when I first saw her in the open bedroom doorway. Her lips parted slightly in a smile that was a bit sad and jaded, as if she'd been through all this before.

"No," she repeated. "It's too risky. It's impossible."

But I moved closer to her, once more letting my hands drift to where I'd already touched her—there, at least, I'm allowed, I thought, since I had reconnoitered that area before—and I felt her tremble. Suddenly, she was the one who glued her lips to mine in a long, deep, lovely kiss tasting of sweet wine, a kiss like none I'd ever given or received before, a taste that made me close my eyes the better to lose myself in it. Her body was plastered avidly against mine, without that calculated distance the college girls always kept. I felt her thighs, her breasts, her belly pressed against me and my hands roamed over her to complete the astonishing feeling of abandon and of unison that flooded through me. Then April pushed me away.

"No," she said, "I was right. It's too risky. You'd better go. They might be back any minute. It's impossible. You've got to leave." Her voice still harsh, she insisted, "Go away!"

That was final, and I knew she was right. Her tone abruptly revived in me the fear of being caught, this time by my teacher and his wife. That would be disastrous. Just imagining the scene sent me scurrying to snatch up my duffel coat from a chair and toss it quickly over my shoulders. I took a last look at April, who hadn't budged from the middle of the room. She wore the same enigmatic smile I had seen when I turned at the sound of her voice and saw her that first time.

I threw open the front door and rushed out into the cold air rising up over the footbridge from the ravine. I raced down the barracks steps in a clatter of wood and galvanized iron that was instantly lost on the wind, and I ran. I fled across the snow, ran until, breathless, I was far away from that line of shacks, until I was past the vacant lot and up on the first hill, where, from the top, I could turn and, in a single, raking glance, take in the ridiculous shacks on their absurd stilts. At the end of the line, in the road edging the ravine, I saw a parked car, a dark blue Ford, that I figured must be April's. That was all I knew about her, and that wasn't going to be enough to help me find her. I knew I had to see her again.

11

SEEING HER AGAIN! AN ACHING YEARNING FOR IT gripped me all that evening. I returned to the campus harboring a secret I couldn't share; telling it to anyone was unthinkable. I was haunted by the sweet-wine taste of that kiss that, I felt, had carried me across the barrier of clumsy puppy love. As if April had taught me more in a single embrace, in that one

meeting of our lips, than whole weekends of flirting
and petting with college dates. That kiss, that
musky savor, that look, that low, veiled voice, that
fleeting moment, that body so close to surrender—
all this had convinced me that a new and promising
avenue was opening out before me, wide, mysterious, but rich and vibrant with life.

How was I to see April again? I certainly couldn't
hide near the barracks and wait to intercept her
dark blue Ford on her way to or from her work for
Rex and Doris Jennings. Too chancy, and I'd be
easy to spot. I couldn't question the Jenningses about
her. I was sure I'd blush at the mere mention of her
name. April!

I kept going back to give Doris French lessons, but
there was no sign of April, and that drove me wild.
I thought of her at night, before I went to sleep,
trying to analyze what had happened between us, re-
calling in minute detail our every movement, my
every word.

Was I in love with April? Maybe she attracted me
because she had taken the initiative; she was the one
who'd invited me to caress her, who had guided my
hand to her hip, she who had kissed me after rebuff-
ing my attempt. She was surely a few years older than
I, and so had subtly subjugated me, and I had liked
that. Other things had come into play: her skin-deep
irony, her arrogance, the breaks in tone that skew-
ered her sentences. These, too, had attracted me along
with the pleasure her lips gave me, the strange high-
lights in her eyes, and the supreme exoticism of her
color. The notion, so seductive to Southern boys, of
love with a black woman simply because she was black
and therefore forbidden fruit did not entice me; her
attraction for me fit into the broad outlines of my

American adventure. It was one more stage in the trail that, day by day, my youth was blazing.

I remembered exactly what Cal Cate had told me that fall in his green Buick convertible: that black women were off limits. I also knew that the boldest students sometimes patronized black whores because it was forbidden. Mom and Dad had forbidden it. Society as a whole condemned such intermingling. I had not been raised to dread these sacrosanct taboos, these poisonous temptations. Yet the danger remained, just as great, just as implacable, because I was living here in the vulnerable position of an invited—tolerated—foreigner, and I clearly understood that there were acts one did not commit in the green and white Shenandoah Valley. One did not cheat, or steal, or lie. One took exams unsupervised; one respected the honor system. Naturally, there was no place in the system for a love affair with a black. "It's too risky," April had insisted, but it was the danger that excited me. I was scared, but more curious about my fear than afraid of my curiosity.

April had also said, "It's impossible." But my pride decreed that it was not at all impossible.

I had discovered sensuality. Aromas and perfumes, voices, caresses, music, colors—everything in America, from my first contact with it, had come to me through the senses, everything that intrigued and attracted me. I don't know if it was America that aroused my senses, like those of an animal prowling through an unfamiliar forest. I don't know if, before that cascade of American discoveries, my senses had ever really exerted their power over my behavior, or if, for some unfathomed reason, as a child I had masked this extreme sensibility. Or whether, and this was more likely, it had gradually been squelched in me as I

grew. Perhaps, now that I was alone and far from The
Others and not quite a child anymore, I was simply
restoring to my senses the rights that had been partly
confiscated from them, was now releasing myself,
freeing myself, discovering myself with all the violence of rebirth.

12

ONE SUNDAY EVENING, ON THE SMALL BLACK-AND-
white TV screen in the lounge at the fraternity house
where I was a temporary guest, we were watching a
popular variety program. The show's host was a newspaper journalist turned television emcee: Ed Sullivan—
horse teeth, fake Bogart look and all. We didn't watch
much TV then, although this was the era in which
television really took over Americans' daily lives and
changed them forever. But in the dorms and fraternity houses on campus, interest was slight.

That evening, however, was different. Watching Ed
Sullivan's show, we caught our first glimpse of a
young rock 'n' roller who, when he sang, writhed in
a way no one had ever seen a white man do before.
Everyone was stunned. This unknown performer (with
the extraordinary name of Elvis Presley) was undulating in a manner so shocking that the TV camera-
man had been ordered to frame him only from the
waist up, never full length. But the show's director had

circumvented the dilemma: sometimes he showed the singer's head and chest, sometimes his legs and ankles and suede-shod feet. Everything but the pelvis.

In the frat lounge that Sunday night, everybody was hypnotized by the singer whose pelvis couldn't be telecast. Not only was his hair outrageously brilliantined, but even his thick, sensual lips seemed to have been bathed in lubricating oil. What shocked us most was the way he waggled his hips to punctuate each verse of his song, especially since you couldn't really see him do it. You could feel it, though; it was easy to imagine what those bumps and grinds represented. He was mimicking the sex act. One of the boys caught on at once, and he broke the startled silence that followed the end of Elvis Presley's number.

"That's easy," he announced. "Anybody can do it."

Whereupon little Herbie Clemson, a fair-haired boy from Alabama, launched into a demonstration that closely imitated Presley's performance, its meaning even more glaring without music. Yells and wild whoops greeted the exhibition.

All the boys in that fraternity were Southerners and proud of it, the kind who pinned Confederate flags to their walls and sang "Dixie" at the slightest excuse. They knew how to dance like the unknown TV singer because most of those Southern kids had been exposed to it back home, in the black nightspots. Nigger dancing, they called it.

In a burst of group frenzy, all the boys in the lounge began bumping and grinding like demented strippers, each trying to outdo the others in suggestive movements. Then they stopped and tried to remember they were gentlemen, but they still couldn't get over the fact that, for the first time, the whole country from coast to coast had seen on the tube what they

had always thought of as the gesticulations of a Southern nigger in heat.

Little Herbie from Alabama couldn't quiet down. He
flitted from boy to boy, whispering like a salesman
for Satan, "Nigger dancin', nigger dancin', who wants
to go nigger dancin'?"

A number of them said they did, which is how I
learned that some of them occasionally sneaked over
to the other side of town, as April had phrased it. I went
with Herbie and his friends in a two-car procession—a
Dodge and a DeSoto—that nosed out into the night
over the snowy campus roads, taking a twisting, complicated route as if trying to disguise our destination
and shake off anyone tailing us.

There was a diner called Steve's—a real diner, in an
old railroad car on blocks—on a low slope overlooking U.S. 11, just past the center of town. It was a
hangout for truck drivers and other forms of hu-
manity we never saw on the campus: hitchhikers, night
watchmen, gas-station attendants, local farmers who
came in their pickups and cattle trucks, and a few
women with weird looks and destroyed faces. Steve's
was a sort of frontier post between the white and black
sections of town. I found out that the ritual was to
stop at Steve's for a couple of beers, to leave as dis-
creetly as possible, and, instead of heading back on
11 toward the campus and the fraternity houses, to turn
sharp right under the railroad overpass. That took
you into neighborhoods that looked exactly like those
in the white town, except that the houses were older,
the streets more potholed, the walls dirtier, and the trees
scruffier.

At that time of night, the feeble light from the
swaying lampposts made it all look sinister and scary.
We drove slowly. I suggested to Herbie that we drive

around before parking outside the club. I didn't expect to see April standing on a street corner, but I wanted to reconnoiter the area. It wasn't hard to spot a small school standing on a sloping street between a dairy store and a record shop.

Moments later we were in a nondescript shack: a few tables, dim light, a fairly big dance floor for a place like that, where black couples were dancing what was not yet called rock 'n' roll and that they termed r 'n' b—rhythm 'n' blues. The music came from two huge jukeboxes, fluorescent orange and green, in the middle of the room. We sat down at an empty table, then bought Cokes in paper cups from a machine, lacing them under the table from the bottles of bourbon we'd brought with us in paper bags.

When we came in, the blacks had eyed us with neither hostility nor welcome. We were tolerated, that's all. There was no question of hustling any of the girls, and besides, they all had escorts. Nor was there any question of getting up and going to the jukeboxes to choose the next number. We'd paid our entrance fee, in return for which a little guy in a baseball cap who was perched on a bar stool just inside the door planted a blue-ink stamp on our wrists; we paid double, he told us, because we were white boys out slumming. We were expected to sit tight, listen to the music, written by no one we'd ever heard of and performed by musicians we didn't know, and watch the couples dance. By comparison with what they were doing on the dance floor, the young unknown we'd seen on TV looked a little clumsy and certainly far less daring.

So we sat nailed to our chairs, casually contemplating the dancers' syncopated undulations, rising only to drop nickels into the Coke machine because the bourbon was going down smooth and fast, its fumes rising to our heads on the sounds of saxes and guitars. Herbie leaned over the table.

"Let's get out of here now," he said, "because in another five minutes they're going to throw us out, and I'd rather go without being told."

We got up and moved toward the door. This time we had to pay an exit fee, again double, to the little guy in the baseball cap. When we were back in the DeSoto, one of the boys complained, "They really take us for suckers. What a racket!"

"Yeah," Herbie replied, "but you saw some black ass tonight. They can't go and see white ass even if they're willing to pay."

They all shut up then. A kind of cloud settled on them, a feeling compounded of conspiracy, satisfaction, and uneasiness.

I thought about April as the DeSoto rolled under the railroad bridge to cross Route 11 and speed back through the snowy darkness to familiar territory. *A car,* I thought. *I have to have a car.*

13

ON A WEEKDAY AFTERNOON AT ABOUT THE SAME time, in the State Theater, the town's only movie house, we discovered another young man no one had prepared us for. Handsome as a Cocteau angel, coarse as a big-city hooker, with a cracked laugh and an androgynous voice, melodramatic and yet natural, he bolted us to our seats. We sat through three straight

showings of *Rebel Without a Cause* to watch him run
a glass of milk across his oddly lumpy forehead to cool
his lust for life, and to watch him wriggle his jeans-
sheathed legs and his torso in its red zipper jacket. When
we met our dates the following weekend, he was all
the girls could talk about. He was so cute, they said.
They were already calling him Jimmy.

In those days it was impossible to understand the hidden meaning of those simultaneous debuts—of a white
vocalist who gyrated like a black singer and a movie
actor who moved across the screen with enigmatic
grace. Only now can we recognize the coincidence of
those two events as the start of an era in which youth
emerged from a long silence to create its own heroes—
bisexual, ambiguous, rebellious, and empty.

At the time we had no perception of this, I least of
all. But what sticks indelibly in my memory was that
first revelation in a peaceful setting of provincial America, those first tremors at a time when my emotions,
my whole youth, were in turbulence. James Dean, with
his strange gait, like a disjointed puppet's. And Elvis
Presley, who had impelled me across the borderline into
Southern black society.

14

I WENT TO SEE CAL CATE.
"Can I borrow your Buick this afternoon?" I asked
him.
"Got your license?"

"Sure," I said, which was a lie, and I showed him
my French identity card, which didn't mean a thing
to him. He gave me the keys and asked me to return
the car in time for him to use it that evening.

It was parked on the gravel in the backyard of the
fraternity house, its heavy, sturdy top firmly anchored to the body. I got in behind the wheel, my
hands sweating. I'd never driven a car in my life.

Taking possession of Cal's magical green machine
set the blood pounding in my temples. I maneu-
vered extremely slowly, trying to imitate all the movements I'd seen Cal make, commenting out loud to
myself on how well the operation was going, just to
reassure myself that it was easy. I immediately felt
what I had already registered as a mere passenger: Cal
Cate's Buick had a smoothness that enveloped you
and carried you to a higher state where you were the
master of events. You were like a prince in a car-
riage, or a dolphin slicing through deep water. Everything was beautiful, pleasing to the eye, the ear,
the hands, the legs. The Buick handled easily, but it
was dangerous for a beginner. The power steering
was so light that you had to be very wary about getting the car back on a straight course when you came
out of a corner or a turn. Every bend looming in the
road made my heart beat faster. An instant of panic,
followed by an equally fleeting feeling of satisfaction
when I got safely through a turn, because then I could
resume my inspection of that wonderful automobile.
The chrome and pearl buttons at my fingertips that
controlled the semiautomatic drive, the power windows,
the vacuum-tube radio, the air conditioner all delighted
me as much as the sofa-size bench seat and the pistol-
grip lever to the left of the steering wheel that controlled the spotlight on the outer ledge of the front door.

I breathed in the smells of vinyl, leather, cloth, and steel, I hummed in tune with the melodious purring that was the only sound you heard from the superpowerful, supersilent motor, and that blended with the almost imperceptible whine of the wind around a closed convertible. This was true music, and I sang along like some benign crackpot. But the countless traps lurking on my first venture behind a wheel, in the snowy streets of the residential neighborhoods and the sometimes icy hills, kept me from relishing the Buick's voluptuousness wholeheartedly. The sight of an approaching car filled me with horror, and I had to learn in a hurry what I needed to know to avoid ramming it. Every time I made it past one car unscathed, I wondered how I'd done it. I talked to myself to whip up my courage, like a rider coaxing his horse. I invoked Cal's name. "Do like Cal," I intoned, "do like Cal, do like Cal." I concentrated so hard on what I was doing that I failed to register that something important had happened: I was saying the words in English; I wasn't even talking to myself in my own language anymore. A few days later, I started dreaming in American, too.

I hadn't borrowed Cal's Buick just for the terrifying pleasure of learning to drive by myself. I wanted nothing to distract me from my primary aim: to see April again. Once I felt able to keep the car going without too much risk, I drove toward the barracks to see if her blue Ford was there. From the road running down to the prefabs on their pilings, I saw no sign of life around the shack where Rex and Doris Jennings lived. I turned around and headed toward Route 11. When I reached the overpass beyond Steve's Diner, I slowed down, dithered, then drove on under it.

By day, "the other side of town" showed a less

alarming face than it had in our nocturnal outing, but
it still looked poor. Few cars, few passersby. I saw fat
women in cheap, rough overcoats and an occasional
man, walking fast, their black faces slightly gray in the
frosty air. The green Buick with its white top attracted attention, so I didn't dare park near the school.
I decided to drive around the block a few times. That
was no less conspicuous. On my third circuit, however, I did spot April's car in a parking lot to the
left of the school. So she was there! I had to find a
way to wait unnoticed. I parked in front of a record
shop on the sloping street that led down to the school.

I went into the shop. A young salesclerk wearing a
greenish-blue jacket with the name Dwayne embroidered on it was sitting behind the counter reading a
movie magazine. He stared at me in astonishment.
What was a white student doing here? I found that I
could lie glibly, even if I was scared to death.

"The other night I came with friends to hear some
music in your neighborhood," I told him. "There
were some tunes I didn't know, and nobody on the
other side of town sells those records. I'd like to find
one or two of them."

"You know their titles? Or the singers on them?"

"No, nothing, but I'd recognize them right away if
I heard them."

Dwayne flashed a condescending smile. "Listen," he
said, "I can't play you every record I got in the store."

"No," I agreed, "of course not."

I walked to the front of the shop and surveyed the
school entrance through the window. Nothing new.

"Tell you what," Dwayne said reluctantly, "I'll let
you hear a few of the current hits, the ones we sell
the most of."

"That'll be great."

On an RCA Victrola that could only take 45s, Dwayne played some records that sounded like the music we'd heard in the shack, but the beat was slower, heavier; a clanking piano was slightly out of sync with a voice that was both syrupy and dusty. The music was so obsessive, so fascinating that for a moment it wiped away the anxiety I had felt ever since entering the black section of town.

The singer was a jowly, fat man with short-cut, kinky hair. On the record sleeve he was smiling at the camera; an embroidered handkerchief stuck out of the breast pocket of a jacket with wide lapels, and on his finger was an enormous, square signet ring. The song was called "Blueberry Hill" and the singer's name was Fats Domino—a name that didn't sound real to me. Dwayne assured me that he and his buddies played nothing but Fats, and he insisted that I hear not only the other side of the record, but other tunes by Fats Domino as well. In my memory, waiting around that afternoon will be linked forever to Fats's basic, rugged piano and his voice—joyous, but with a sad, arid undertone, as if he had some fatal affliction of the throat, or a soul overflowing with the blues.

Suddenly, through the shop window, I saw April's Ford come out of the school parking lot. I nodded my thanks to Dwayne and rushed out, leaving him standing nonplussed at the counter beside his pile of unsold 45s. Just as I reached the Buick to follow the Ford, I glanced at my left-hand mirror and saw a police car top the crest of the hill. I started up slowly, petrified at the thought of being stopped by a patrolling cop. Swallowing my fear, I drove slowly along the street. To my immense relief, I saw the patrol car stop in front of Dwayne's shop.

I trailed the Ford as it headed toward the railroad

overpass. Within moments it had crossed the town
and, ascending a street I had never taken before, reached
the hill that rose to the barracks. Our two cars were
alone on the road. The Ford stopped a few yards ahead
of me. I braked, too, and watched as April got out
and walked back to the Buick.

Looking furious, she motioned to me to lower my
window.

"What is all this?" she asked. "Are you crazy?"

"I wanted to see you again," I said.

She seemed to hesitate. Her voice softened.

"Don't you know you don't do things like this
around here? You don't realize it, but anybody for a
hundred miles around can recognize this fat-ass car
you're driving."

"I wanted to see you again," I repeated.

She burst out laughing. "You've really got nerve,
haven't you?"

"Don't stand out there like that. You'll catch cold,"
I said.

"No, I'm going to my other job now. Goodbye!"

She started to walk off, then turned back. The old
irony and defiance had resurfaced in her face.

"Mrs. Jennings is home," she said. "If you want to
wait for an hour, I'll meet you next to the barracks,
in the ravine. You can drive down. You'll find the road.
I guess you're smart enough for that."

15

THERE WAS NO MORE FEAR AT ALL.
There was something perilous and secret that I was living through utterly alone. There was a whole series of obstacles I had faced from the moment I first climbed into Cal's car, and that I had overcome. Now, at the bottom of the rocky ravine, which I reached by maneuvering the Buick down a steep, pitted, icy road, I was waiting for the final test. And I was firmly determined to overcome it, too. So I sat there, both hands clenching the wheel, my stomach knotted and my eyes shut while the jowly black man's piano pounded in my head with the ebb and surge of my desire.

16

WE MADE LOVE ON THE WIDE BACKSEAT OF THE Buick, as I'd hoped we would. It was brief, and it was endless, and all the sensations I had felt when April first kissed me washed over me like music.

90

She arrived there in a little over an hour. I hadn't
counted the minutes. When I heard the sound of a
car engine over the noise from the radio and the blasting wind that sometimes shook the Buick's top, I
opened my eyes and saw April's blue Ford parked in
front of me. She got out, opened the passenger door
of the Buick, and sat down facing me with her legs
tucked under her. She was wearing heavy white cotton coveralls with a hood that hid her hair and made
her look like a boxing champion in training. But the
bright redness of her mouth and the brilliance of her
eyes, the perfume she exuded, made her even more
desirable than if she'd been wearing a dress.

She removed the hood, shaking her glossy black curls
into shape, then undid the laces holding the top of
her coveralls together to reveal a man's pink button-
down shirt under a crew-neck sweater. In fact, she
was dressed the way white college girls dress when
they're not on display, when they're studying in the
evening—bobby socks and tennis shoes, with scarves
around their necks and glasses on their noses. That
charmed me even more.

She questioned me, calmly and purposefully. "How
much time do you have?"

"I have to return the car tonight."

"It's not yours? Matter of fact, that's probably a good
thing. It's too showy."

In our temporary shelter I listened to her and looked
at her anxiously, tensely, hungry for her.

"Yes," I said, "maybe."

She had stated the rules to follow, the orders to obey
even before we'd made a move toward each other.
That didn't surprise me because everything that was
happening was unprecedented for me; I went along
with it all, feeling rather as if I were embarking upon

a new ritual. And even before this one had led to anything at all, April also outlined the procedure for our next meeting.

"Next time we can meet here in my car," she said. "That's the best way. It's absolutely safe. You can just walk over."

When I didn't answer, she added, "I come to the barracks twice a week. Tuesday and Friday afternoons."

"What if I want to see you some other time?"

"You can't. You're certainly not going to go wandering around among the Negroes again. You want to get yourself expelled? Elsewhere? I'm not going to meet you in your dorm with all the little white boys in it, and you are not coming to my house."

"Where do you live?"

"With my parents and a passel of brothers and sisters and grandmas and grandpas. Full of Negroes, those houses are, lots of people, lots of noise. Not at all the kind of place to do what you and I have a mind to do."

Those last words spurred me to move closer to her. She smiled conspiratorially, and her voice changed. Authority, efficiency, sarcasm, too, disappeared; her face took on a frail, vulnerable look.

"I got cold out there," she said. "Warm me up."

Then I took her in my arms, or perhaps she had opened hers, and we sat that way for a long time without moving, without kissing, holding each other close, feeling each other tremble, breathing faster. Cheek to cheek, lips to ears, registering our heartbeats and breathing in the scents of each other's skin, hair, neck, the hollow of a shoulder, until we couldn't stand it anymore and our hands moved, to breasts, bellies, lips, thighs, groins. Then we kissed, rekindling the long, chaotic sweetness of that first kiss but going further, fiercer, and all the savor I had guessed at the first time, the full taste of April, came back to me so brutally, pierced so deeply into me, that I was almost frightened.

She pulled loose from me, straightened her legs and, panting, said, "Let's do it now."

We scrambled over into the back and lay down on the seat. The Buick seemed like a boat now, and I had the feeling I was lying on a bunk in a cabin, with the silent sea around us. She wriggled out of her suit pants, making me a gift of the brown velvet skin of her legs, and I thought it was lovelier than any gift I could have dreamed of.

I remembered the shouts in the yard of the freshman dorm in autumn when the boys came home from their Saturday-night dates and asked each other how they'd made out and whether they'd *done it*. The realization flashed into my mind that I could never talk to anyone of what I was about to do, but at that instant it didn't matter anymore. Because I *had* done it.

17

I DROVE CAUTIOUSLY BACK TO CAL'S FRATERNITY house with the windows wide open to let the icy late afternoon air dispel the odor of our lovemaking. I parked the Buick in the same spot from which I had set off earlier. Like a thief wiping away his fingerprints, I made sure there was no trace left of April, no trace of me; with a punctiliousness I hadn't known I was capable of, I performed the rites of this clandestine relationship, of this new life within my life that had already become another life.

I walked across the campus to the buildings and the friends to whom I remained a foreigner. Day after day I did everything I could to be like them; did I really understand that what I had just experienced had widened the gap between them and me? I may not have been conscious of it, but I somehow adjusted to it; my meeting with April aroused my instinct for concealment, for calculation, prescribed a new way of structuring my day and setting my priorities. I reorganized my life.

It had never occurred to me that I might not see her again. When we separated, nothing was said about another meeting, no time was appointed, because that had already been settled, and because the need we seemed to have for one another would dictate our behavior. On future Tuesdays and Fridays I'd be in the ravine. I might have to borrow Cal's Buick again or maybe I'd have to wait, shivering with cold, huddled against the rocks out of the snow and wind, until April's car came nosing down the steep road. But I'd be there, and I knew she would be, too. I knew it wasn't all going to end with one meeting—yet I couldn't be sure.

Sitting on my bed in the dorm, while the Austrian bent over a book across the room to finish some homework, I wondered how I could bear to wait three days and three nights before seeing April again. It was too long, I thought. I was already frantic to make love to her. I considered borrowing another car from another student belonging to another fraternity, but when I silently reviewed the list of possibilities, I realized that Cal was the only one I could ask who wouldn't pester me with questions, and that I couldn't ask him too soon or too often. I had to be cautious, wily, had to behave like a wolf in a woods that bristled with traps. But compulsion strained against reason: I even thought of walking down to Steve's Diner, having a bowl of soup, then, when night fell, marching under the railway bridge in search of April. I was sure I would eventually spot the blue Ford parked in front of her house "full of Negroes," and that I could figure some way to get her out of there. It was stupid, unrealistic. The thought of seeing that patrol car suddenly reappear finally tamped down my impatience.

I forced myself to calm down. I lay down, closed my eyes, and relived the love scene on the backseat of the Buick. Throughout that crucially important day I had thought that making love to April would be that last lap of my obstacle race; I had driven myself on to win it, to triumph. Now that the day was over, I thought differently about it, and the very notion of triumph seemed wrong. Instead I thought that there were moments of happiness and beauty in life, that I had experienced one of those moments and would experience others, and that between those interludes, which would have to remain secret, there was the rest of the time, the rest of life. The only thing I could do when one of those moments occurred was to savor it fully and deeply, but that could not be called a triumph. There was no such thing as triumph or success. Only moments, some of them simply happier than others, and these had to be grasped as you grasp at luck, that rare bird that flies above you and that you can only seize by leaping into the air with outstretched fingers. I had to live life by hurling myself toward heaven, with my hand forever outstretched.

18

THE FOLLOWING TUESDAY I SET OUT FOR THE BAR-racks on a tide of longing for April—to touch her, kiss her, to talk to her, and to hear the mockery blend with the tenderness in her voice. I ran across the empty lot, weaved warily between the piles to avoid being seen by Professor Jennings or anyone else I knew, and arrived much too early. Daylight simply wouldn't do for these meetings, I now fully realized. It was too risky. April got there at the agreed time, and we made love in her car.

This time I kissed her immediately and it was I who undressed her, punctuating each movement with a kiss or a caress. This time I was the one who set the pace of pleasure, and she who responded. We used the backseat of the Ford, a narrower, more workaday car than Cal's aristocratic Buick. We fell easily into our places and positions, allotting the space as before: the back for making love, the front for undressing, re-dressing, talking. It was a little like moving from one room to another in a house. There was a room for carnal knowledge, for stifled cries and mutual exploration, bodies entwined, her yellow eyes never releasing mine, not even when she came, moaning softly, staring at me still when I climaxed and when I told her how perfect it had been.

Then we shifted to the front seat, with the radio turned low, a place for words and for confessions. If we'd had to clock the time spent in the chamber of love versus the time in the conversation room, the talk would surely have won hands down, for we made love quickly, driven by desire, but haunted, too, although we didn't talk about it, by the thought of danger, of transgression. The fear of being caught in the act.

But we didn't clock ourselves. We had other things to think about. It was better, we agreed, to meet at night, better to avoid the ravine as our sole rendezvous; otherwise we would attract attention sooner or later. April told me of several possible spots. We set after-dark times for meeting and figured out how I could reach the places on foot if I couldn't borrow Cal's Buick.

April was twenty-one, three years my senior; to me

the gap seemed disproportionate. She was a brilliant young woman with a rich gift for words and a penetrating mind. Having already run up against a good number of life's obstacles, she had developed a keen sense of the relativity of things. April had dropped out of a black college in Maryland because her parents could no longer pay her expenses; Dad was out of work, she'd been told, give it up. So she'd come back to her hometown and had easily landed a job as an assistant teacher in the school in the black neighborhood. She did a lot of work on the side—not just for the Jennings family—to accumulate money to return to college and get her degree. And then she'd go north, to try to find more freedom than she had in the South. She cleaned house for several of the teachers at my school, soaking up snatches of the life on our campus.

As she talked, I realized that her life at college had not been so different from ours. Except that blacks seemed less snobbish, less uptight than we whites were. She did not like being labeled a "Negress," and she never uttered the words *black* or *colored*. *Negro* was the preferred term in those days.

April's clear-eyed awareness of the limits imposed on her by her race had reinforced her tendency toward sarcasm, her love of irony, her gift for sardonic phrases. Small creases of hardness occasionally framed the corners of her mouth, but she fought the temptation to grow bitter. She refused to let that first setback cow her into resignation. Everything hinged on money, she said, on dollars and cents. She had learned that the hard way. Well, she could earn money, she'd make out, return to Maryland. She needed a year more of course work to complete her degree.

"And I'll tell my sorority sisters I slept with a white college boy, and they won't believe me."

"But you won't tell them."

"No, I won't tell them. But if I were going to, it'd be easier for me than for you. You can't whisper it to your Saturday-night dates, to your pretty blondes, your Southern belles. Can't you just see it? They'd shun you like the plague."

She burst out laughing. And I laughed with her.

Then, after a long pause, she murmured, "You'll see. Someday you'll be ashamed of what we're doing. Just you wait: you'll end up being ashamed."

I didn't really understand her. I looked at her and saw someone so mature, so much more experienced than I, so serious that, instinctively, I almost asked her if I was her first white college boy, if she hadn't already stepped across that dangerous line. But I didn't dare. I kept the question locked up inside me. Then the night blotted it out. We saw each other two nights in a row after that, then the Christmas vacation began, and I left for Texas.

19

BOB KENDALL AND I DROVE SOUTHWEST THROUGH Tennessee and Arkansas, where we stopped for the night. In Little Rock, to be exact, where we stayed with an alumnus of the college, a friend of Bob's parents. He was a big guy, damned by too much money and too much alcohol. He took us to an endless eggnog party, and we both left the next morning feeling sick as dogs.

I had been fascinated by the eggnog ritual—the silver ladle dipping into the big, brimming silver punch bowl, then tipping the pale, unctuous liquid into what looked like teacups. The stuff had seemed so harmless, so easy to drink, especially with the severe cold outside. Unfortunately we woke up feeling nauseous and gummy, as if we'd been swallowing hot, sugared tar.

We drove to Texas in a straight line, only two states to cross, but you cross them from end to end. This was my first really long trip by car, and I loved it from the start: the map spread over my lap, the changing landscape, the Appalachians and the Ozarks, cities and towns with strange, musical names. And the stops at the Howard Johnson's. And the stretches of superhighway—in those days, the country had not yet been imprinted with its matrix of dull, stultifying interstates and expressways. We frequently changed highways, often using small farm-to-market roads.

There were valleys and mountains, woodlands and plains. We drove past dams and stud farms and grain elevators and airfields. Bob and I followed our progress from county to county by reading the license numbers around us and listening to the local radio stations that played music I never tired of.

And I immediately fell in love with the open road. It was during that first excursion into the heartland that country music was revealed to me, with its lovely nostalgic tone, its catchy guitar and fiddle tunes, the nasal twang in which the singers told of everyday things straight out of confessional magazines and the headlines of the more risqué newspapers: love affairs with waitresses and divorces and broken childhoods, the gnawing of time and the bad things people do, hot coffee in the morning and dust in your eyes at night when the truckers miss the hard curves and crack up because they gotta get there on time and the boss won't put up with their being late. All this piled on a steady beat like the rhythm of a train in the night. The singer we heard most often in those days was Hank Williams, but Lefty Frizzell was my favorite; his hoarse voice belted out a song so that it sounded like a confession, something warm and intimate. Like Bing Crosby, he understood what a microphone was for, and he used it shrewdly, seeming to sing—no, to talk—to a lone listener, to you, personally.

We were always changing radio stations, because those local transmitters only carried over a range of fifteen or twenty miles. Consequently we were always moving from one song to another, although they all had basically the same inflection. Out there country music was just about all that was being broadcast. Yet at one point I again heard the black piano player Fats Domino, and he not only sang, but someone interviewed him—a local disc jockey, between a town called Puma and another named Only, on U.S. 40. "What do you call your music?" the deejay asked him, and Fats replied that he didn't know what name to give it. The whites were starting to talk about something called rock 'n' roll, but he, Fats, had never done anything but rhythm and blues. The deejay also talked about rockabilly, but to me it was all the same thing. Because I recognized Fats Domino in the middle of a Southern night, that led me to thinking about April, and I couldn't get her off my mind for most of the rest of the trip.

April and the music, the South, the road—all that imprinted itself on me like a landscape on an empty canvas. It still haunts me, even now.

The music of the 1950s was dumb, simple, primitive music that asked no questions about the meaning of life. It was not written by thoughtful people and it certainly wasn't made to be analyzed. There were no magazines to dissect the lyrics and the music; nobody wrote page after page to explain the hidden meanings that Fats and Lefty were getting at. Everyone's identity was well defined. Boys were boys and girls were girls and the word *romance* meant that someone was bold enough to buy flowers for his girl. On a dance floor, boys led and girls followed. Later, in the sixties, no one led anymore, and no one followed. It was everyone for himself, and by then people were trying to classify things, and they found a name to categorize the sound Fats refused to identify, but by then it was all over. Innocence had disappeared. From the moment people tried to define the simple popular arts, from the moment the judges, critics, and scholars appropriated all that and ingested it and digested it and dished it up again, it wasn't the same anymore. It was spoiled. Like that Christmas eggnog in Arkansas, it gave you an overwhelming urge to puke.

20

As soon as we reached Bob's mother's house —Bob hadn't told me there was no Mr. Kendall around—we went to bed and slept for twenty hours straight, which was about as long as we'd been driving and we couldn't keep our eyes open any longer. Bob's mother waked us singing a Christmas carol. She was a tall, lithe brunette in a red silk bathrobe. Bob looked a lot like her. And they both wore garish ornaments on their fancy clothes. They were bound to each other by an amused view of life. A subtle complicity seemed to unite them, and they approached the world and its people with the same frivolous air. They gave the same impression that everything was an excuse to smile or to laugh.

I never saw Dallas. The Kendalls lived in Irving, the city's wealthy residential suburb, and I never set foot in the city itself. In the distance, across the vast, flat, greenish-yellow prairie on which Irving, Texas, sat, you sometimes glimpsed a few high rises, but nothing else. I saw only the bright, neatly mown lawns and the huge luxurious houses that all looked new. We went from residence to residence, from party to party. We went to bed late and got up at the beginning of the afternoon to devour a late brunch. The day unwound idly, lazily, Bob and his mother playing cards, me lis-

tening to music, until evening, when we got ready
to go to another party. As evening neared, excitement
bubbled up into giggles from Bob and his mother,
and they floated off into a kind of private intoxication, acting giddy even though they hadn't drunk a
drop. They sparkled.

Every day, and every night, was Christmas. On the
well-trimmed lawns, giant, garlanded Christmas trees
shone with lights that the owners of those palatial
homes never bothered to turn off, not even in full
sunlight, for December down there was warm and
sunny. After dark, the landscape resembled a forest
dotted with gigantic, multicolored pines, and those trees
of lights functioned as landmarks guiding us toward
the mansion where that evening's party was under way.
There were always lots of long, bulky, brightly colored cars—Cadillacs, mostly—parked along the gravel
driveway leading up to the main house. On the porch
decorated with lighted bunches of mistletoe, holly, and
the state flower—the yellow rose—our hosts wel-
comed us with real Texas hospitality.

Bob and his mother introduced me as their Christmas houseguest. "He's from Paris," they would say.

"Really? Paris, Texas? Which one?"

The reply was unvarying, which was how I learned
that there are several towns called Paris in Texas and,
more important, that Texas is a nation, and that its in-
habitants scarcely imagined that any other place existed beyond its frontiers.

Honoring the Christmas houseguest was ritual, so I
was coddled, questioned, borne from group to group
in an uninterrupted babble of voices, shaking hands with
bejeweled old women and solidly built, horsey girls
flanked by their escorts, husky young jokers who tow-
ered over me by a head. Nothing important was said.

Folks wondered who you were, what city you came
from, where you were going, if this was the first time
you'd been here and if you liked it, and once you had
answered all these questions, the group seemed to
melt away and you were left alone until your hostess
took you quickly by the hand and led you to another knot of guests who fired off the same fusillade
of questions.

Just as punctually the hostess or her daughter or
her cousin came and scolded you sweetly: "Why, you
haven't eaten a thing. . . . You're not drinking. . . ."

And they filled a plate for you with turkey and cran-
berry sauce and chestnut purée, or pecan and raisin
pie, which you washed down with bourbon or with
that horrendous eggnog that I had learned to mistrust. Beyond the buffet table set up in adjoining ground-
floor rooms, I would see Bob and his mother, all
smiles, also spinning from group to group. Bob
would turn and give me a friendly, worried wink as if
to inquire: *Everything okay? You having fun, at least?*

I nodded approval. By this time I had worked out a
series of standard replies to the elderly ladies' standard queries, and I had met other Christmas house-
guests from all over the United States who, like me,
were doing the rounds of the parties in the wake of
their host families.

Among the out-of-towners was a very pretty girl
named Jessica, who flirted openly with me. She was
from Louisiana and she had long, widely spaced doll's
lashes and a line of bright chatter. On more than one
occasion she led me away from the buffet and invited
me for walks in the garden, or to sit in the lounge
chairs on the terrace facing the lighted swimming pool.
Jessica wanted me to hold her hand and kiss her. It
was hard to keep on saying no; it would have been

insulting. Our encounters grew into a standing joke that Bob and his mother artfully embroidered.

"Go ahead and kiss her, for God's sake," Bob advised me after one party.

"Absolutely! Why won't you kiss that divine young creature?" his mother asked as she drove us home in their huge Cadillac Eldorado. Mrs. Kendall's fingers touched the steering wheel ever so lightly. Her nails were so red, so heavily coated with polish, that they seemed almost to bend under the weight.

The Eldo was enormous, a new model equipped with such novelties as a panoramic windshield, tailfins as sharp as spurs, and deep seats made to wallow and doze in. We drove home along the branch road that linked the main residential districts, bypassing the inner city. Bob sat in front, beside his mother. I couldn't see his face, but I sensed that he was mugging to egg his mother on. She went along with him; they loved to kid around that way, in constant interplay, seeming to feed on each other's pranks and laughter.

"I asked around," Mrs. Kendall said. "The girl comes from one of the best families in Shreveport. I don't see why you won't give her that kiss she's yearning for. It would just be common courtesy."

"Mother's right," Bob said with a chuckle. "You ought to listen to her."

"I don't want to insist," his mother went on, "but if I were you, I'd kiss that girl."

Bob twisted slightly around toward his mother and I imagined his mischievous eyes encouraging her to *keep it up, keep it up!*

And so she did, stringing out a silly, endless patter. "I'd kiss her because I don't really see what you have to lose, except for your reputation as an Old World gentleman. That's the truth, and I don't mind re-

peating it. That girl wants a kiss and you don't really
have any choice. You'll have to acquiesce, especially
since you haven't exactly brushed her off, as far as Bob
and I can see. You just keep on cooing like a Gal-
veston Bay pigeon, although I must say you're taking
your own good time about it. If that's your strategy, I must admit it's pretty neat. That divine Jessica
is just dying for you. So when you finally do give
her that kiss, she'll flip! She'll go back to the great state
of Louisiana a new woman!"

When she reached the end of this monologue, Bob
burst out laughing. "Great stuff, Mom," he told her.
"You really had him going, there."

"Thank you, dear," she replied. "I must say I out-
did myself."

And they both laughed without looking at me. It
wasn't malicious laughter, though; they weren't trying
to exclude me from their fun. And the Eldorado slid
silently past the lighted rows of giant Christmas trees
toward the Kendall house that waited for us, empty in
that endless prairie.

21

W AS REFUSING TO KISS JESSICA MY WAY OF REMAIN-
ing faithful to April? When we had separated, the day
before I left for Texas, she had kidded me. "Well, so
you're going to meet some blonde Texas beauties,
right? Seems they're all blonde there. And you're

going to preen and strut for them, I know. They'll love you. They're just gonna melt."

April's voice was low. I held her hands. It was night, and the Ford was parked with its lights out in a blind alley behind a municipal parking lot a few yards from U.S. 11. I was about to walk back to the campus and April had turned her car around to head to her home. I had managed to make her give me a phone number where I could reach her at least once in the two weeks I would be away.

"Be better if you don't call me," she said. "We'll kiss, we'll part, we'll miss each other a lot, and we'll see each other in two weeks. Be faithful to me."

On the drive down into the heartland, I'd thought about those parting words. *Be faithful to me.* I remembered them in the Kendalls' car, and again the next morning when their black maid served our brunch. To me, being faithful didn't simply mean resisting Jessica's advances. It also meant respecting people whose skin was the same color as that of the girl I loved. Once I knew April, I no longer looked at blacks as I had before. Until then, in the pure white world of the Shenandoah Valley, I'd been blind to their very existence. So when Bob gave an order to the maid, I tried to detect in his voice the note of condescension that April told me she invariably heard whenever a white person addressed a black.

"It's a part of them," she said, "they can't help it, it's part of them. They don't even hear it themselves. They don't listen to themselves." And she had added, "That's why I kissed you that first day. You looked so alone and guilty, I felt sorry for you, but what really hit me was that you talked to me without that tone in your voice—*their* tone—and you can't imagine the impact that can have."

The Kendalls' maid was named Charlayna. She was an overweight, graceless, motherly woman with a low forehead who clomped around heavily on her thick legs. I listened to Bob, but I couldn't hear the tone April had cautioned me about and that she hated so. He was friendly toward Charlayna, sometimes adopting the playful repartee he used with his mother. But one evening when I thanked Charlayna for ironing the only white shirt I'd brought with me to Dallas, and which I had to wear nearly every evening, Bob stared at me. He then whispered in my ear, in French, "Why do you talk to Charlayna that way? You're *funny*."

I thought he might have heard something in the gratitude I'd expressed to Charlayna that betrayed my relationship with April, and I was afraid he'd make fun of it as he did of everything else. My fear made me uneasy. I was in for a much more uneasy time of it a few days later.

In the middle of that hot, idle afternoon, Bob announced, in a voice that brooked no argument: "I'm sick of playing cards. Let's go for a ride. Mom's lending me the car."

He shook the keys at me, and off we went in the huge Cadillac. "We'll pick up my buddy Fred," Bob said. "Then the three of us'll go get us some black pussy."

The expression was so crude that at first it didn't sink in. We stopped at a nearby house for Fred, a tall boy with a crew cut and nondescript looks, then the Eldorado took off in a direction I had never been in before. The landscape changed: the neat lawns gave way to a wasteland of sparse weeds and stones; the houses were less showy and more squat. We crossed two freeways and finally reached a rundown motel with yellow walls and a flashing blue neon sign that

announced VACANCIES at every second blink. There
wasn't another car in sight, not a passerby.

"We'll go in first and settle on the prices," Bob told
Fred. He looked at me. "Then we'll come back for
you."

"Bob," I said, "I don't want to."

"You don't want a nice black mama? They're good,
you know. Last time we had one as big around as
Charlayna, with a nice, plump black pussy. Doesn't
that speak to you?"

"No," I said, "I'm not in the mood."

"You wait here for us," Bob said. "We'll go dicker
over prices. By the time I get back, I bet you'll be
in the mood."

They got out, and I watched them walk to the door
of a cabin that opened onto the concrete parking lot.
The ritual seemed cut and dried: they knocked twice
at the door, a black man in an undershirt opened it,
and all three of them went inside. A few minutes later
they came out—Bob, Fred, and the pimp—and went
next door. On his way Bob flashed me a *sit tight* signal. I guessed that they had settled on the prices and
were now going to inspect the merchandise, for a moment later Bob emerged, followed by a matron in a
pink housecoat whom he asked to turn and face the
car. He was showing her to me. She seemed heavily
made up and ageless. After a few seconds she went back
into her room. Bob and Fred came out to the Eldorado
while the black man waited at the open door.

Bob bent over and spoke to me through the open
car window.

"They're offering us a cut-rate deal, if that's okay
with you. Twenty bucks a shot, but if we all take
the same chick, it goes down by five bucks each time.

Which means you can pork her for ten dollars—if you're willing to go last, after Fred and me."

"I'm still not in the mood," I replied weakly.

"Or," Bob continued, "if you'd rather, there's another nigra, same style, same room. So you don't have to go with the same one, but in that case we each pay the full rate."

"I'd rather not, Bob."

"You don't have the money, or you don't want to?"

"Both."

"I'll buy you one, if you like. Here's ten bucks. It's my Christmas present to you. Twenty, if you like."

"Look, Bob, I keep telling you. I don't want to. I can't, that's all, I'm not in the mood."

"Scared you'll catch the crud? Not to worry, I've thought of everything."

He took a small, flat, colorless, rubbery-looking object out of his wallet and held it up to me.

"Thanks anyway," I insisted, "but I'm not in the mood. I can't do it."

Exasperated, Bob waved away the discussion and turned his back to me. He and Fred rejoined the pimp. I saw the boys hand their money over to the black man, who stepped aside to let them enter the room where the woman was waiting. He went back to his own room, and I waited, watching the hands jump on the big, opalescent dashboard clock.

Disgust seeped through me. I wanted all this to end. I wanted us far away from this dismal place that not even the December-afternoon Texas sun could brighten. I wasn't thinking of April. All I could think of was how embarrassed I felt toward Bob and his friend, and I vaguely feared that my refusal would sour the good mood that, so far, had pervaded my stay in the Kendall home. And since I was grateful to Bob for his hospitality, I blamed myself for disappointing him. I certainly didn't blame him. His down-to-earth bluntness throughout that scene hadn't really shocked me; I figured it must reflect the upbringing that he and Fred had been given by other men, by their fathers, and that this upbringing was normal in their region, their time, their social circle.

It also seemed to me that I had jumped from one foreign land to another, and that the difference was dizzying. What a universe separated that sweetly comforting campus in Virginia, with its gentlemen students' code of manners, from this miserable blotch of cow pasture surrounding Dallas, this desolate and faintly threatening motel. This wasn't the first time since my arrival on this continent, for which nothing had prepared me, that I'd felt my stomach go hollow, my head spin, that I'd been teetering on a precipice. No sooner had I grown used to one color, one accent, one landscape, than other colors, other music, other settings shook up everything I'd learned. Between the moments of beauty and happiness I thought I'd found, then, were these abysses and this emptiness, this nausea, this gut fear and feeling of belonging nowhere, of being cut off from my roots in limitless, omnivorous America.

Then I thought about my family—of my father, with his white hair and protective authority; of my mother, with her inexhaustible reserves of indulgence and her encouragement of everything I attempted; of my oldest brother, whose charm and maturity I admired; of the shy, withdrawn brother several years his junior; and, finally, of my third brother, my youngest brother, of whom I had at first been jealous and whom I now cherished. I reviewed our games, our coded language, our signals of recognition, our meals together in the comfortable apartment on the rue de Longchamp in Paris—that whole family world that, until now, had shielded me from all wounds.

Now I was alone and picking my way along the rims of one precipice after another. Sadness swept over me. I longed to see my brothers and my parents again. Yet, at the same time, I saw clearly that I had begun a journey, and that I loved travel too much ever to consider turning back.

22

Bob SHOWED NO OVERT DISAPPROVAL OF MY DE-cision at the motel, but his attitude toward me changed abruptly. The adjective *little* recurred frequently when he talked about me to his mother: "our little friend," "our little Frenchman," "the little fella." And when he introduced me to the hosts at the parties we were subsequently invited to, it was with a slightly apologetic smile, as if he were no longer very proud of his Christmas houseguest. His friend Fred was there sometimes, and I thought I saw them snickering and whispering to each other when they looked at me. I realized that I had to act fast if I didn't want to lose the two boys' respect. I didn't want to endure their barbed jokes forever.

On the eve of our return to college, Mrs. Kendall's turn finally came to repay the countless invitations

we had received to the neighboring mansions. Throughout the day, Bob, his mother, and I worked to make
sure all was in order in that house overrun with cater-
ers, florists, decorators, and extra help. To me it was
especially trying because I sensed an invisible wall of
disappointment and distrust rising between Bob and
me.

So, while we were moving the table from the main
dining room into another wing of the house, I remarked to Bob, "I hope you've invited Jessica."

"Naturally," he said. "Why?"

"You still think I ought to kiss her?"

There was a marked pause before he replied. "If you
can, little man, if you can." Now he wasn't even con-
cealing his scorn.

That made me more determined than ever. The party
that evening was an explosion of noise, of singing,
and that piercing Texan exclamation: *yaa-hoo*. This was
the last of the holiday blowouts; tomorrow the children of those privileged families would return to their
colleges and universities; the fathers would fall back
into their business routine; and the mothers would return to their club meetings and their good works, or
they would leave for the beaches of Mexico to rest up
from that exhausting period that had left their com-
plexions muddied and their hair brittle. So everyone
drank more than he had the previous evenings. The
bourbon and eggnog did their work: groups dissolved
as quickly as they formed, and you could already hear
the splashes of fully dressed men diving into the pool
to sober up.

Amid all the din, I went over to Bob and, since the
noise volume rose as the evening progressed, I shouted
into his ear, "I'm going to your room with Jessica.
Come up in ten minutes and you'll see for yourself
if I could kiss her."

I saw a gleam of excitement in his eyes. Turning my back to him, I walked straight over to the girl from Shreveport in her filmy pink dress with white ribbons. She was sipping a mint julep and, from the way she stood weaving on her feet, I could see she had already drunk too much.

"Jessica," I told her solemnly, "the time has come." I was also more than a little tight.

"What?" she asked. "Time for what?"

"Time for us to . . . kiss," I announced portentously, "alone, far from the madding crowd."

She batted her doll's eyelashes and gazed out at me from under them. "What a divine idea," she said. "I've been waiting for this."

We went upstairs, carrying our drinks, and I steered her into Bob's room, carefully refraining from locking the door or turning on the lights. We drained our drinks, gauging each other like a pair of duelists about to cross swords. She seemed ready for anything.

"Jessica," I intoned, "do you really want me to kiss you?"

"Oh, yes, I adore to be kissed and kissed again. I like it to go on and on."

She smelled of mint and shampoo. I took her in my arms and we kissed standing up against Bob's bed. Jessica was a necker emeritus. She had a cool, pointy little tongue that she darted into my mouth and just as speedily withdrew while keeping her parted lips pressed to mine. She went on like this—quick, repeated little licks, like a cat cleaning its coat. It was exasperating, because I wanted to hold on at least once to that deliciously flickering thing that I never had the time to savor.

To maintain the offensive, I pressed her down on Bob's bed. She didn't protest. She merely heaved a brief sigh. I stopped kissing her for a moment. Jessica had shut her eyes and seemed to be waiting to be possessed; her low-cut dress revealed swelling breasts; ribbons floated in disorder around her legs, which she had opened when she lay down, having carefully hiked up her skirt. I had felt no desire for her when we entered the room and I'd been mentally counting the minutes, hoping that Bob would burst in to observe that I was no less a man than he. But there was still no sign of him. And now that Jessica was offering herself, and her teasing had so excited me, I was caught up in the spirit of the moment. I wanted her. Catching fire, I sprawled on top of her, trying to imprison her mouth, my hands foraging through the ribbons and the petticoats in a sudden frenzy. When I met no resistance from Jessica, I tried to speed things up.

Then, suddenly, she started violently and bit my tongue so hard and so deliberately that I recoiled with a yelp of pain. There I was, standing with my tongue hanging out of my mouth, bare-assed, my dick poking stiffly out above the pants around my knees—and I heard Bob and Fred howl with laughter. I looked behind me. The two boys were standing in the doorway. They had stepped aside to let Jessica race out, and now they were hugging themselves in an ecstasy of laughter. My tongue hurt too much for me to defend myself from ridicule. Bob came up for air long enough to advise me to get dressed and go and bathe my bloody mouth.

"Well, well," he sputtered, his eyes dropping to my cock, "you're a damn fast worker."

Despite the laughter still erupting from him and Fred, I now knew that I would hear no further innuendos about my virility from these two Texans.

The next day, and throughout the drive back to Virginia, I had trouble talking; Jessica's teeth had drawn blood, and my tongue was badly swollen. I had to submit to Bob's wisecracks and his arch glances, but in fact he was highly pleased with my performance. He had told the whole story to his mother before we left, which had given them a whole morning of jubilant complicity. She had hugged me as if I were her second son. "Drive carefully," she admonished us.

Then we left, with Bob's eyes lingering in the rearview mirror on his mother's dark, slender image, wrapped in her red silk bathrobe. Before the Kendalls' splendid home vanished from sight in the prairie behind us, Bob murmured softly, mysteriously, "You know, Mom has Cherokee blood in her veins."

I wanted to ask him about the father who was never seen, never mentioned, about that absence that I had thought weighed so heavily in that huge house. But something told me to avoid the subject. Bob said nothing more about his mother. He switched on the radio, and that was how my Christmas in Texas ended.

23

I WENT BACK TO THE BARRACKS. APRIL WASN'T THERE. The ravine was empty. From a booth on the campus, I called the number she had given me and that I hadn't dared dial from Bob Kendall's house. There was no answer. I toured the parking areas where we'd huddled on our last three nighttime meetings. No sight of April's blue Ford.

Had something happened to her? I wondered. Had she and her family left town? How was I going to find out? Our pact of secrecy prevented me from going near her home or the school where she taught. This went on for several days. I couldn't keep my mind on my classwork. I fell behind in my lessons. I slighted the extracurricular activities I had forced myself to participate in: the International Relations Club, the *Student Gazette,* and so on. At the fraternity house where I had my meals, I lost touch with the other boys, arriving just in time to sit at the end of the table and bolt down my fried chicken without saying a word to my neighbors, then leaving before coffee was served.

No one made the slightest effort to hold me back. Americans are profoundly social animals; they extend their friendship to whoever seems to want it. It's like tennis: if you don't hit the ball, no one will return it to you. I felt that April's unexplained silence was a crucial event that I could not share with anyone at all, and this reinforced the tragedy of my situation. Perhaps I enjoyed being blue and dragging my despondency around the snow-clogged campus. Perhaps I wanted to get used to what I thought was the start of a deeply melancholy life. But it didn't last.

Several signals lighted up to show me that I was not meant to suffer like young Werther, that I hadn't come to America to wrap myself in a romantic mantle of unconsoled gloom. No longer would I play the Hamlet of the freshman dorm.

24

LIKE ALL THE OTHER STUDENTS, I HAD RENTED A box in the small post office that stood atop a low rise on Lee Avenue, opposite the Lowitz menswear store. Mine was No. 13, and that day there was a letter in it from my family.

My oldest brother, having graduated from reserve officers' training school, had been sent to Algeria, where what was not called a war but a police action was spreading. He was a second lieutenant in a marine regiment, commanding a small fort on a remote hill south of Oran; no week went by for him without a skirmish, or without coming under rebel fire. He wrote my father that a friend had committed suicide by shooting himself in the throat with his rifle, and that the man's brains had spattered the room's ceiling and walls; he did not say why his buddy had done this, but my parents couldn't sleep for thinking about it.

They had enclosed a picture of my brother in their letter; he was wearing a dented kepi and a dark canvas jacket on which his officer's stripes stood out. The nose he had broken years before in a rugby match looked sunburned. His face wore a raffish expression, a look of defiance; it was one I'd often seen, but the constant presence of death had drawn an indefinable veil over it. There were two young men beside him in the photo, and a cross drawn in ink on the back of the print meant that one of them was already dead.

I tried to imagine my brother in that country which, until now, we had known only through our geography books, but I couldn't begin to guess what he was going through. I never dreamed that this conflict he had been thrust into would become that of a whole French generation. Nor did I consider that I, too, would be caught up in it someday. I didn't begrudge him his dashing image, either, although I knew that henceforward my parents would be thinking mainly of him and his constant confrontation with death rather than of me and my foray into America.

I had always loved and admired my brother. Although we were separated by a mere three years, I had felt when he reached manhood that I could never catch up with him; I, after all, was just a complex-ridden, introverted, graceless teenager. Physically he had matured quickly, and I had looked up to him as the first of us boys to confront and conquer those unexplored regions of voice changes, long pants, the right to make phone calls, to smoke cigarettes, to take exams, to fall in love, to be free.

While our parents had never encouraged open rivalry among us, the mechanisms of stimulation and competition were set in motion very early on. As children, my brother and I fought a lot. Sometimes we bloodied each other, and he always won. He was the tougher guy. I didn't know what my other brother, the one who was born second, thought of all this, but I knew I had often felt sick with frustration, silently swearing that someday I'd beat him. For longer than I could remember, I had secretly tried to overtake him, or at least to impress him, to make him admire me, to make him blink first. When I, in a systemwide competition, won a coveted one-year scholarship to a school in the United States, one of the things I felt was jubilation at flying over my older brother's head. I had become the American, the one who was about to travel to the end of the world. And he would have to stay home and wait like my other two brothers to read my letters for news of my tribulations and my triumphs.

Yet here he was now, sleeping on an army cot in a shack atop a rock, under the threat of a bullet or a knife at his throat. What this stirred in me was no feeling of jealousy, but a sharp spasm of love, and of fear for the safety of this cherished brother. This response upset all my calculations. Suddenly enough clarity shafted into my inexhaustible narcissism to give me some detachment; I could stand beside myself like a stroller beside his shadow and think about what was happening to someone else, and compare that with what I was going through. My little romance with April took on an air of absurdity, and a terribly adult thought occurred to me: things weren't as serious as they seemed.

25

OLD ZACH RECEIVED ME IN HIS OFFICE, WHICH WAS hazy with Amsterdammer and Bull Durham smoke.

He was the liberal arts dean, in charge of the literature, history, and journalism departments, all the things I loved and had elected when I first arrived at the college. Almost everyone called him by his nickname, but his full identity was Zachariah Wilhelm Gilmore.

Adorned with a splendid mane of white hair, he was one of the living legends on campus. It seemed that he had always been there, and that he would be forever. He was part of the landscape along with the Doric columns and the rolling lawns. Entire classes of freshmen had dreaded and adored him because he meted out justice fairly and with humor and, to everyone's delight, cultivated his persona of an impenetrable yet accessible giant. He was the only dean whose office door was, literally, always open. When you passed his office, if you glanced through the wisps of pipe smoke and over his secretary's head, you would see the stooped figure of Old Zach, in one of his indestructible light gray suits, listening to some student explain his problems. Puffing on his pipe, his eyes all but hidden behind quadrifocal glasses, he would clear his throat and dispense wickedly well-worded advice.

He was an eccentric. He had lived part of his youth in the Montparnasse of the Twenties, with its great colony of American expatriates. During World War II, Old Zach had worked in an unidentified section of Wild Bill Donovan's Office of Strategic Services. He had come home loaded with medals, but no one had yet heard a full account of his exploits. He had maintained contact with what was known as "the world of intelligence," and made occasional trips to Washington for meetings on unspecified subjects about which no one on our small campus ever learned anything. When he went to the capital, Old Zach did not stay at a hotel, but at the Cosmos Club, the most exclusive in the city, a haunt of intelligence veterans and barons of politics and finance. We knew this because on one of his trips, he took along a few students whom he had turned over to the editor of a major daily to learn the arcana of newspapering while Zachariah Wilhelm Gilmore went about his mysterious business.

His stay in Montparnasse had left him with a weakness for anything Old World and, particularly, French. I didn't see much of him outside of class, but he had taken a liking to me, especially after I gave him an authentic French beret at the onset of winter. It was a real beret, very round, very French, a caricature of a beret, wide, black, and malleable, that I had sent for from home; Old Zach proudly wore it every day. He was a sight to behold as he rolled cautiously down the snowy hills from his house on his big, black bike to pedal along the campus paths with his pipe in his mouth, his heavy glasses sitting low on his long nose, the beret screwed down on his mass of white hair, his long arms and long legs straining under the gray fabric he invariably wore. His vanity forbade him ever to don a raincoat, overcoat, or cape, so that no one ever saw him in anything but a three-piece suit. Old Zach, whose opinion meant more to us than anyone else's, the covert hero of the secret wars, the sage with the antique vocabulary who, as far as any of us knew, might once have been an expert at torture and sabotage. *Old Zach* . . .

He directed me to a seat and studied me wordlessly for a moment. Then, in his cavernous, gravelly voice, he announced that he wanted to talk to me about me.

"I've been watching you for quite some time," he said, "and I have come to the conclusion that something is wrong."

He waited for me to respond, but nothing came, which didn't seem to surprise him.

"I don't know what it is," he finally went on, "and I am not going to try to find out. But it is obvious that you are not yourself. Your grades are deteriorating; your attention wanders in class; you are even less diligent in your work at the radio studio and the *Student Gazette*."

How much did he really know? Wasn't his claim to know nothing simply a shrewd method of interrogation? He said very little; I said nothing at all. He sucked on his pipe, emitting curls of blue-gray smoke. Then he did something you didn't often see: he took off his glasses. Suddenly he looked like another man, a more awesome Zachariah, less dean and more inquisitor.

"Come closer," he ordered, "as close as you can. At two inches I begin to see."

I had to get up, lean over his desk, and peer eyeball to eyeball at him. His eyes were two small, black dots sunk into his flesh like a pair of nail heads, two black fleas in those gelatinous whites. It was both terrifying and hypnotic; you were a prisoner of those two

round, hard, dead-looking points that seemed to sink
into your soul like steel drill bits pulping the crum-
bling wood of an old cabinet. In his legendary past,
had he already used this trick to interrogate spies? I was
paralyzed.

A moment later Old Zach pushed me away, none
too gently. He motioned to me to sit down again
and, very slowly, he repositioned his glasses on the
bridge of his nose. Then he started talking again,
weighing his words in that silent office where I could
no longer distinguish anything clearly; the power of
Zach's eyes and the weight of his words had blanked
out everything around us.

"I'm going to tell you something very simple and
very fundamental," he said confidentially. "It is this:
Don't spoil it. Don't spoil your year."

He took a breath, then went on, articulating his
words as if he were dictating a telegram. "You are
spoiling what may be a unique period in your life, an
interlude of inestimable value. What you are experi-
encing here is priceless."

And, as if he thought he had not decoded the message clearly enough, he added something that was to
stay with me for a very long time: "Do not give that
dark streak of weakness and baseness that's in all of
us the satisfaction of making you a failure."

He waited for the words to sink in, contemplating
their effect on the young man facing him. I couldn't
find anything to say, and I had the feeling he expected
no reply. When he decided that enough time had
passed, underscored by enough silence, he set his huge
carcass in motion.

He stood up and shook my hand briskly. And I took
leave of Old Zach.

26

OF ALL THE SIGNALS I RECEIVED THAT WINTER, THE most insidious was probably the one flashed by April herself.

I did see her again, in the ice-sheathed ravine beside the barracks. I had been going there faithfully twice a week, waiting despite the cold and blizzards, and April had finally returned. She was as beautiful as ever; the sight of her eyes, iridescent gold, made my heart pound as it had the first day. She wouldn't make love with me. She wanted to talk. She answered my questions with a kind of smiling detachment; she had been very busy at her little school after the holidays; cousins from Delaware had been visiting at her house. Mostly, she said, she wanted to find out what I'd do if she didn't show up.

"I really expected you to seek me out at home or at school," she said.

"I promised I wouldn't, ever again. You always said it was too risky."

She laughed.

"Sure," she said, "but if you'd really wanted to see me, if you had really wanted me, you'd have ignored the risk."

"But we swore to it!"

"Well, now, if I'm following you correctly," she

126

went on, "your reputation on campus seemed more important to you than our . . . relationship. That it?"

I couldn't understand where April was leading me. What kind of an act was this?

"You put reason before lust. And after all, why not? I also wondered if you hadn't met another girl, some beautiful white girl in Dallas, or maybe here after you got back."

"Of course not," I protested. "There's never been anyone but you."

"Just the same . . . just the same . . . You certainly must have been having a fine time in Dallas if it didn't occur to you to phone me, not even once."

"It was difficult," I said. "I was in someone else's house."

"You don't have to make excuses."

I had the impression she was playing with me. Her voice was softer, more melodious than usual, as if she wanted to envelop me while still keeping her distance. Gone was the hoarse whisper that accompanied our rapid lovemaking on the backseat of the Ford, when, with her mouth close against my ear, she taught me the raging, naked language of the sex act. And as we reached climax—for we reached it together, and that was another thing that linked us so tightly—her voice would go more raspy and cracked, more primitive. Today April was talking at a different pitch, and I finally grasped that she was playing with my emotions, looking for ways to make me feel guilty so as to strengthen her hold on me.

"I expect," she murmured, "that since you've been back you've been dating again on Saturday nights."

"That's right."

"And I guess you're already wondering who you're going to take to the Fancy Dress Ball. Which Southern belle have you picked? You must have one in mind."

There were three big dances during the school year, one per quarter. The Fancy Dress Ball at the beginning of Lent cut the winter in two. At this stage in our college life, most of the boys had developed close enough relations with girls in the nearby valley colleges so that they could make plans: reserving a room in town for the girl and her chaperon; registering the girl's name with the only decent local florist so that the traditional Florida orchid could be delivered fresh two hours before the dance began; and saving up enough money to meet the expenses of this important event, which lasted two days and one night—the night of the ball itself.

But I had no date in mind, and I was starting to feel the same anxiety that had assailed me before Christmas, the same fear of ending up alone, separated from my friends, missing out on one of those great occasions that weld a class together. April knew all this. "At my college in Baltimore we had the same rituals you have," she'd once told me. "We Negroes went through all that, too. We're as American as any white. And we've learned to imitate whitey in everything, even society games."

Knowing the inner rhythm of our campus life, she was also using this new barrier between us, belaboring me for the betrayal I was inevitably going to inflict on her by lending myself to such *games*. This was a cruel pose that she abruptly dropped, suddenly breaking off her act.

"What's between us is completely offbeat," she said calmly and soberly. "You know that. Well, you don't really know it. But I do. And no matter how strange our relationship is, I'm not strong enough to resist ordinary impulses like jealousy and possessiveness and all that nonsense."

Now her voice rang with conviction again. I even thought I caught the familiar tone of our old intimacy, a reawakening of our collusion.

"Please forgive me," she then said. "I'm behaving like a bitch."

Her lovely face puckered. All my defenses crumbled.

"No you're not," I said faintly.

She moved closer to me. Her lips parted, red and moist. "You still want to?" she whispered.

"Naturally," I said. "What do you think?"

"Let's do it," she murmured breathily, and those three furtive words stirred all my old yearning to touch her skin, to plunge my fingers into her richly musky hair, to taste that honeyed mouth, and melt into that alien body.

And so I did, with heightened passion because April had so skillfully manipulated me that I had wavered again and again between my guilty conscience and my fear of losing her; she seemed more desirable because I had thought she was slipping away from me, and because her crowning confession of weakness had convinced me that she was more intelligent than I. My lovemaking was rougher and more voracious and hurried and despairing. "It's lovely," she said, "it's lovely, as if we were going to die as soon as it's over."

Yet, inevitably, I was left with a taste of bitterness and ashes—a new sensation, which I recognized with surprise.

Walking alone along the campus path, I kept telling myself that April and I were together again and that I had scored a victory, but the rest of me seemed to have suffered a defeat. I had been a puppet in her hands. I had finally realized this, and a voice within me said I had no right to make love to her again, yet

I would. Again and again. We'd promised each other we would. We had separated on words uttered as both a kiss and an order: "You'll be here, huh?" And I hadn't said no. It was night, a cold night; she had dropped me off at the other side of the empty lot and I had walked back across the paths shivering in my old black duffel coat that flapped around my legs without really protecting them. I was hungry, too; making love had left me hungry and all I had on me was fifty cents and it was too late to grab something at the co-op, the only place I could have eaten for that price. It occurred to me that I was going to have to earn some money.

27

MONEY WAS ASSUMING GROWING IMPORTANCE IN my life. American money, dollars.

I needed dollars to dress better. I'd arrived on the campus at the start of the school year with a trunk my mother had packed with my Paris high-school-boy clothes, and I had thought that would do me for a year. But I had quickly realized that in the complicated society I now inhabited, each season imposed its special uniform. There were fashions and styles and currents to which everyone bowed, and if you wanted to belong, you had better wear certain ties and certain fabrics, certain colors and certain cuts. In winter you had to have tweed and flannel and cashmere or lambswool.

I wanted to throw away the old duffel coat I had
bought at a British navy surplus store in Pigalle, but
I needed dollars to buy new clothes at Neal W. Lowitz,
the shop that dictated Ivy League style for all the campus gentlemen: a heavy, straight-cut, tailored overcoat, dark blue with dark blue buttons and lined with
black baize. It cost a lot of money, but everything at
Lowitz's was expensive and everything there was
good-looking.

The entire store breathed of rich young men. Two big
chandeliers lighted the racks of jackets and slacks. The
parquet floor gleamed. There were piles of button-
down Oxford shirts on the walnut-wood shelves. The
Virgin Islands shaving lotion smelled of dollars.

Neal W. Lowitz was a short, plump, bald Jew with
a bulging pate who was always dressed like the most
elegant of his elegant customers. He offered various
forms of charge accounts. His big ledger opened wide
to you and you had only to choose among the shirts
and shoes and scarves, and sign the book. At the end
of every quarter, Neal W. Lowitz sent you his bill, and
that brought you down to earth with a thud. Southern college boys' daddies were always ready to pay the
freight for sonny's sartorial whims, but mine wasn't.
Yet I wanted to be as well and warmly dressed as the
gentlemen around me; I, too, had heard the siren call
of appearances, and I needed American greenbacks to
satisfy what was both a new taste for clothes and a
vital need to conform.

I also needed money to pay my share on weekends
when we took our dates out for giant pizzas. It was
out of the question for our dates to spend a single
penny; on a night out, boys paid for the movies, the
popcorn and candy eaten there, and the little bunch of
flowers purchased after the show. On the way back

to the fraternity houses, boys would chip in to buy booze at the state stores, as well as soft drinks and ice. We all shared the expenses of fraternity parties.

None of this had been included in my scholarship, which covered only my tuition—steep at a private college even then—as well as my room and board in the dorm, and my books. In the scholarship awarded by that international jury, no provision had been made for the costs of social life. And my father, who had given me some money at the start of my great adventure, hadn't planned for these extras in his budget, either. I could never have imagined what sort of tribe I was being initiated into, or what customs I would be called upon to observe. You needed money for your laundry and upkeep, money for scents and oils, money to stay in the race. Everything was expensive. Everything tempted me. I discovered American-style consumption and, without plunging head over heels into it, since I couldn't afford that, I was nevertheless its willing victim.

The dollar had made its impression on me. I had witnessed its power. I became instantly used to this currency, to the childish simplicity of its subdivisions, the smell of its paper, the green and white colors of the bills that happened so oddly to coincide with the prevailing hues of the valley into which I had been transplanted. In a purely carnal way I had felt the dollar's omnipresence in our daily lives, its fundamental necessity. And since I was always a bit shorter on dollars than most of my fellow students, I had developed a love-hate feeling toward money.

Last, but not least, I needed dollars to buy gas for Cal's Buick, when I could manage to borrow it from him for my nocturnal meetings with April. I finally decided I needed dollars, lots of them, to buy a used car, for the conclusion was luminously clear: acquiring an automobile would solve a great many of my problems. I didn't want to rely on Cal when I saw April, but I wanted even less to have to rely on April's car. Nor did I want to go on tramping through the snow after dark, climbing up and down hills, shuddering with cold in my expatriate-schoolboy clothes. Because I felt strongly, even if I couldn't analyze why, that my predicament was partly to blame for the position of inferiority in which April had placed me.

The Ford was her home. She received me in it. I entered it and left it. Each time we parted, I was left standing alone on the sidewalk, in the snow, while April drove off at the wheel of her home—a humble abode, true enough, but more than sufficient. April could get around in her Ford. She could come—or not come—to the icy ravine or to the empty parking lots where I stood and waited, chilled to the bone, with my hands rammed into my pockets. I was at her disposal. And if I had wanted to visit someone else, that Southern belle she had predicted would come into my life someday, I couldn't have done it because I had no independent means of locomotion—in a country where space plays such an essential part. I needed money to conquer space.

I needed to earn money to be free to love who I wanted to love. As, where, and when I wanted. To pursue my journey.

I had to get *organized*. Discovering that I was sensual was not enough. I still had to organize my life. Sensuality and organization: a contradictory combination that struck me as I trudged back through the frosty darkness across the deserted campus to my dorm room. I realized with some asperity that desire couldn't run its course unless it was supported by effort, just as a thoroughbred horse won't race without a jockey to ride it.

By the next day I had worked out a program to amass funds. I put it into effect without delay. Aided by my favorite teacher, Rex Jennings, and his wife, I succeeded in widening my circle of customers for French lessons. Soon a dozen faculty wives were coming to my classes in the tiny barracks home three times a week.

In addition, Old Zach's influence landed me a job working several nights a week as a copyboy at the town newspaper. I cut off and delivered copy from the wire service Teletypes, sorted out the stories from county correspondents, and heated coffee for the two night deskmen. The two men, in turn, prepared copy for the pages that would be set up early in the morning and inserted into the full afternoon edition.

I knew that, modest as they were, these two regular sources of income could give me some standing at the local bank. I wasn't making any great waves, and it would take a lot of French lessons and many extra hours at the paper to buy that dark blue overcoat from Neal W. Lowitz—and even more to acquire my own car. But I hoped I could impress the fiscal powers. I was earning money. Maybe I could float a loan.

28

THE NIGHT EDITOR AT THE *VALLEY NEWS* WAS NAMED Jack O'Herlihy. He had worked for a long time as a United Press police reporter all over the South, especially in Chattanooga, Tennessee, where he had remained for several years. Then, in answer to an ad recruiting staff for the *News,* he had abandoned the police stations to work for this peaceful, prosperous paper in this tranquil valley where the opening of another mile of interstate expressway was news of cosmic significance.

I never knew why O'Herlihy made that move. The eyes in that fortyish, slightly alcoholic face were sunk in dark circles, and behind them something had irreparably snapped. He had a Southerner's courtesy and gentleness, and he seemed only to enjoy talking to people younger than himself. He said little to the two night deskmen, whom he nicknamed Heckle and Jeckle, after the two garrulous crows in a series of movie cartoons. On the other hand, Jack took obvious pleasure in explaining to me what was wrong and what was right in the copy I brought him.

"Sit down there," he'd say without looking up from the typed pages before him.

He used a red pencil, one of those copy pencils so thick and oily that they are wrapped in paper that you peel off the way you peel an orange. Jack worked over every line, meticulously crossing out, cutting, changing.

"That's too long, see? They used an unnecessary adjective there, too. No adverbs, no adjectives; short, clean sentences. You have to write cleanly, understand?"

He handed me the edited copy, peering at me over his half-glasses.

"Clean doesn't mean flat," he said. "It means terse, incisive, forthright, precise." He smiled. "My God, I used four adjectives to describe one. I'm getting weakminded. Now go have that retyped and then come back and see me. And bring some coffee. There's something I want to say to you."

What O'Herlihy had to say to me was annoying, but instructive: "You little gentlemen at the college are lazy devils. You're asleep. Have you got the slightest idea of what's happening in Charlottesville, only a hundred miles from here? You're hopeless, all of you."

He waited for me to ask, "What's happening in Charlottesville?"

"What's happening is that one of this country's rare geniuses is delivering a series of six lectures at the state university, and you don't know it. In any case, it doesn't seem to have made a dent on campus life. I certainly haven't noticed any stampede toward Charlottesville. Oh, I admit a lecture series isn't as fascinating as girls. But there are thousands of girls around here, whereas this country has only a handful of geniuses."

He paused, relishing the suspense now that he had played on my curiosity.

"Who is this genius?" I asked.

Like a true Southerner, Jack beat around the bush a bit more before furnishing a reply.

"If I remember correctly," he said, "this genius still has three more lectures to give. A young man with a little curiosity in his soul would be well advised to get a move on, even if he has to cut classes—even if he doesn't show up here for work one evening. I know his boss would gladly overlook that. Just so the young fella hustled over to see and hear the great man."

Another pause.

"Especially since it's you Europeans who keep proclaiming that the man's a genius. In this country writers aren't always recognized—as they are where you come from. Here they're isolated, lost in the desert. The great novelists—I'm not talking about the ones who write best-sellers, I mean the ones who put all their madness and passion and insight into what they write— these great novelists aren't always read and admired as they should be. Of course, being read and admired isn't all that important. What counts is having written."

It occurred to me that Jack was talking about himself now. He gazed blankly over my head, into the darkness at the other end of the city room.

"Everybody tries to tame the beast," he said, "to root it out of himself and trap it in his typewriter, get it on paper. You can ruin your life that way."

I didn't say anything. Questions were out of place now.

"You can mess it up a dozen times, but nothing prevents you from starting over again. Nothing."

He dropped his head, then quickly looked up at me. "Faulkner. That say anything to you? He's tamed the beast more times than most have. William Faulkner. You hurry over there, kid. If you don't have a car, there's a fine train out of Buena Vista every morning."

I didn't have the effrontery to ask him why he wasn't going, too, and a second later I was glad I hadn't,

for before turning back to the copy on his desk, Jack
told me he had in fact just come back from Charlottesville, where he had managed the rare feat of in-
terviewing Faulkner. The article was scheduled for
next Sunday's paper.

29

HARRY RIDDLE WAS ON THE PLATFORM UNDER THE
ocher-colored girders of the small, wood-roofed Buena
Vista station. His being there only half surprised me.
For a few minutes we pretended not to see each other.
It was obvious that he, too, was on a pilgrimage to
Charlottesville and that, like me, he was pretty proud
of himself for it, which explained why he had chosen the anonymity of a train instead of driving. That
way, when he got back he could brag about it to the
young freshmen who so admired his culture, his glib-
ness, and the ambiguity of the persona he affected.
When we finally dropped our little act on the platform, Harry admitted he would rather have been the
only man on campus to have gone and heard the great
author. But the fact that I was his sole competition
wasn't too bad. I didn't have his influence over the
other students, and I did not control the network he
had artfully woven through the fraternities.
  Riddle had his men in each of the fourteen fraternities on campus, thus breaking with the convention

that each fraternity was a house unto itself, with its own ritual, its own rules, its loyalties and its enemies, and, most of all, a unanimous pact of silence toward the outside. Silence concerning every detail of a house's internal life: quarrels, power plays, scandals, and the way these were dealt with.

Harry had an implicit power of seduction over the young men he attracted because the honesty of his sexual proclivities forged a deeper and more abiding bond than any temporary loyalty that they might pledge to a purely social institution like a fraternity. So Harry was informed of every wisp of gossip, every minor fluctuation in a house's mood. This gave him enormous pleasure. He had devoted his four years on campus to organizing his personal Mafia; he liked nothing more than to feel that he was in on everything, that he could influence even those faculty members who were open to his skillful proselytizing.

"We're the real power here," he boasted to me on the train that morning.

At a time and in a place that viewed homosexuality as a stain to be hidden like a skeleton in a closet, Harrison Riddle was bold enough to show his colors. For this he was admired by those who dared not, or could not, or who did not recognize those colors as their own. The others, the straights, hated Harry, or vaguely feared him because he was a force to be reckoned with; the arrows he could loose in the clustered ranks of our small community could wound.

"It's infernally cold this morning. That young creature over there must have the most horribly shivery thighs."

He said this in the avid, burlesque tone he always used in speaking of students younger than he, and whom he always vaguely feminized: "the darling," "the young creature," "the little dear."

On one of the wooden seats covered in brown plush at the end of our long, whites-only compartment sat the young creature in question: frail-looking, red-haired, wearing a lightweight tan raincoat better suited to less rigorous weather. The person's features were so delicate that, after careful scrutiny, I remarked to Harry that he'd made a mistake. What he thought was a boy was in fact a girl. Her hair, which would have been unusually long for a boy, seemed short and shaggy for a girl, especially a college girl— for a college girl she undoubtedly was. It was as if she'd taken a scissors and hacked off the hair at her neck and around the ears and had snipped away the locks that always adorned our dates' brows. Added to her total lack of makeup—no lipstick, no rouge or mascara—this made the girl in the raincoat look as if she were recovering from a serious illness. She was reading a thick book, the title of which I couldn't make out from where I sat. She kept looking up from her book and staring at me, forcing me to lower my eyes. She was beautiful.

I thought I'd seen those eyes somewhere before, that chin, that nose, but I couldn't remember where. Harrison Riddle, in any case, lost all interest in her the moment he realized that she was not a handsome boy. That's how the trip went, through the snowy countryside to Charlottesville. The girl in the tan raincoat left by the rear door. We lost sight of her for a moment, then encountered her again at the only taxi at the station entrance.

Imperiously Harrison blocked the girl's way and got into the cab. He waved me in with him and quickly told the driver, "The university, please."

The girl turned to me and spoke in so faint a voice that I had to lean over to hear her.

"I'm going there, too," she said. "Can I share your cab?"

"Certainly," I told her.

Harry scowled petulantly, but the girl's stumbling thanks gave him no choice, and he shifted his heavy body against the far door so that the three of us could fit on the seat. Then he barricaded himself in sulky silence, breaking it only to declare to rather than ask our passenger: "Of course you came to hear Faulkner's lecture."

"Of course," she murmured.

No one said another word throughout the ride. I felt the girl beside me shiver now and then in her light raincoat, as if she were cold or hungry or sleepy, but I had no chance to inquire about her health. The ride to the university was very short.

There was a small but dense crowd around the entrance to the auditorium in the university arts building. We had only to follow the students—boys and girls, since the state university, twenty times the size of our school, was coed—to the only open door. Before it were posted two young men who kept announcing, like guides in a museum lobby, "Students and faculty of the university, please show your identity badges. Nonschool auditors register for the waiting list at the other end of the lobby."

With the easy gesture of a member of some exclusive club, Harrison took a folded sheet of paper out of his coat pocket and flashed it under the nose of one of the monitors.

"Oh, certainly," the young man said after he'd read the note. "Go on in, please."

Around me, people were crowding calmly but persistently. On their faces I could read satisfaction or anxiety; this was clearly the event of the year at the university. Every indication sharpened your eagerness to share in this august occasion: the meticulous filtering of the guests, the hurried arrivals of elderly gentlemen who were obviously school worthies, the continuous but never ill-mannered babble echoing under the high ceiling. No news of Harry. I glanced across the lobby at the people who had signed up on the waiting list. Among some thirty hopefuls standing there impatiently I saw the girl in the raincoat; she smiled at me with the reserve she had shown in all our brief exchanges. I reflected that she might have made this whole trip for nothing, and so, in another few minutes, might I. Just then a guy with a shrewd face and big blue eyes pushing toward me through the crowd of latecomers nodded at me to move away from the auditorium door.

"I'm a friend of Harry's," he told me with a conspiratorial air. "Here's his pass. Show it at the very last minute so the monitors don't recognize it."

He handed me the precious note and went back inside. I backed off, turning away from the flurry around the entrance and marveling at Riddle's ability to maintain contacts and exert pressure even in another school. When I read the pass I was even more impressed. Typed on the letterhead of the dean of arts of the state university, it said: "Please admit the bearer of this note. He is a *Friend* of the university." The signature was illegible.

A bell rang, as though summoning a theater audience to the start of a play. The buzz in the lobby reached an acute pitch. I walked over to the girl amid

the loud protests of those who were not being allowed in.

"Want to come with me?" I asked her. "We can try
to get us both in on this pass."

"Thanks a lot," she said. "Thanks. This is the fourth
time I've come and I still haven't heard him."

It turned out to be easy. I showed Harry's pass to
the monitor who hadn't seen it the first time, and
when he looked questioningly at the girl, I took her
firmly by the arm and said, in my thickest French
accent, "She is my sister. We just arrived in your country yesterday on the *Queen Mary* and we drove all
night from New York to hear Monsieur Faulkner."

The monitor, jowly, pink, and chubby, made a sort
of bow. In singsong French in which he took a certain pride, he replied, "Mademoiselle and monsieur,
you are more than welcome in our university."

We were in. The auditorium was an amphitheater,
and someone pointed us to an empty space in one of
the last rows, on the steps that bisected the hall. I spotted Harry Riddle sitting like a potentate in one of the
front rows, surrounded by a handful of young men,
including the conspirator who had delivered his pass.
I wigwagged my thanks to him, which he waved ma-
jestically away. Fortunately, he didn't register that I
had used his largess to get the girl in, too, because I
knew he'd have hated that. But he was too immersed in the pleasure of being at the very heart of
things to notice her sitting beside me.

I had let go of her arm, and she shivered once or
twice as she had in the cab. Yet she didn't seem ill.
As I peered at her as we settled uncomfortably on the
steps, the blurred outlines of another face began to
take shape in my memory, the face of the girl she resembled and whom I had met before. But when? And

where? Something told me I would eventually super-
impose those two faces, and that they would blend
into a single image.

William Faulkner slipped quietly into the amphitheater carrying three books under his arm. The atmosphere suddenly congealed into respectful silence.
Contrary to custom, he did not stand behind the lec-
turer's chair at the left of a small platform. Instead
he sat down at a table on the dark brown plank floor
in the middle of the hemicycle at the foot of the platform, facing the fascinated spectators. A pitcher of water and a glass had been set out on the table.
He put his three books down carefully, as though
they were antique vases he was afraid of breaking.
His movements were as slow and erratic as his walk,
the movements of a man whom, it seemed, nothing
could hurry, not because he was stubborn, but because his mind was elsewhere. He had his own rhythm.
He appeared unaware of the world around him. Not
once did his eyes meet his listeners'; it was almost as
if he were doing everything he could to delay the moment when he would have to look up and see those
three hundred faces, would have to open his mouth
and articulate words. He had on a worn but handsome gray herringbone-tweed jacket, heavy gray flannel slacks, dark, ankle-high boots, a pale button-down
shirt, and a knitted tie. The tie was colored a garish
red, contrasting with the rest of his outfit.
Everything about him suggested remoteness. Or perhaps he was slightly sleepy, or crushed by a kind of
boredom, or embarrassment, as if he were wondering
what in the world he was doing there, among all
those strangers. He looked like those rare photos that
usually appeared on the back cover of his books. But

those pictures bespoke someone opaque, dense, almost massive, whereas Faulkner that morning seemed to me puny, frail, removed from reality. We were ordinary human beings, spectators won over in advance; he belonged to a different world, for he bore in him the immeasurable magic of what he had written and the enormous prestige of his loneliness and his struggles to spill his obsessions into words.

The girl beside me silently handed me a small pair of opera glasses that she had taken out of her raincoat pocket. Through them I could examine more closely the mask worn by this man who, along with two or three other writers in our century, had succeeded in giving a metaphysical dimension to action novels.

His yellowish-blond mustache looked like an old shepherd's. Puffy, pinkish bags swelled under dark eyes that were veiled by some gossamer film of damp mica and that looked unremittingly annoyed. Wrinkles rippled on his forehead, cheeks, chin, like trickles of rain on drought-ridden clay soil. He had a prominent, slightly aquiline nose. From that handsome face ravaged by whiskey and sleepless nights radiated a charm that was not merely the product of what we knew about him and his work, but of his looks themselves, of what those looks expressed. If you didn't know who he was and he happened by you in a bar or on a train, if you saw him sitting in a church pew, he would catch your eye as firmly as he did in this auditorium.

Now his words filled the intolerable silence. His voice was soft, so wan and weak that I sensed a kind of simultaneous movement of three hundred bodies leaning forward to hear him. We recognized the inimitable accent of his native Mississippi, part of the South we lived in, yet not the same South at all. He spaced out his sentences, pausing regularly between remarks. It was just possible he did this to catch his breath. It was more likely that he was choosing his terms carefully. Or he may simply not have been cut out for teaching.

This was not, properly speaking, a lecture, but part of a course in comparative literature, a series of critical analyses—of other writers' works, naturally—so the references he made to what he had said in his three previous appearances went right over my head. Besides, I had trouble following some of the analogies he drew between American authors whose books I had only just begun to study, or of whom I had never heard.

Around me, mainly below me since, from my place in the back, I could see the whole amphitheater, students were conscientiously taking notes. When their heads were not bent over their lined yellow pads, they were strained forward to catch the thin trickle of sound from the man in the red tie.

What must be called Faulkner's reluctance for public speaking made me wonder why he had agreed to give the course at all. He didn't really seem to like being there, though he never departed from the courtesy, the suave patience that people in the deep South have. Had he finally given in to pressure from his old friend, the dean of arts at the university, to whom he may in some drunken moment have made a rash commitment? Or had he simply agreed to spend four weeks in Virginia to make some money, in the same way that he'd make sporadic forays to Hollywood to work on the screenplays of whodunit movies? People said he was always trying to make a buck, that his publisher was stingy with advances, and that his roy-

alties from abroad, where he was probably more famous than he was at home, had long since been
swallowed up in running his farm.

O'Herlihy had asked him the question when he interviewed the author, and got no answer. In fact, Jack
had told me, he hadn't gotten much out of the great
man, and what Faulkner did say was not really suited
to a newspaper article. How could a regional paper pub-
lish Faulkner's few remarks on the incoherence of life
and the white man's disintegration, remarks that had so
dazzled O'Herlihy that he had repeated them to me
without having to refer to his notes?

I thought of all this as I observed the novelist's par-
simony with word and movement, and I concluded
that it didn't matter if I didn't really understand what
he was talking about, or even if I didn't take notes.
What counted was the event itself. I would certainly
have more incentive for plowing through those novels haunted by time and remorse now that I had seen
their author and heard his weary voice insisting, as
he sat bolted to his chair with his legs crossed and his
freckled hands lying like dead things on his knees,
that you cannot explain what constitutes the soul of a
book.

Barely an hour had elapsed when he suddenly stood
up in mid-sentence, murmuring that he felt a bit dizzy
and needed to rest; his auditors would please forgive
him, but anyway he had given them enough mate-
rial so that they could write the papers they were to
submit to him at their next session. His glance again
directed anywhere but at his audience, he picked up
the books he had leafed through during his lecture,
nodded almost imperceptibly to the assembly, piv-
oted, and, his back to the auditorium, walked out
with the same slow, disembodied step, amid the same

silence. Not a single comment was heard on the elegant but unexpected fashion in which he ended his lecture.

"Beautiful," sighed the girl beside me.

In the sudden commotion that arose when Faulkner closed the amphitheater door behind him, the girl snatched her opera glasses from my hand, muttered a hasty goodbye, and ran down the steps to the exit. I was still bewitched by what had happened in the past hour and, indifferent, I let her go, although I was a bit taken aback by her cavalier manner.

30

Harry Riddle told me he was spending the day in Charlottesville and that a friend would drive him back to school later. I went off alone to the station.

The girl in the raincoat was on the train, in the same seat at the end of the compartment, and I sat down opposite her. This was the first time I could scrutinize her face calmly, and not in profile, as I had before. I saw an ill-disguised gleam of willfulness in those lively eyes, and the way she held her chin suggested determination, the stamp of someone who doesn't like to lose.

"Mind if I sit here?" I asked.

"Not at all," she said, her tone reserved.

She closed the book she was reading. I vaguely noticed a Germanic-sounding name I didn't know. She slipped the book behind her back and contemplated the toes of her shoes as if to dissuade me from starting a conversation. I was not to be put off that easily.

"How far are you going?" I asked.

"I get off at the station after yours," she replied. "I assume you're going back to the gentlemen factory."

"You can call it that, yes," I said. "And if you're getting off at the stop after it, that means you're at Sweet Briar."

She repressed a laugh. "You have remarkable powers of deduction." She bit her lip in remorse. "Sorry," she added, "that just slipped out."

She straightened up, plunged her hands into her raincoat pockets, her face washed clean of treachery. Her boyish-cut hair looked like the helmet of a medieval knight about to go on crusade.

"It slipped out," she repeated. "I used to be like that. But I'm trying to curb the dark side of my nature. I've said farewell to arrogance."

She spoke quickly, like a child at confession, and suddenly I recognized her. At last I recaptured my first image of her, full-face, when she had worn her hair long and wavy and had terrified and dazzled me on the campus of her school. Of course, that's who she was! My recollection of the tip of her pink tongue between her pearly teeth had haunted my first nights in Virginia; I had thought about her for days on end: *a lovely, dangerous girl at Sweet Briar College; maybe you've got a chance with her and maybe you don't*. The man-eater, the queen, the girl who made my buddy Cal Cate, the football hero, blanch and writhe in humiliation. She had smelled of peaches or apples then, and it was autumn, and with her bright smile and

haughty bearing she had symbolized to me the perils
and charms of the American girl.

Now it was winter, and we were in a nearly empty
railroad car traveling through a frozen white plain. I
was no longer quite the person I had been, and neither was she. What had happened to her?

"I know who you are," I said.

"I doubt it," she replied. "I don't even know that
myself."

"I do. I know your name. Your first name, anyway. It's Elizabeth, and I met you a few months ago
at your school."

Her face, bare of makeup, twisted faintly in derision.

"You behaved then," I added, "like the queen of
the campus."

She was more interested now. "It's taken you all this
time to recognize me—since this morning, on the
train?"

"Yes."

"You didn't even recognize me in the auditorium?"
she insisted.

"No. That seems to please you."

"And how. Because it means I've really changed."

"You've changed, all right. You're not the same at
all. You'd even fool Cal Cate now."

She frowned. "Cal Cate? Oh—yes, of course. All
that seems so long ago."

"Do you remember me?"

"To tell the truth, I don't," she said.

I told her my name and asked hers, since all I knew
was Elizabeth.

"Don't you think," she retorted, "this conversation
is thoroughly pointless?"

"Yes, I do," I said, a little annoyed.

I looked out the window at the ice-sheathed pines
and cedars flitting past us. She leaned toward me.

"I apologize again," she said.

"That's too glib," I said.

"What?"

"That's right, it's too glib. You pretend you've said
farewell to arrogance, and when I believe you and
try not to deliver a pitch—you know, young man picking up a girl on a train—when I try to establish a
friendly relationship with you, what do you do? You
throw a dirty crack at me every other second and then
apologize. Uh-unh, that's just too phony."

She thought about it, then nodded.

"You're right," she said. "If that's how I come across
to you, it means I'm not actually cured yet, and that
really bothers me."

"Cured of what? Have you been sick?"

"I . . . I don't much want to psychoanalyze myself
in front of you," she said. "I don't even know you."

"What difference does that make?" I replied. "We
can learn to know each other, can't we?"

"I'm not interested in flirting with boys anymore.
All that's over."

"Who's talking about flirting?"

She gave me a long look, and then she smiled a genuine smile in which, if you made an effort, you could
see what had made her so egregiously feminine. Now
something had given it a new look, a sort of serenity
—edgy, but serene nevertheless.

"Don't hold it against me," she said, "I've lost the
habit of talking to boys. I've wanted so much to say
farewell to my horrible—ho-rrrr-ible—arrogance that I
don't even trust myself to talk to people anymore.
The humility I seek can only come through silence."

I was wondering if she had found all these catchphrases

in the mysterious German book her noticeably frailer body was pressing against when I suddenly realized the train was beginning to slow down. I didn't want to leave Elizabeth. The time had swept by too fast. I talked faster. I wanted to know more about her, and about the radical change in her appearance. By what metamorphosis had that flawless, sovereign, radiant creature been transformed in only a few months into this bizarre, shivering girl trying to punish or destroy herself? I wanted to touch her.

"You certainly dropped me like a hot potato at the end of Faulkner's lecture," I remarked. "For someone who preaches humility—"

"I knew you'd throw that up to me, I knew it! I can't tell you why I acted that way because if I do you'll think I'm completely twisted."

"No I won't," I said. "Absolutely not. Please tell me."

"No," she said, "I want to remain as smooth as a pebble in a river."

She looked vaguely through me. I felt I was losing her attention.

"At least tell me what you thought of Faulkner's lecture," I pressed her, trying to revive the conversation.

"You disappoint me," she said. "You don't talk about experiences like that off the top of your head. You absorb them, let them grow inside you, slowly, like a plant."

"You're right," I said. "Thanks for the lesson."

To my surprise, tears suddenly welled in her eyes. She began to shiver again, and she stammered, "I wasn't trying to teach you a lesson."

The train was moving slower and slower. And the closer we got to the station at Buena Vista, the more

I feared that the fragile thread I had stretched between us would snap.

"Never mind," I said, "it doesn't bother me at all. I even think what you just said is very fine."

But she wouldn't let go of it.

Her voice muzzy with tears, she tried to hold back. "It's awful," she protested, "your thinking I was trying to teach you a lesson. Awful! I don't teach lessons to anyone anymore, believe me. Not to anyone."

"Elizabeth," I said, "you haven't understood me."

She seemed to relax, and her trembling diminished. The train pulled into the station. I had cut three classes to attend Faulkner's lecture, and my twelve students were waiting for me in the barracks. I couldn't stay aboard and ride with the girl to the next stop. Yet neither could I detach myself from her and the riddle she presented.

"May I see you again?" I asked her.

She didn't seem to hear me. Resignedly, this time, she repeated, "You can see that relationships between the sexes always turn into a confrontation. It's always a case of who will win the battle of arrogance. Oh, I do hate arrogance!"

"May I see you again?" I insisted. "Will you give me a date?"

The train had stopped. I had to get up.

"I don't know what the word means anymore," she said, her voice flat.

"Please, Elizabeth, stop playing games."

"I'm not playing games."

"Neither am I," I said. "But I would honestly like to see you again. Listen, trust me, I'm not like the other boys at my college. We won't call it a date. We won't go out. I won't try to hustle you. We'll just talk. We won't even have a drink at a fraternity house. Okay?"

She smiled sweetly at me. "The train's going to take off again. You'd better get off."

I stormed out of my seat. "Well, so long," I said, "and please don't thank me for getting you in to hear Faulkner. If I'd known I was dealing with a pretentious little snob, I wouldn't have gone to the trouble."

On this graceless note, I jumped down onto the platform. As the train began to roll, a black conductor deftly slammed the doors, one after another. I wanted to wave goodbye to Elizabeth, but she was sitting on the far side of the car and I couldn't see her. That didn't bother me too much. I knew where to find her, and I'd made up my mind to do just that.

31

THE NEXT DAY I RECEIVED A LETTER FROM ELIZabeth. The handwriting was clumsy and closely written, compact, the words and sentences jostling each other in the middle of the page like a schoolboy's scribble. What caught my eye were the adverbs, which she had underlined, on nearly every line.

> The reason I dropped you, as you put it, at the end of the lecture was that I was *frightfully* afraid of owing you anything at all and, therefore, of having to be

engaging toward you, walking *amiably* to the station
with you, chattering *foolishly,* of forming some vague,
artificial relationship with you that would *certainly*
have ended up with your asking me for a date, which
I couldn't refuse, since you'd been so *insipidly* kind
to me.

I admit this was *disgustingly* selfish and petty of me.
Tactless, in fact. But I haven't entirely managed to
stamp out my manipulating, calculating instincts, on
which I've *absolutely* declared total war. And it all
turned out to be *utterly* pointless anyway, since I did
see you again after all, and you *naturally* asked to see
me again. But since you also left with a remark I
thought was *frankly* petty and, in fact, tactless, I guess
our two pieces of tactlessness *mutually* canceled each
other out.

All in all, I'd like for us to get together again, but it
would *definitely* have to be along the lines you pro-
posed. It mustn't be a date.

> Sincerely yours,
> Elizabeth Baldridge

At the bottom of the lavender-gray page: "You're
probably different from the others, since you didn't
once call me Liz, a contraction I detest *excessively*."

The letter enchanted me. I went through a dozen
drafts before coming up with an answer that satisfied me.

> I do not think you have a thoroughly twisted
> mind, but the only way to make sure is to have tea
> with you, which I will certainly do after I come
> and fetch you Sunday afternoon at 4:15, a time you'll
> agree does not fit at all into the ritual of dating.

I also added a P.S. with which I was especially

pleased: "Even in the clearest streams, all the pebbles
have two sides."

I chortled as I read over my metaphor, then I ran
deliriously to mail my letter, my feet hardly touching the ground. I was to meet April an hour later, in
the ravine behind the barracks.

April had predicted all this, I reflected, and she was
right: I'd already stopped being faithful to her. With
that innocence that haunts young hearts, I was convinced that my love life could not support two affairs at the same time. Besides, I was driven by some
deep-seated prohibition against lying to April. We had
nothing in common. Nothing but the backseat of a car.
Nothing: no social activity, no contact with other people, no mutual experience of life—a movie, a meal,
money problems, moods of the weather or the town.
We had never shared a moment in a real room, sat together at a real table, or lain together in a real bed.
We had never tested one another against the outside
world. We had not changed, never aired our opin-
ions before friends. Our relationship was formed out
of the single reality, raw and naked, of our sexual
attraction. We'd never had to mislead each other or anyone else. The subtle arrangements, the gradual slide
toward lies and omissions that other couples—adult or
not, who are immersed in a social system are subject
to—had not touched us; it did not lead us, as it does so
many others, to hypocrisy, compromise, and willful
misunderstanding. Since we were not social animals,
lying was useless and we never resorted to it.

So I felt I ought to tell her everything as soon as I
got into her car, before I kissed her or touched her.
But I hadn't sufficiently reckoned with our mutual hun-
ger. I made love to her first and hurt her afterward,
the way grown-ups do.

For a moment she said nothing. Her mouth, usually so prone to sarcasm, tightened briefly at the corners, and her head dropped. Then she raised it again. "I appreciate your honesty," she whispered. "Anyway, this kind of thing can't last. Or it ends in something vicious, or in shame."

"You used the word *shame* once before," I said. "The first time we did it, in the Buick."

"You see? I was wrong there. At least we've avoided that."

A wave of affection flooded through me and swept me toward her. I tried to take her in my arms. The sadness in her voice, the frailty that suddenly seemed to afflict her limbs, made her dearer to me just when I announced that we were breaking up. This awoke a glaring and characteristic weakness in me: I felt guilty. First you hurt someone, then you say you didn't mean to hurt them, and then, seeing the extent of the devastation, a sudden quirk of egotism makes you say let's forget this happened, let's act as if no one had ever been hurt. Let's go on as we were before.

April was too inured to pain to let herself be dragged onto this kind of merry-go-round. If she had tried to hang on to me, she could have. But she cut off any retreat and pushed me away firmly.

Her voice hardening as she spoke, she insisted, "If you hadn't done this, if you hadn't made the break, sooner or later I'd have told you we're through, that this can't go on, we can't spend our time fucking in a car in winter at the bottom of some crummy ravine." And she added, just as severely, "We're lucky I'm not pregnant. You were never very careful." She laughed harshly. "Cat got your tongue?"

It was true. I couldn't say a word. I wasn't very

proud of myself, yet I felt a cowardly relief that I couldn't understand.

"Maybe you were scared you'd knocked me up," she said. "What would you have done, huh? What would the poor little foreign student have done? How would you have handled that particular problem? For that matter, what would I have done? Did you ever even stop to think about it?"

"You're not, are you?" I murmured, hating my own pettiness.

She laughed again. "No, not to worry. There's no danger I ever will be, either."

April had occasionally said things, made veiled allusions that led me to suspect she'd had an affair like ours not long before I met her. It had been so easy for her to set up our meetings. At least twice she had referred to danger if our interracial mating were ever discovered. And she was so familiar with what went on at my college; I couldn't attribute all this lore to her maturity alone, to the few years she had over me. Had April already made love with a white student in the small town's empty parking lots? What had really happened? Now that we were on the point of ending that indefinable thing that had been our thing, I blurted out the question.

"No," she said, "nothing like this ever happened to me before, any more than it did to you. But I'll tell you the God's truth: I'd always wanted it to happen, I thought about it a lot, and when I saw a chance for making my wish come true, I didn't hesitate a second. You were pretty daring, too, but I'd been waiting for you without your knowing it."

She ran a pearly-tipped finger along my cheek. It made a slight scratching sound in the cavernous silence in the Ford.

"My little winter love, you were such a pushover. I could've done anything I wanted with you." Then she laughed, and rested her hands on the steering wheel. "Within limits, of course."

I kept still, focusing on the brown hands whose paler palms opened wide when we made love. She would close them little by little; then, when we reached our climax, both her hands would open and spread like a bird's wings. A poignant feeling of regret shook me, as I'm sure it did her. What had possessed me to tell her I was attracted to someone else? What need had I felt to demolish what was between us, and which was ours alone? I had no assurance that a single meeting with Elizabeth could ever lead to what April and I had experienced with our first embrace. Everything, in fact, pointed to a difficult relationship with what seemed a highly neurotic girl who, so far, at least, had shown only the most cursory interest in me. Neither my curiosity about Elizabeth nor my scruples about always telling the truth to my secret lover could explain my break with April. Other factors had brought me, obscurely and instinctively, to the ending we had now reached.

It was still too soon for me to foresee the need for April that would probably beset me later on—*need* in the sense that drug addicts understand the word after they've kicked the habit, when their bodies cry famine because it hurts too much to pry the monkey off their backs. Well, maybe I'd never experience that need after all. I wasn't thinking about that now, at any rate. But it was too late to try and save the impossible relationship that had filled the hidden hours of our lives. April had found the right words. It was all summed up in that terse, trite phrase that men and women use to justify whatever is ending, whatever is slipping away from them because it's ending: *it couldn't last.*

"Let's go," she said. "I'll drop you on the other side of the barracks, at the edge of the empty lot."

It was night. The Ford's headlights pierced the shadows in the ravine, then lit up the road that ran to the empty lot; I would shortcut across it, through the ice-crusted snow, to reach the sleeping campus.

"Don't kiss me," she said. "And let's not talk anymore. Let's just remember the beauty of it. That's something no one can spoil. Goodbye."

She kissed me lightly on the forehead.

"Goodbye," I said weakly.

Getting out of the car took an effort. I felt empty, with no links to the realities of the night, the cold, the pits in the snow. I watched the car's rear lights moving away from me. Then, briefly, they stopped. April had probably braked. Was she trying to spot me in the rearview mirror? At that distance, in that darkness, she couldn't possibly see me. I started running as fast as I could toward the car, running toward April. But the lights moved off again, and the car disappeared around a bend.

32

WHEN OLD ZACH WALKED INTO CLAY HALL THAT morning to deliver his Journalism II lecture on "Propaganda and Psychological Warfare," the expression on his veteran spy's face was even slyer than usual.

"Gentlemen," he said, settling his gray-clad frame into the Louisiana blond mahogany rocking chair that was carried into every classroom he taught in to pamper his deformed spine, "gentlemen, we feel called upon to comment today on an event of some importance."

He stopped and glanced along the rows of seats, heightening the suspense, his eyes unfathomable behind the thick lenses of his celebrated glasses. He always insisted that before we came into any of his classes, regardless of the day's subject, we scan the newspapers and listen to the radio news on the local station, WTEW, which picked up the network news, informing us of what was happening in the rest of the world, not just in the state of Virginia.

Old Zach invariably began a class with a series of questions to test our ability to synthesize events, and to gauge how well we separated what was meaningful from what was superficial. He called this "the morning sifter."

"For once," he said, "I imagine you all agree on what I consider the most vital piece of news on this day now getting under way."

Hands rose, but Old Zach declined to call on any of the students.

"The house I live in," he said as he began rocking slowly in his beloved chair, "is a very big house, as some of you may know, and I've been lucky enough to acquire a few acres of scrub and woodland that I deliberately refused to landscape."

We listened, captivated as usual by the mere sound of his voice, the rhythm of his sentences, but we couldn't see what he was getting at.

"Throughout the year I frequently see at least three types of fauna in this natural preserve. First, there

are the insects: the gnats, bees, bumblebees, mosquitoes, fireflies, and just plain flies. Then come the
birds."

He paused and, to our astonishment, let loose a kind
of tremolo of jubilation.

"The regular assortment," he went on, "consists of
crows, slate-colored juncos, purple finches, Carolina
wrens, white-throated sparrows, blue grosbeaks and
evening grosbeaks, goldfinches, mud hens, robins,
cardinals, yellow-shafted flickers, blue jays, and crested
tits. Wild geese sometimes pass overhead, and ducks
and herons land on Lake Leverty, just beyond my land.
Mrs. Zach and I have even flushed a few ruffed
grouse that sought refuge in our woods and that fled
as we drew near, making a *phut-phut-phut* sound as
they went."

His long arms rose to imitate the birds' frantic flight.
We were more and more puzzled about where Old
Zach was taking us, but we followed him without a
sound, enchanted by his flair as a storyteller and the
music of his pure Southern accent embellishing the
names and colors he mentioned.

"None of this," he said, "has anything to do, of
course, with the quarrel brewing this morning between the Democrats and the Republicans over the islands of Quemoy and Matsu, off the coast of For-
mosa. Nor has it anything to do with the latest dis-
closures concerning the vicuña coat given to the
president's special assistant, Mr. Sherman Adams,
whom I have often had the privilege of meeting, but
whose awkward acceptance of that little gift will probably cost him his job in the long run, *and* his power,
which, as you know, was enormous."

He coughed, took one of his pipes out of his jacket

pocket, and filled it with tobacco that he first rubbed between his fingers in a pigskin pouch.

"The third type of fauna," he said after this long pause, "is composed of what, having referred to the birds, I must now call the beasts. And I must say that I have occasionally been disappointed by the paucity of my reserve. True, there are squirrels, hares, nutrias, skunks, peccaries, mice, moles, frogs, toads, raccoons, shrimps, and a few reptiles. We have no rattlesnakes on our land and I killed the only copperhead we ever found the instant I spotted him."

Some of us were beginning to squirm in our seats, not because we were bored, but because the digression, which had already taken up part of our class hour, intrigued us and forced us to concentrate harder than usual. We were waiting for the penny to drop, if it was ever going to. Old Zach had now lit his pipe and taken three puffs on it, wreathing himself in a dense enough cloud of bluish smoke to make him appear more remote and mythical than ever. But he still gave no hint of when and how he would end his delightful account of the creatures inhabiting the valley we were growing up in.

"You also see deer," he said, "who come to feed on the ferns. But that's about all the animals there are. However, somewhere in the vicinity, near a pond, lives a tribe of gray foxes, and I'm not sure they haven't chosen to live among us out of a curious impulse toward mimicry. You all understand what I mean."

We laughed. One of the nicknames we gave Old Zach was "the old gray fox." And with his long, crafty-looking nose, his undulating walk, and his obsession for the color gray in everything he wore, there was something about him of the animal with which he now seemed to want to buttress his thesis.

"Over the years," he said, "the foxes have established a prudent but highly courteous relationship with us. I have observed that, among their other characteristics, the foxes never cross the stretch of lawn nearest the veranda, which I will call the civilized section. Whether it's the father or the mother or any cub of however recent a litter, they always swing wide around our house when they want to move from east to west. They respect our territory. With, nevertheless, one exception. Year after year I have confirmed this strange violation of their immutable rule, and the dates—I'd even say the times of day—coincide perfectly. The day always comes when the fox emerges from the spinney on the eastern side of our land and marches straight up the lawn, stops twenty feet away from our windows, and stares at us for a while. Then he resumes his lordly progress toward the shrubbery and woods on the west side."

Old Zach took a breath and, like the accomplished actor he was, remained silent a few seconds longer than he had to.

"In performing this unusual but fatidical annual rite, my neighbor the gray fox is telling me something. He is sending me a message. The newspapers haven't reported it, so you haven't been able to pick it up in your press roundup."

He stepped up the pace, his face lit with an intense joy in living.

"But if you don't agree with me that it's this morning's most sensational news, you are not worthy to figure among my students. For you do not yet know the real value of things."

He stood up, as though to leave the room. Yet the hour was far from over.

"Gentlemen," he said solemnly, "this morning the gray fox crossed our lawn from east to west and we looked at each other through the veranda window. That means that an irresistible event is happening, more pregnant with consequences than the trouble in the Far East or the scandals in the White House. And, like all good headlines, it can even be expressed in a very few words: *spring is here.*"

With that, he gathered up his papers, and, with an enthusiastically stagy wave of his hand, walked out, as though prompting us to follow him out of Clay Hall to sniff the new fragrance that had pervaded the campus for some hours now—but which we had failed to identify.

PART THREE: SPRING

33

THE ASSISTANT MANAGER OF THE PAXTON COUNTY Bank was a bald man with endless legs and torso whose thin voice didn't square at all with his ex-basketball-center build. His face was neutrality incarnate. Nothing moved on its skin, pink as a veal cutlet.

"I understand," he said after hearing me out. "I understand the repayment schedule you tell me you can maintain. But I don't get what you want the money for."

He had glanced through my bank statements, squeaking approvingly at the weeks of regular entries in the receipts column, the money I'd earned from giving French lessons and working nights at the *News*. Not many withdrawals; I had cut down radically on all but essential spending. I wasn't rich, but my position was healthy.

"At this rate," the assistant manager remarked, "you're going to wind up with a nice little balance, enough to warrant a loan. There's no real reason why we shouldn't grant you one. We often extend loans to students to help them meet their expenses while they're waiting for their families to replenish their accounts. But that's as far as it goes. Your case is different, since you're a foreigner and nobody's feeding deposits into your account—not regularly, at any rate. But you are earning money and you are solvent."

His ponderousness took on an edge of agitation when he asked, "What do you want this money for? A bank, my dear sir, has to know what it's getting into."

"It's simple enough," I said. "I want to buy a used car."

"Ah," he said. And, pleased at having received an answer, he repeated, "Ah."

A light finally went on in the two big, round eyes he swiveled to meet mine. He had found his next question. "And what are you planning to do with this car?"

When I had told Bob Kendall that I was planning to request a loan, he had warned me: "Remember, when you go see the banker, you don't have to tell him the truth. But always make him think he's smarter than you are. All the guys at school know him. He's a big, bored hulk who loves to sit around and gossip with the students."

So I told the assistant manager, "With a car I can commute between jobs a lot faster, which will save me time and energy."

"Ye-es," he said, encouraging me to keep going.

"And in that case I might even find a third job."

"What for?" he threw in quickly.

"Er . . . to make more money so I can pay you back faster," I said lamely, running out of arguments.

"Ah." And he scrutinized me again while digesting what I'd told him. "Let me get things straight," he said in that chirpy voice I couldn't get used to. "You are earning money to qualify for a loan to buy a car that will enable you to earn more money and repay your loan faster. That right?"

I nodded, unable to decide if Kendall had been wrong and this so-called big hulk wasn't really a monumental nitpicker. Or maybe I was dealing with the dim-

mest man of the century. Or maybe the assistant
manager of this small branch of the Virginia State Bank
just liked to do business at this pace. Maybe, after
all, he was bored to death behind his big desk, bored
with staring at the photos of himself as a basketball
star that he had tacked to his buff-colored office walls.

"That still doesn't tell me why you wanted a car in
the first place," he said.

He leaned back in his chair, his veal-pink cheeks
glowing redder as he chewed over the question and
approved its soundness.

"Because," I replied instantly, "you have to."

He frowned. "You have to what?"

"In America you have to have a car."

I was a trifle annoyed at having to put such a truism
into words. But he burst into laughter that was as
shrill as his voice, a staccato, satisfied sort of laugh.

"I like the way your mind works," he said. "It's logical. And you're absolutely right. How long have you
been in this country?"

"Since the start of the school year," I said.

"You're absolutely right, and it's something we can
really be proud of. The automobile has done a lot
for our way of life. It's changed the face of the nation."

Impressed by the scope of his pronouncement, the
assistant manager fell silent. What he'd said had a
practiced ring, as if it had already been used at some
convention, or at a local Rotary Club meeting. He
was proud of it and he peered covertly at me to see if
his thoughts had made the proper impact on me. I
nodded obsequiously in agreement. At that, he relaxed, leaned toward me, now entirely friendly.

"You ever been bowling?" he asked.

"No," I said, disconcerted by the question.

"You ought to try it," he murmured enthusiastically. "It's a lot of fun."

"Sure," I said, showing as much interest as I could muster.

I suddenly felt that I was doomed to accompany this bald, lanky, baby-skinned bore and his friends to share in the indescribable joys of bowling. I'd seen the town's only bowling alley once, while out with a bunch of students, and I'd seen its customers: fortyish men in shirtsleeves drinking beer and munching pretzels, hicks whose days were uneventful and who launched their bowling balls conscientiously, intently, with the look of people who were doing everything they could to mask the emptiness of their lives. The spectacle had taught me a vague but repellent lesson, and while I couldn't pin it down, I knew I'd had a brush with the Great American Boredom.

I was lucky. My young wits had been honed exclusively by contact with my teachers, some of them less brilliant than others, but all of them open and outgoing, always ready to converse with us, all of them aiming at the same goal: to help us develop our minds. As a bonus, there was that splendid genius, Old Zach. What's more, I was living with boys from the best families in the South and Southwest. Every moment so far had been a source of surprise, of excitement, of discovery. The cocoon around our superb little college kept us from entering a parallel world, one inhabited by what the statisticians call the average American. The kind of men I had watched sending big black balls rumbling down pale, polished alleys to pulverize rows of white, reinforced-plastic pins.

The assistant manager of the Paxton County Bank belonged to that world I had glimpsed with such dread. Evenings, in heated discussions in the dorm and the fraternity houses, we swore we would never let ourselves be trapped in that world, that we were meant for far better things. Our American literature professor had quoted a line by Thoreau: "The mass of men lead lives of quiet desperation," but we had not really understood how true that is. Could the saying be applied to the assistant manager of the Paxton County Bank? I didn't think so, because that tall, bald veal cutlet exuded well-being. Or had Thoreau stopped too short? Perhaps his line should have been amended to add: *and don't know it.*

Luckily I was not dragooned into going bowling. No doubt the assistant manager thought the interview had gone on long enough and there was nothing left to say. The face he showed me was approving.

"I'm always glad to meet a young fella like you," he said, rising and sticking out his thick hand.

"Me, too," I said.

"And of course," he continued as he ushered me to his office door, "you have many semesters ahead of you to pay us back in, since as I understand it you're still a freshman and we can count on having you as a customer for three more good years."

"Of course," I said, trying to keep my voice steady.

That was a lie: an approximate date, distant but inevitable, already loomed to wrench at my heart—the date when my boat sailed back to Europe, sometime that summer. So soon! It had been the second lie I'd told in the interview. If I'd been totally honest, I'd have told the assistant manager I wanted a car so that I could go and see Elizabeth at Sweet Briar whenever I wanted to. And that I wanted to buy Cal Cate's green Buick because it was convertible, and because spring was here.

34

SPRING MEANT YOU PUT DOWN THE ROOF OF YOUR
car and roared off with your hair blowing in the
wind; your destination was the natural bridge at Goshen
Pass, where you'd dangle your feet in the icy waters
of a trout stream. Spring meant that at Neal W. Lowitz's
gents' store you could buy whimsically stylish straw
boaters in yellow straw with black bands, and multicolored madras Bermuda shorts, and red cummer-
bunds to go with the cream-colored monkey jackets
to be worn to the big spring dance everyone was already talking about; it would go on all night, and
the Dorsey Brothers' band had been hired to play
for it.

Spring meant that the black cherry trees were abloom
with white flowers, not so white as the dogwood
blossoms, the Virginia state flower, not so white, either, as the white splendor of the hawthorns and the
hollyhocks and the giant magnolias. The redbuds, or
Judas trees, also typical of the Shenandoah Valley,
gave tiny but dazzling flowers of a vivid pinkish purple. And the air on the campus was heady with the
scent of the cucumber trees and the tulip trees. Some
mornings, when the aroma was overwhelming, you
saw a few seniors in their blue-and-white-striped Haspel
cord suits sprawled on the pale green grass with their
heads resting on belted stacks of books and their faces

to the sky; they knew that graduation day was only a few months away, and that they would then leave that blessed enclave for good. So they tried to melt into the earth and the lawns, into the scents and the sky, soaking up all these evanescent splendors.

The radio played new songs that matched the season's mood: "Tender Trap," crooned by Sinatra; "Unchained Melody," introduced by Roy Hamilton, who also had sung "Don't Let Go," probably the first rock tune ever recorded in stereo; "Memories Are Made of This," tossed off nonchalantly by Dean Martin. Nice tunes.

Fringed hammocks appeared on front porches. Discreet election posters went up on redbrick walls advertising candidates for student-body president. From the playing fields far off beyond the viaduct came the crack of bats against baseballs. Those sounds blended with the *thok, thok* of tennis volleys and a clashing of hockey sticks. The Notables Glee Club, twenty-eight boys who had bombed in their first concerts the previous fall, was now playing to packed houses, as if the students and their dates, the teachers and their wives, felt a more pressing need for music, and a need to congregate to absorb it.

To this poignant beauty in which I was wholly immersed was added an upsurge in the quality of my schoolwork. I was at last starting to catch on to the subtleties of the language and to glimpse the benefits to be derived from the courses I'd been advised to take when I registered. Old Zach and his corps of teachers, assistants in the School of Literature and Journalism, had propelled us into a program bristling with challenges and experiments. Tolerance was the key word: we did what we wanted to do. We put on our own radio shows, which were aired at off hours by the local radio station. We converted news items into scripts for plays. To us was assigned full responsibility for the *Student Gazette,* the four-page sheet we printed in the basement of Clay Hall, and for which I was given the title of assistant editor. The history of the great battles of the Civil War gave me a real understanding of how torn the South had been. And I could now speak in Eco-Pol I on the consequences of the great drought in Oklahoma in the Thirties. I could call everyone I saw and greeted on the campus by his first name. The student body was small enough so that, after one semester, I knew every face. I was part of it all now. I belonged, as they said at school. Even if I wasn't like them.

In fact, that difference had stopped being a handicap and had become an asset that earned me invitations to all the fraternities (I was not a member of any clique). I went to the cocktail parties given by the professors' wives, too; they liked to invite this foreign student who had settled so neatly into the school mold, and whose French lessons helped fill those afternoons which, for this circle of ladies, could be so hollow. Now I was capitalizing on my specialness. One learns to please. One likes to perform, to profit from a situation that gives foreigners the stance of actors whose importance to the play doesn't emerge until the end of the second act. Their novelty, their lack of roots in the drama that everyone else shares, sets them apart from the group. I had been there since the previous fall, but suddenly, in spring, here I was being discovered, and I enjoyed it immensely.

I had used my bank loan to buy Cal's green Buick convertible. This was a major undertaking for me, the act of an adult. Cal had been generous enough not to profiteer during this season, when cars sold at premium prices.

"Take good care of it," he had solemnly admonished me. "It may belong to you now, but it'll always be *my* Buick."

And a few days later he was showing off in the latest model, a 236-horsepower, two-colored Roadmaster, red and black, with the first transmission in automotive history to be based on airplane engines. To Cal, Buicks were *the* cars, and when he handed me the keys to his old one he earnestly repeated the slogan that had boosted the brand's sales that year to record heights: "When better cars are built, Buick will build them."

Whereupon, on an unwonted and scarcely American impulse, he kissed me on both cheeks.

I felt free behind the wheel of my first car. That was the word: I was a free man.

All this is what spring meant. But there was more— for I brought to my activities at school and in love the frenzy of someone who knows his days are numbered.

35

ELIZABETH BALDRIDGE TOOK A SIP OF TEA, THEN PUT the cup down.

"I knew it," she said. "This tea is putrid."

"What do you mean, putrid?" I said. "I tasted it. Seemed perfectly all right to me."

"No," she said flatly, "it is not all right. It is absolutely putrid."

"Really? You could have fooled me."

She looked amazed at my ignorance. Elizabeth was dressed in a kind of shapeless, washed-out yellow jacket, a full chambray skirt that hung down to her ankles, and brown ballet shoes with worn soles. She was wearing no more makeup than she had when we met on the train from Charlottesville, and her hair, cut short and ragged, was beginning to grow back in jagged tufts. A scarf worn halfway back on her head struggled with only partial success to hide that unruly shock of hair. Needless to say, the scarf, like everything else she had on, looked like a Salvation Army handout. For our first outing, which was not a date, as we had again agreed when I picked her up at her school, she had taken great care to erase every trace of femininity.

"The water's putrid," Elizabeth explained. "It's not spring water. And the tea was obviously made with one of those odious bags they buy in job lots at the local supermarket."

"Tell me about the milk and sugar," I said with exaggerated suavity. "Tell me they're fake, too."

"Don't give me any crap," she retorted. "I refuse to follow you down the path of sarcasm."

For our first conversation—that was what our meeting had to come down to, a conversation—we had chosen a thoroughly innocent tearoom near Sweet Briar. The place had charm. It was empty—only one other table was occupied, by an elderly couple, and we sat with our backs to them—and looked out on a quiet street lined with hazel trees. It was a silent, restful place that suited what I'd anticipated would be a sensitive rendezvous with this girl who so intrigued me.

"I won't fence with you that way," she went on, "because it invariably leads to emotional involve-

ment. Cats scratch first and caress afterward. We're not
cats."

"No," I said, "that's true."

"At least we agree on that. I remember distinctly
your promise on the train: 'I won't try to hustle
you.'"

"Yes, of course," I said. "I remember that very
well."

But I already felt like reaching my hand across the
small table and taking hers. She seemed so vulnerable. Seeing her trembling in Charlottesville and again
on the train had aroused in me a feeling for which I
was unprepared. Tenderness? Affection?

"You seem disappointed," she said.

"Not in the least. Everything's fine. I'm very glad
to be here."

"It's . . . difficult, though, isn't it?"

"No more so for me than for you," I said.

"I mean it's difficult to avoid putting on an act. Even
if you are different from the other boys—and you
are or I'd never have agreed to see you again—you've
been corrupted just the same by the way the two
sexes playact toward each other. I'm sure you've learned
it all and that you go along with it now."

"You're wrong," I said. "I had all kinds of trouble
understanding the dating system and fitting into it."

"But you did go along with it," she said. "Oh, don't
worry, no one escapes from it."

"Sorry to contradict you," I said, "but *you're* the one
who wrote to me. I was tremendously surprised—
and pleased."

She gave me a sweet, hesitant smile, but said nothing.

"Anyway, even if I hadn't gotten that letter, I'd have
come looking for you. If you really want to know,
that's why I bought a car."

I was afraid I'd gone too far too fast, that I'd confessed too much. But she didn't object.

"You might have picked a less garish color," she said. "Bright green! That's terribly outré. It's . . ."

She searched for a better adjective. In her letters as in her conversation, Elizabeth's use of language set her apart from other girls her age, from the trite, routine words they used.

"It's positively Californian," she finally ventured.

"What's that mean?"

"It means being so emancipated from taboos that you slip over into vulgarity, knowing it's vulgar, but not caring."

"You know California?"

"No, but I know its diametrical opposite."

"Where are you from?"

"You see?" she said indulgently. "There's where you're different from the rest, and why you amuse me. Haven't you guessed? Don't you recognize my accent? I'm an Easterner, of course—New England. I brought this putrid accent along with me from Boston."

"I'd never heard a Boston accent before," I said, "so how could I have guessed? What do your folks do?"

For a moment she trembled as I'd seen her do before, but not since we'd entered the tearoom. The seeming ease of her conversation and my feeling that we were beginning to reach some sort of real exchange vanished when I asked the question. She stiffened to control her shuddering. She'd gone pale.

"Pay no attention to my passing bouts of weakness," she said. "It's my body defending itself in the war I'm waging against it. Sometimes I'm not sure it's going to hold up."

I tried to interrupt, but she hurried on.

"I won't answer your question about my parents for two reasons. The first is contractual."

"Contractual?"

"That's right," she went on, even faster now. "We agreed on a sort of contract between us: no boy-meets-girl act. So all these hollow, mealymouthed questions like where are you from and what does your father do are banned from our conversation. They're not in the contract. Is that clear?"

"All right, if you say so."

"The second reason is that I refuse under any circumstances to describe the putrid and putrescent putrefaction of my family environment."

She fell silent, withdrawing into herself. And I was clumsy enough to say, "Elizabeth, do you realize that since we started talking here you must have used the word *putrid* at least seven times?"

Her face crumpled like a smashed doll's; its very structure dissolved. Between clenched teeth she murmured, "That's because everything is putrid. Everything!"

She suddenly stood up. With her went the table-cloth, sweeping the teapot and our cups and saucers off to shatter on the floor. The tea drooled away. In unison the elderly couple uttered a shocked murmur. The black waitress ran out from behind the cash desk. Standing there, Elizabeth looked as if she were about to faint. I hurried around the table, took her arms, and led her toward the toilets.

"There is a distinct possibility that I may puke," she whispered.

We got to the ladies' room, a small compartment furnished with a dressing table and a hassock, separated from the toilets proper by a door covered in flowered wallpaper. There Elizabeth could sit down without my holding her. She shut her eyes, pressed her hand to her heart, and took a few breaths.

"Wait for me outside," she said at last. "Gentlemen aren't supposed to be in the women's rest room."

"You sure you're all right? I couldn't care less where I'm supposed to be or not be. I want to help you."

"Thanks," she said, "you're sweet. It's all right now. I'll join you in a moment."

I went back into the tearoom, where the waitress had already cleaned up the mess on the floor. We were alone; the elderly couple had presumably fled. The waitress told me soberly, "That young lady doesn't eat enough."

"You think not?"

"Absolutely," she said. "It's plain as the nose on your face. How about I make her two or three nice slices of French toast? We can even put some honey on them."

"I don't know," I said. "I'm not sure I ought to force that on her."

"We can always try," the waitress said, bestowing a reassuring smile on me.

"While you're at it," I said, "make us another pot of tea—but not with tea bags, if that's possible."

I sat down at the table, which the waitress had also tidied, having changed the tablecloth and set out fresh cups and saucers. She worked briskly and efficiently and walked out to the kitchen humming, as if the incident and the extra work it caused her gave her genuine satisfaction.

I waited for Elizabeth. "This girl," an inner voice told me, "doesn't have what you're looking for." When I'd first arrived in this country, I'd been attracted, almost obsessed, by girls who were really stacked, as we used to say—the ones whose hips, hair, figure, and complexion expressed everything that was rich, opulent, smooth, appetizing, honeyed, voluptuous

about America. Like a greedy kid in front of a pastry-
shop window, I'd wanted every one of those cream
puffs.

I had doubtless changed since then. Had my affair
with April given me a taste for a different kind of
person, for difficult and peculiar situations? Elizabeth
had been an imperious and beautiful girl, a regal figure when I'd first seen her the previous fall. Now, although she still had her slender elegance and the
distinction inherent in her every movement, her grace-
ful walk, and the delicate tracery of her face, she was
nothing at all like the beauties the magazines saturated
us with. She had willfully destroyed her natural
beauty, had grown a lot thinner; she was pale, and pe-
riodically shaken by that alarming trembling. This
didn't repel me. Just the opposite: Elizabeth whetted
my curiosity, stirred my compassion. Her vocabulary, her way of talking heightened my interest in her.
I did not know how to go about kindling a friendship with her or, better still, a love affair, but I didn't
try to plan it. I just waited.

She returned at the same time as the waitress, who,
with some pride, brought us a platter heaped with
French toast and a jug of Appalachian honey. Elizabeth's expression was calm now. There was a hint
of color in her cheeks. She motioned to me to sit down
while she resumed her place across the table.

"What are these astounding victuals?" she asked,
pointing with her chin at the French toast.

"How do you feel?" I asked her.

"A shade less putrid than usual," she replied.

"Careful," I said. "We don't use that word here
anymore."

She hid her mouth with her hand and bubbled with
laughter. I began laughing with her and soon our hi-

larity filled the still miraculously empty tearoom. The waitress, apparently delighted by the change in the atmosphere, brought us a pot of tea.

"Taste this," she said firmly.

Then she left us alone.

"I think that woman's marvelous," I said. "You ought to try what she's made for you."

Elizabeth poured some tea, sipped it, seemed to like it. She nibbled at a piece of French toast, with elaborate circumspection at first, then, as she realized how good it was, with bigger and bigger bites, almost voracious mouthfuls.

"Wonderful," she said. "I haven't consumed anything this remarkable in centuries. Or anyway, to put a fine point on it, since my last meal three days ago."

She stopped talking to finish the first slice of toast and immediately lit into another, embalming it with a dollop of clear honey.

"Forgive me for not providing you with anything but the sight of a human being feeding," she said, "but I was taught never to talk with my mouth full."

"Don't worry about me," I assured her.

She finished the second slice without another word. There were still two slices left on the platter, and she set about demolishing them, too, suspending her onslaught just long enough for an occasional gulp of tea. Not until she had eaten every bite did she shake her head, as if to recover her aplomb.

"Selfish creature that I am!" she exclaimed. "Self-centered wretch! I only thought of myself and you haven't eaten a thing."

"I wasn't hungry."

"Stop playing nursemaid," she said. "You are too exemplary and too altruistic, too restrained and too patient. You're not yourself. I must be getting on your nerves."

"Certainly not."

"You see how hopeless I am, how utterly corrupt, and how little I've really reformed? All we've worried about is little me and my anorexia and my private little melodrama, but not at all about you. For over an hour I've forced you to share the horrors of Elizabeth Baldridge's daily life. We haven't once talked about you."

"We will next time," I said.

She looked at me, in her eyes a gleam of that coquettishness she had used so artfully in the recent past and which she had tried to root out of herself, but which crept back in unawares and was probably natural to her.

"Because there's going to be a next time?" she asked.

"We can make a new contract now," I said, trying to imitate her way of expressing things.

Elizabeth smiled and stood up, walking with me to the cashier's desk, where our marvelous waitress awaited us. The check (including property damage caused by Elizabeth's fit of nerves) was so trifling that I called for a recount, but the waitress wouldn't hear of it. We left promising to be back for another orgy of French toast, honey, cinnamon, and real tea.

It was six o'clock. A cool breeze off the pine-covered hill caressed our faces as the Buick convertible glided slowly toward Elizabeth's college. When the school's pointed roofs came in sight above the trees around a bend in the road, Elizabeth said, "Let's stop in that parking lot. I don't feel like going back just yet."

I swung the car over to the right and stopped on a stretch of weed-spattered gravel under a row of live oaks and sycamores.

"We don't even know that waitress's name," Elizabeth said, laughing. "It must be Wilma. I bet her name's Wilma."

I laughed, too. She rested her head, with its mop of red hair ravaged by some insane scissors, on the back of the leather seat and breathed a long sigh of well-being.

"If only I could live so simply all the time," she said. "We were so peaceful. But my mind is a welter of confusion. I feel so terribly confused."

Silent, diaphanous tears trickled down her cheeks. I couldn't tell if they were caused by the serenity that seemed to have filled her, or by the thought of the confusion she said was preying on her. All through that afternoon with Elizabeth I had felt as if I were inching forward on thin ice that might crack under me at any moment.

Now, in the silence in the car under the trees, I thought we'd reached more solid ground. So I asked her the question I'd been trying so hard to hold in: "Elizabeth, what's happened to you?"

36

Elizabeth Baldridge's mother was a purebred Bostonian so proud of her daughter that from the girl's first years in school she had mapped out a program for success and social grace designed to guide her little darling safely to the status of Most Frequently Photographed Girl in New England and, if possible, in the United States. Elizabeth's mother had enjoyed the same satisfactions, the same eminence in her youth; no question of her daughter failing to follow in her footsteps.

In her first year at Sweet Briar, Elizabeth, experienced in all the rules and all the secrets of what is called the social whirl, had kept pace with the schedule for progress her mother had drawn up for her. She'd even stolen a march on it: elected the Most Promising Beginner of the Year by her classmates, Elizabeth had not only maintained a straight-A average, but had also won a two-week trip to Paris in a contest organized by a local modeling agency. There, despite the vigilance of a professional chaperon, she had lost her virginity in the arms of the photographer accompanying the three prizewinners to record their discovery of the Old World. The incident did not figure in the career plan laid down by her mother, so Elizabeth never dared to tell her about it. She had hated that escapade. She had hated herself for succumbing.

It had been a mess: the man had been both brusque and inane. And it had left Elizabeth with a repugnance for the whole physical side of courtship—flirting, holding hands, necking, and all the other rites; she had devoted her second year at college to avenging her wound on anyone in pants and a blazer, on all the college boys who danced attendance at the door of the sorority, where she already reigned supreme, to beg her for a Saturday-night date. Her mother had once dictated to her the sovereign commandments for converting men into whatever she wanted them to be— victims, bank accounts, docile future husbands thoroughly apprised of what the slightest hint of rebellion would cost them.

"You have to treat 'em rough," Mrs. Baldridge had counseled, "until they get down on their knees and

implore you to stop. You have to wrap your rough-
ness in velvety charm, in irresistible femininity. You
must be distinctive and fragile and rare, like an orchid. Except that the edges of every petal, every leaf
on the flower must be made of sharpened steel."

And she'd added: "Attack right away, at the first encounter. Make them feel your authority immediately.
You're driving the horses."

From her early teens, Elizabeth had observed her
haughty mother apply this philosophy in her every
action, in the daily scenes of family and social life over
which she presided. The girl had no trouble following Mommy's precepts because she never came up
against any serious obstacle to her conquest of the
world.

Elizabeth took part in every campus activity. She was
admired, respected, feared by the other girls. Then,
at the beginning of winter, as she reached her junior
year at college, this whole splendid edifice collapsed
like a building dynamited from within.

She had noticed the first crack, the first fault, one
evening after she'd returned from Christmas in Boston: a sudden, stunning feeling during a particularly
plush dinner—so she told me later—of being surrounded by "a pack of monkeys" and that she herself
was "one of the she-apes." It was weird: she was sitting there, in a dark velvet dress that set off her emer-
ald eyes and auburn hair, and beside her she saw a
vile little monkey. The conversation went on. She heard
herself talking and laughing, but that's how she saw
herself, as an animal in a grotesque zoo.

The feeling had persisted all through the evening.
She left the dinner disturbed, but not frightened. Then
she did something her mother probably had not included in the battle plan mapped out for Elizabeth's

conquest of the social heights: she began to think. She began looking at herself, listening to herself, reviewing her life to date, and from then on she thought of it as pointless playacting, the perpetual and vain pursuit of an undefined objective. Buffoonery.

She told me that one of the things that distressed her deeply was that she could find no explanation for this sudden metamorphosis. She waved away the episode of the photographer in Paris. True, nice girls in those days did not so early or so easily surrender that virginity whose preservation a whole culture decreed to be sacrosanct. She had done something enormously stupid. But that hadn't given her nightmares. Besides, Elizabeth had decided long ago, before being "tainted," that experiences of the body, the senses, the flesh were minor. You rule a body as you do the rest.

Her confidence in that body and its maintenance, in her moral soundness, in the unyielding arrogance with which she had been consistently inoculated since childhood, the personal resources she believed unlimited—all these dictated a simple line of conduct: to go on as she had before. She thought it unseemly, even absurd, to consult a doctor. She refused to talk about all this to her mother or her father.

On the third day of the semester, Elizabeth had a second hallucination.

She described the scene to me as it had unfolded during ceremonies inaugurating the school's new concert hall. The president of Sweet Briar had invited the Richmond Chamber Orchestra, which played a few selections before the six hundred girls at the college, members of the faculty, deans, and department heads. It devolved on the girl who was the most poised public speaker, the most attractive, the most certain to succeed—in short, on Elizabeth Baldridge—to read a brief paper on the influence of music on manners and civilizations.

The speech ran to three typewritten pages. Elizabeth knew it almost by heart, but she occasionally glanced down at the text on the lectern before her. She turned over the second page and, before beginning the third, looked up at the audience—and saw six hundred monkeys staring back and silently making faces at her. The apparition was appalling, unbearable. She riveted her eyes on the typewritten page without looking up again, finished her speech, and went immediately to her room in her sorority house.

Elizabeth peered at herself in the bathroom mirror. She decided that the only way to avoid ever encountering those monkeys again was to make radical changes in her appearance, then in her behavior. First her appearance, the adornments of her beauty: the artful architecture of her hairdo, the makeup, the accessories to seduction, the earrings, the nail polish—all that was *putrid* to her. Without a moment's hesitation, she hacked off her hair with a big shears she used to cut reproductions of great paintings out of art magazines.

Having destroyed the appurtenances of her beauty, Elizabeth went to bed and woke up the next morning with a temperature of a hundred and four and a case of double pneumonia. She made the other girls swear they would not alert her family. She asked to be admitted to the college dispensary, emerging one week later and some twenty pounds lighter. She resolved to cancel all her social activities, to hack them away as she had her auburn hair.

"I cut off dating, too," she told me. "No more dates with any boy on any pretext, no more opportunities to attack, no further occasion to make myself hated. No more teasing, never again the game of arousing and provoking boys, dominating and breaking them."

Elizabeth fell silent.

I hadn't said a word during this recital. Now I asked, "Have you seen the monkeys again?"

"No, and I don't intend to."

"But how'd you explain your behavior to the dean and the teachers and your friends? How did they take all this?"

"I didn't explain anything. I said I needed to breathe. I must have disappointed them terribly. I have a strong feeling they'd rather I didn't come back for my senior year next fall. The dean tried to talk to me. I lied and told her I was saving my strength for the up-coming exams and didn't want to distract myself with a lot of pointless trifles. 'But, Elizabeth,' she insisted, 'social life is no trifle.' I replied that she was surely right, but that I wanted to come up for air for a while. We agreed to talk things over again later, and I asked her to give me a reprieve. I especially asked her not to notify Boston."

"Boston? You mean your mother?"

"Yes," Elizabeth said. "My mother doesn't know anything about this. I haven't seen her since Christmas. She'll probably have a fit when she sees me. It's going to be abominable. I don't know how I'm going to avoid that. Maybe I should just not see her again, ever. But that's not what worries me most now. What matters is how I feel and how I'm going to erad-icate what I was. After that I can decide what to do."

"How do you really feel?" I asked.

"Rotten," she said, laughing, "absolutely rotten. Haven't you noticed?"

"Then why won't you try to get help?" I said. "Why not go and see a doctor?"

"Because."

It was getting dark. And cold.

I thought I could get in one other question before
we separated: "What made you suddenly decide to
tell me all this?"

She thought about it for a moment. Her head came
up from the headrest and she shook herself like a
sleeper trying to wake up.

"Let's go back," she said.

I eased the car onto the road and drove slowly until
we reached the lawns of Sweet Briar College, which
were flecked with the dying light of day.

"I don't know," she said finally. "Maybe because
you happened by at the right time and you have
something that all the twerps who feed me their silly
line don't have: you know how to listen. Or maybe
what makes it easiest for me to talk openly to you is
that you're a foreigner. You'll sail away home soon.
It doesn't hurt to confide in someone who's just passing through."

She waved all these explanations away. "I'll get out
here," she said. "Thanks for everything. It was nice
because we managed to break through the playacting."

"Can we get together again?" I asked her.

"Do you want to?"

"Of course, very much."

"Wilma's French toast was delicious," she said. "We'll
have to go back and have some more."

Her answer delighted me. We had reached Elizabeth's sorority house, a Jeffersonian Classical building just like the fraternity houses at my school. Before
opening the car door to get out, Elizabeth turned to
me and stuck out her face in deference to the rite that
punctuated all dates, the quick good night kiss. Then
she instantly drew back, anxious to avoid one of the
standard ingredients of the dreadful *buffoonery* at which
she'd been so dazzling a performer.

Her sudden retreat—the conflict within her between the old habit of faking and the new demand she made on herself for truthfulness—made her smile because she saw I'd understood.

"Confusion," she said, "all is confusion."

She waved goodbye, opened the door, and walked up the path leading to the veranda. I sat there watching her, hoping she would turn and wave again, as custom also prescribed, but it probably didn't occur to her. Her shoulders were hunched, her ankles seemed almost too frail to bear the weight of that exhausted body hidden under the exaggeratedly long skirt and shapeless sweater. In the distance, in the now full darkness and under the dim light over the veranda, Elizabeth looked like a scarecrow that the slightest puff of wind could blow away.

37

On my way back, in that Buick I'd bought for the sole purpose of making a play for the girl at Sweet Briar, I felt unspeakably weary, as if my body had been drained of all its strength. Thinking about it, I realized that it was Elizabeth who had left me feeling so hollow. I had concentrated so hard on her confession, straining not to talk about myself, to submerge my own self-absorption. I had made a tremendous effort to avoid being clumsy and spoiling the climate

of confidence that we'd established. Now that I'd at
last gotten a clear picture of the breach that had
opened inside Elizabeth—although I couldn't begin to
diagnose why it had happened—I felt emptied, flat-
tened, helpless.

The feeling didn't last long. But it surprised me. This
was the first time it had hit me so intensely. Did you
really have to forget about yourself so completely before others could reach you? This was new, proof
that there is no love worthy of the name without some
sacrifice of one's precious and stubborn egotism. It
hadn't been like that with April. Now, for the first
time, I was less captivated by what had happened to
me than by what had happened to the other person; a
crack had developed in what, until now, had been
my smug self-contemplation. A small floodgate had
opened in the dam; the valves were shuddering under the pressure; the water could run both ways now.
For the first time, my heart did not throb for me
alone.

For the first time . . . People who talk so authorita-
tively about youth often forget how important everything is to the young. Everything. Because they have
forgotten their own pasts or because their senses have
grown fossilized, these people make youth appear an
easy, insignificant, frivolous succession of events.

Nothing is insignificant or facile between the ages of
sixteen and twenty. With the passage of time, though,
so much can be diminished or forgotten: the first time
you fall in love, the first time you're lied to, the first
time you make love, the first time you lose an illusion, the first time you encounter beauty, and ugliness.

Adults and life finally condition you to accept the
old precept so vital to survival: blot things out and

go on. But nothing can ever really blot out the first time, any more than you can entirely expunge the bloodstain of lost virginity from the immaculate whiteness of a sheet.

38

I DECIDED TO INVITE ELIZABETH TO THE SPRING Dance. She was the partner I wanted. I knew it wasn't going to be easy, that winning her consent would take some careful plotting.

The Spring Dance became the main topic of conversation on campus. Everywhere students drew up lists, named subcommittees to help the main committees; everyone was feverishly organizing and planning. After the dance would come the cramming for the finals, then graduation, and then the ending I didn't even want to think about. In June the campus would empty out; everyone would go home, the other undergraduates for the summer, me for good. But between now and this ineluctable end to a college year rose the prospect of the dance.

Who're you taking? Where'll you stay? Which party are you going to? Will the Dorsey Brothers' band dare depart from its standard fare of comfortable, danceable swing and play some rock 'n' roll?

Behind all these questions—their frivolousness swept away by the febrility with which the students, especially the freshmen, asked them—lay a hope: that the occasion would live up to its reputation.

Old hands said it was the key event of the year. Some of them had welded their fates to a girl's at the dance, or exchanged oaths of loyalty and constancy with their best friends; during the long weekend of which the dance was the pivotal event, conversations with members of the faculty who received you in their gardens and on their front porches were often turning points that set a boy's whole professional future. For the teachers were more candid with us over that weekend than ever before. Everything and everybody seemed like voices in harmony.

I plunged fervidly into this atmosphere, but I didn't understand it then. Only later did I recognize it as evidence that our small college's character was anchored in something undefined, something that had never been inscribed in the bylaws of that historic institution, but which was as immutable as the shapes of the Blue Ridge Mountains walling the green and white Shenandoah Valley. The molding of minds there followed the rhythms of nature: autumn was a mutation, winter a struggle, spring a flowering. My own life on the campus had vibrated deeply to those rhythms.

But these truths never entered my mind at the time. I merely drew up a balance sheet of my performance at previous dances. My record had been pitiful. At the Openings, the October dance that kicked off the school year, I hadn't dared ask Sue Ann, on whom I'd had a crush at the time, to go with me. I just rented a tuxedo so that I could circulate along the Promenade, the gallery over the big gym where the dances were held; from there, empty-armed and empty-hearted, I watched the couples whirling below me.

For the second big dance of the year, the Fancy Dress Ball in February, I never even left my room. I was

then deeply immersed in my affair with April and
hadn't felt like attending the dance. I remembered that
gloomy evening in the deserted freshman dorm. Even
my roommate, the Austrian with the homely face I
couldn't stand, had found a date to suit him. I didn't
want to feel alone and forsaken that way again. I had
a car, friends, money in my pocket; I wanted to enjoy
those important moments that made up the daily fabric of life on the campus to which I now felt so deeply
bound. I had decided that Elizabeth would go to the
dance with me. And since I had achieved everything
I'd set out to do so far, I was sure I'd win this round
as I had all the rest.

"What you're asking," she told me, "is almost insulting."

"Really? Why?"

"Why? Because it means you're dismissing everything I told you last time about my boycott of the
social farce—which you acted as if you agreed with.
You weren't listening to me. I am absolutely crushed.
I really mean it, I'm crushed. Pulverized. You are a
pulverizing young man."

We had gone back to the tearoom. It was more
crowded than it had been the previous Sunday. The
waitress was named Althea, not Wilma, but between
ourselves we went on calling her Wilma. She had put
us at the same table, where we could sit with our backs
to the rest of the room. Elizabeth had ordered French
toast, which I chose to see as an overture.

"Listen," I said, "I'm not trying to drag you into
any kind of farce. This'll be my one and only dance
of the year and after that I'm leaving, so it won't create any obligation on your part. It won't mean anything to you. And I'd be thrilled. There's no commitment, no contract."

Elizabeth had taken some pains with her outfit this time. She wore a white blouse with a round collar and a tailored skirt of dark blue linen, and she had knotted the sleeves of a pink cardigan around her shoulders. I found her lovelier and less vulnerable, as if she'd recovered some of her old strength. And she admitted that her week had been, on the whole, "relatively positive."

"I managed to finish three meals out of six," she said. "I didn't light into anybody, and no one provoked me. I didn't let on about my feelings at all when my mother made her weekly phone call to check on her meritorious daughter."

In her distinctive diction and with humor that may or may not have been deliberate, she repeated the conversation between *Boston*—meaning her mother—and herself as she sat at the phone in the vestibule of her sorority house. To imitate her mother, she took on the eminently snobbish accent of the New England upper crust. For her own replies, she adopted the crisp, superior voice of the girl her mother had always thought of her as being—that tone of innate authority and seeming indolence that only the rich can master. Elizabeth used her empty teacup as the telephone receiver and the saucer as the mouthpiece.

"Liz dear, how are you?" her mother had asked.

"Fine, Mother."

"How are we doing, Liz?"

"Couldn't be better, Mother."

"No, dear, I mean how are we doing with our theatrical rehearsals and the photo contest and our invitations to the spring dances. Who've we decided to go with and how are we going to turn down the other young men who've asked us without damaging our relations with their families?"

"We'll do what we usually do, Mother."

"Of course, Liz dear, but you're not answering my questions. How are we doing on all the fronts I've just mentioned?"

"Mother, darling, don't worry, everything is under control on all fronts."

"I'm delighted to hear that, dear, but don't hesitate to call me if unexpected problems crop up. I know you're perfectly capable of handling anything that might arise, dear, but I want you to remember that no matter how busy I am I'm always here to consult with you about the strategy to follow. Or to revise, if it comes to that."

"No revision necessary, Mother."

"Then I'm doubly delighted, Liz dear. I must say, though, that I'd have preferred a detailed report with dates, names, and family backgrounds instead of these reassuring but rather vague answers you've been giving me."

At that point Elizabeth broke off her recital. Re-creating that conversation had amused her. She had enjoyed making me laugh, but suddenly her face seemed to cloud over at the memory of her conversation with *Boston*. She closed up.

"Please forgive me," she said. "I don't feel like being funny anymore. Let's change the subject. What *were* we talking about, come to think of it?"

"You were telling me that, on the whole, you'd had a relatively positive week."

"And you?" she asked.

"Me? I was asking you to go to the Spring Dance with me."

"Oh yes, that's right," she said. "My God, you really are stubborn."

"You have nothing to lose," I pointed out. "And since we were talking about strategies . . ."

She picked up the saucer she'd been using as a mock
telephone and hotly interrupted me. "I don't have any
more strategies, I don't know the word *strategy*. I don't
know anything about that putrid vocabulary of war
and tactics and aggression and attack. I'm not the one
who used that putrid term *strategy*. That was Boston. That was my mother. It was Boston!"

Her voice grew shrill. For a moment I thought she
was going to start shouting. I took her hand under
the table. "Come on, now," I said, "take it easy. I'm
your friend."

She didn't pull back her hand, and she lowered her
voice.

"Are you really my friend? Aren't you just trying
to seduce me?"

I gave a snort of laughter; down deep inside I knew
I didn't want her.

"What are you laughing at?" she asked.

"I was thinking how wrong you are to mistrust me.
I'm not trying to put the make on you, I've already
told you that. I just like to be with you."

"That," she said, "is incomprehensible. I'm no longer
of any interest to a normal boy."

"Well, then I'm not a normal boy."

"A logical conclusion," she said, "as monumental
as the faces on Mount Rushmore."

She laughed, and when I laughed with her she took
my other hand under the table and told me with tears
in her eyes, "We get along fine, don't we? Don't you
think it's positively astonishing that we've reached
this stage so soon? I do wish I'd known you before I
got so sick. We'd have had some wonderful times."

She fell silent, withdrew her hands, bit her lip.

"But I'm not sick," she declared. "I'm not sick, am
I? Tell me I'm not. I order you to tell me I'm not."

"You're not sick," I said.

"It's the rest who are sick," she said. "Sick of the rat race, the race for boys, for success, for appearances, for first place in everything. Isn't that so? Isn't it? Aren't I right?"

"I guess you're right," I said.

"You don't sound very convinced."

"Sure I am," I said. "In a way, I think you're right."

I shut up then because I didn't know if I was lying to her. I understood her phobia, but I couldn't give her false encouragement. When I'd arrived in the States, I had wanted more than anything else to fit into the system—as defined at college, as defined in American society with its complicated patterns and its rites of passage. I had fit in; I had succeeded. I'd been accepted and I liked that. The extraordinary hatred that this girl from Boston's high society had conceived for that system probably stemmed from her childhood, from too far away for me to fathom. You'd have to have been raised, as she was, in that closed, patrician society to be able to gauge her repulsion, her determination to break the mold fashioned for her by her mother.

Part of me endorsed her rebellion, but another part of me rejected it. I was drawn, moved, slightly fascinated by this pathetic and unpredictable creature, and I had grown to love her for her folly and fragility. She was like no one else I'd ever known. I wanted to comfort her, listen to her, protect her as I would a bird with broken legs and severed wings. I loved her, I had to admit it. I realized that when I looked at her elegant, tortured face across the table. Therefore, I couldn't lie to her and tell her she wasn't sick; I had just discovered that I loved her precisely because she was sick. To avoid lying, I renewed my invitation.

"Come to the Spring Dance with me," I said. "Please."

I saw a gleeful coquettishness awaken in her eyes and course across her face.

"My God, what'll we do there, you and I? Dance? Do you even know how to dance?"

"No," I said, "I dance like a three-legged hippopotamus. No sense of rhythm. When I dance I'm always out of sync with the music. It's one of my weaknesses."

"So what do you do at a spring dance when you're a three-legged hippopotamus?"

"You say to hell with everybody else," I said. "Hippopotamuses have a right to be happy, too."

She seemed to think it over, then decided she admired my persistence and my insolence. "You really want me to go that badly?" she asked.

"I want you to go with me. This will be my first and last American dance."

Elizabeth raised an admonitory finger. "Careful there! No romanticism. You'll say anything to get your way. You're a dangerous man."

"No I'm not."

She smiled.

"Let's change the subject. What've you read lately that wasn't too putrid?"

39

I FELT LIKE SEEING APRIL AGAIN.

The thought stole over me insidiously on my way
back from Sweet Briar, after I had dropped Elizabeth off at her sorority house. Elizabeth had finally
agreed to be my date for the big Spring Dance weekend, and I should have been happy. Yet when I left
her at the end of that spring Sunday afternoon, a fresh
wave of dissatisfaction pummeled me.

Something about Elizabeth checked the love I thought
I felt for her. I sometimes had the impression she was
playing with me, manipulating me, that she delighted
in her sickness. To erase that feeling, I'd have liked
to go to bed with her. But as I eyed Elizabeth's some-
what broken form at the top of the front steps to the
sorority house, she seemed so slight—almost ethereal—
that I knew it would be months and months before
I could even kiss her. I might never reach the point of
caressing her, of taking her in my arms. The notion
seemed both farfetched and vulgar; it was like one of
those insults Elizabeth accused me of proffering, an
insult to her vow of purity, to her withdrawal, to her
struggle against her body. I imagined that body gone
so thin, almost skeletal under the bulky, floppy clothes
she wore. Was Elizabeth sexy when she was naked?

Then I remembered April's thighs, remembered her
breasts in my hands when we made love, hungry for

each other on the backseat of the Ford, and I felt a re-
surgent need for her vitality. I wanted to taste her
mouth and surrender mine to her. The sweet-wine taste
of her moist lips returned to my memory like a temptation, faint but persistent.

The days were getting longer. I reached the edge of
April's neighborhood just as the light of the orange-
pink sun began disappearing behind the roofs. Those
houses formed the first line to cross when you came
from the white side of town. Where did April live? She
had never given me her address.

The Buick arrived almost on its own at the short,
sloping street on which her school stood. I knew there
was no chance of finding her there, since this was Sunday, but I thought the street where I'd waited for her
one winter day would serve as an observation point
and that luck would take me from there. It seemed
logical to park my car at the same spot, in front of
the small record shop, also closed now, where I'd first
heard the hoarse, winning voice of Fats Domino against
the wonderful background of his clunky piano. This
was the main drag, and I hoped against hope that April
would come through on her way home.

Four kids in red baseball uniforms were using the
street as a playing field. A car went by now and then.
Everything was peaceful. The ugliness of the neighborhood, which I hadn't seen since the previous winter, seemed almost beautified by splashes of white and
yellow and green in the trees and bushes surrounding the school.

I felt no frenzy in my yearning to see April again.
I just thought that if she happened by, it would be nice
to take her to one of our old hangouts. There I could
exorcise my longing for her that was like the longing
of a weaned child. I was already smugly savoring

those sexual joys that I never doubted she would wholeheartedly grant me. And, too, I felt the excitement
that gripped me every time I entered forbidden territory.

A shadow suddenly darkened the right side of the
Buick, blocking the fading sunlight that had warmed
my cheek. Something massive crashed down into the
passenger seat beside me. I saw a flash of tan serge
before I looked up at the huge, boisterous form in-
vading my car. It was Sheriff McLain, Big Jim McLain.

Fear knotted my guts. McLain wore the same Sam
Browne harness he'd worn the first time I'd seen him,
in that brief encounter in the dormitory corridor after
the suicide of Buck Kuschnick.

"All right, Mr. Snotnose," he said in his thick accent, "how about your tellin' me what you're fuckin'
around here for."

The butt of his revolver stuck out of the holster plastered against his bulky left thigh; his gleaming nickel-
plated sheriff's star was pinned to the expanse of pearl-
buttoned shirt that stretched across his chest. Sweaty
blotches stained his uniform at the armpits and gave
off an acrid, nauseating smell that blended with his reek-
ing breath. He was chewing a big plug of tobacco
that dribbled its brownish juice along his lower lip.

"You're gonna have to tell me," he said, "here or
at the station."

I felt paralyzed.

"All right, let's have it," he growled, his voice still
even. "You're smack in the middle of Nigger Town
and that's no place you oughta be. I'd like to know
some more about that."

He spoke slowly, seeming to relish my discomfi-
ture, my terror. I took my freshman student card out
of my jacket pocket.

"Yeah," he said, "seems to me we've run into each
other before. You're the foreign student."

"Yes," I said, "that's right."

"Yeah," he said, as if to punctuate his thoughts.

He stopped talking, swung his big body toward me, and seized my shoulders in his huge butcher's hands, forcing me to face him. His eyes were a strange shade of green, and the glint in them was shadowed by the broad brim of his Stetson. Its brown leather chin strap hardened his brick-red face.

"Let go," I said. "You're hurting me."

"What the hell's a little gentleman from the white college doin' fuckin' around on this side of town? Huh? And a foreigner at that."

"Let me go," I said. "I haven't done anything illegal."

"On a Sunday evenin', too," the sheriff went on, ignoring my protest.

I felt I had to say something to stop him from digging into my shoulders. "I got lost," I said. "I missed my road and wound up here and I'm tired so I stopped for a minute. I was just about to leave when you showed up. There's nothing wrong with that. You have no right to push me around like this."

He removed his hands from my shoulders and smiled wickedly.

"Was I pushin' you around?" he asked, feigning surprise. "Are you injured? Want to file a complaint?"

"No," I said, "it's okay."

"Yeah," he said. "That's better."

He fell silent again. I was still scared. In the Buick's rearview mirror I could see the patrol car with the light on its roof parked just behind us. How could I have missed hearing it come up? How could the sheriff have walked forward to my car without my spotting him? He must have cut his motor at the top of the hill and coasted down behind me. But why hadn't I noticed anything? Despite all the clanking hard-

ware he wore—handcuffs, whistle, revolver, hobnailed
boots—I'd been as surprised as a thief caught red-
handed when that big form loomed up beside me. I'd
probably dozed off. The sunset, maybe, the late-
afternoon air; I'd just gone blank for a moment.

"Here's what we're gonna do," the sheriff finally said.
"I'm goin' to get in my automobile and pull out ahead
of you and you're gonna follow behind me and we're
gonna leave Nigger Town. We'll park on the campus and you'll get into my automobile and I'll take you
for a little ride. There's somethin' I want to show
you. Okay?"

"Okay," I said, baffled by what this giant cop was
up to.

I followed his instructions, alarms clanging in my
mind, my legs like water, my body weakened by fear
and guilt. I imagined the worst: interrogation at the
police station, a summons from Old Zach, a growing scandal. But the same inner voice that had so often guided my escapades, that voice that had always
exhorted me to do what I'd thought was beyond me,
told me now: *Relax. He doesn't know a thing. Get hold
of yourself. You can lie as well as the next man. You must
maintain your standing. The guy's just an asshole. You're
as tough as he is. He's trying to scare you. Keep cool. Don't
be a baby.*

I repeated that last admonition out loud: "Don't be
a baby."

Alone in my car, in that cozy compartment where I
had so often talked to myself, the words changed as
my confidence oozed back. They became more com-
bative, more determined to throw off the lawman's
hold on me: *You're not a kid anymore.*

40

THE KID I TOLD MYSELF I NO LONGER WAS GOT OUT of the Buick, opened the passenger-side door of the sheriff's Dodge, and climbed in beside him. The patrol car moved off toward the hills overlooking the campus. The sheriff didn't say anything, just continued chewing his tobacco, driving slowly. His piercing eyes flicked over the paths and lawns bathed in the moonlight that had surreptitiously dissolved the orange dusk of what had been a glorious spring day. We were in full darkness now. Driving at a leisurely pace through the residential district near the college, the sheriff was taking me toward the barracks, where the teachers lived. I didn't register that right off; I was late in recognizing the place I knew so well, because McLain had taken a road opposite the one I had so often followed during the winter of my clandestine love affair with April.

Not until we had come out on the other side of the barracks, on what looked more like a track than a road, did I realize where I was. All my strength spewed out of me. McLain, still silent, stopped the car above the ravine and shone his spotlight on that basin of dirt, that sinister-looking gulch where April and I had staged our secret meetings. Fear surged through me again.

Don't say anything, I thought, don't do anything.

Nothing can happen as long as you keep your mouth shut. This is a test, a trial. You mustn't lose or give in.

Beside me, the sheriff seemed to be waiting. The silence in the car was broken only by the sound of his chewing and the slight metallic clicking of all his policeman's gear whenever he moved his powerful body. That went on for quite a while. Then he started talking slowly and softly, as only Southerners can, and the bigger and stronger and more muscular they are, the more murderous that softness sounds.

"I come here a lot at night," he said. "Usually take the track we just came over. Nobody knows that track. And I wait. Sometimes nothin' turns up. It's like huntin', you know—sometimes nothin' comes in sight. Other times I do see somethin'. Or somebody. Then, after a while, I leave."

He looked at me. "Did you want to say somethin'?"

I shrugged.

"Once," he went on, "only once last winter, around five o'clock in the afternoon, I thought I saw a green Buick, the automobile you're driving, down in the ravine. I was just fixin' to go on down and check it out when I got a radio call, an all-points call, and I had to hustle on back to U.S. 11 to set up a roadblock —some fellas who'd been robbin' farms up in Maryland had crossed the state line. It took me the rest of the day and part of the night, too. When I got back the Buick was gone, o' course. How long you been drivin' that automobile?"

"I bought it this spring," I told him.

"Uh-huh," he said, "sure."

He spit a long jet of dark yellow saliva through the open front window. "When I saw that same Buick today over in the coon neighborhood, I got to thinkin'.

Hey, I said to myself, I've seen that Buick somewhere before. You ever come here? In your automobile, I mean."

"No," I said.

"Of course, anybody has a right to roam around
here. There's no law against it. This is a free country."

Don't answer him, I thought, don't let him drag you
into his game. All you have to say is *yes* or *no*. He's
trying to get a conversation going. Don't fall for it.
That's what's dangerous.

"On the other hand, while there's no law against
wanderin' around among the nigras on a spring Sunday afternoon, we do have customs here, boy. And
custom says you don't go messin' around with them
shit-kickers under any circumstances. See what I mean,
boy? It's not the law, but it's our custom."

The sheriff's eyes never left me. With his hat still
screwed down on his head, the strap slightly damp
with dribbled tobacco juice, his face was more awesome than ever, there in the darkness of the car. I
thought I could read an amused, suspicious question
in his eyes, as if he were searching for something.
He went on in the same soft, slow, deceptively lazy
voice.

"And custom, boy, is a lot more important here than
the law."

After that statement, with which, probably unwit-
tingly, Sheriff McLain had summarized the deeply
rooted code of the South, silence once more settled in
the car. I remained stubbornly closemouthed. He
waited.

An obscure inexplicable temptation welled up in
me—a temptation to confess. I had never told anyone of the secret of my affair with April, of my love-

making with a black girl. It weighed on me like a
steel bar. I hadn't felt in the least guilty at first; I wasn't
a Southerner; I wasn't even an American. Their rac-
ist heritage had never touched me. But the secret had
nevertheless bred a vague feeling, the beginning of a
troubled conscience. And the more deeply I was as-
similated into this country's life and traditions, the
more sharply I understood the audacity, the madness,
in fact, that had ruled this whole episode in my life.

Maybe Big Jim McLain was offering me relief. He
was a big, rough man, but reassuring, too, because
he was an old hand at playing good-cop-bad-cop; he
elicited rather than demanded the truth. He circled
around and around the problem, sniffing at the enigma
he knew I harbored. He enjoyed it. McLain was a
born hunter. I could feel two opposing instincts clashing inside me: a desire to confess, a duty to keep
silent.

The conflict was brief. In the contest between desire
and duty, my pride tipped the balance, along with
the loyalty I felt toward April. We had sworn to say
nothing to anyone, under any circumstances. An oath
is sacred. While I had told myself before to stop being
a baby if I was to face the ordeal the sheriff was in-
flicting on me, now I congratulated myself for pre-
serving intact a child's purity of heart. A secret is a
secret, and a child would rather die than betray one.
In that respect, children are stronger than adults. I
was stronger than this strong sheriff. I knew then that
I would keep the memory of April for myself alone,
that it would form an indestructible kernel deep down
inside me, at that depth at which you never betray
yourself; it would drive me to overcome fear, anxiety,
loneliness. At last, now, I could open my mouth; I
was ready to put on any kind of an act.

"Did you catch them?" I asked confidently.

Big Jim looked puzzled. He looked at me blankly.

"Catch who?"

"The robbers, of course. The ones from Maryland you were telling me about. You put up a roadblock for them last winter. Did you get them?"

He let out a surprised but self-satisfied guffaw.

"Hell," he said, "I'd forgot all about them. Sure we nabbed 'em, what do you think, boy? There was a helluva lot of shootin'—three police units we had, from three different states, you see. Turned into a regular shootin' gallery. It was worth the wait. We weren't savin' money on bullets, let me tell you. Jesus H. Christ, they came out of that automobile cryin', on their knees, beggin' us to stop shootin'. Sonsobitches were shittin' their pants."

He huffed, seemed to reflect for a moment, then added: "I know cops who've waited all their lives for a shoot-out like that. What a night that was, my boy."

"I can just imagine," I said.

I was surprised at my own fawning; it wasn't, I found, so hard to do. I even got kind of a kick out of it.

"You can't imagine it if you didn't go through it," he said sententiously. "One thing I can tell you, though: hassles like that one give a man an almighty thirst. We really tied one on afterward."

He switched on his engine and threw the car into reverse. "I could go on and on," McLain said, "but I got to be headin' back."

He drove me to the campus. All the way back the sheriff fiddled with his radio, checking with head-quarters in case there were any calls for him. I realized he'd cut off radio contact during our visit to the ravine, and I shuddered thinking about it. For that meant

he had really planned our excursion as an interrogation, and he didn't want anyone disturbing him during it. Now, with the car full of the radio's ceaseless
crackling, I figured the danger was past. Suddenly
McLain was no longer a silent, menacing presence.
When we reached the campus parking area where I'd
left the Buick, he stuck out his big hand. I thought
it was all over.

"So long, my boy," he said.

"So long, Sheriff," I replied happily.

I don't know why, but a word escaped me, one word
that was almost a confession. "Thanks."

He winked at me. "What for?" he shot back.

I hesitated. I had to go on lying.

"For telling me about your gunfight. It was fascinating."

McLain smiled maliciously—a connoisseur's smile.

"A flatterer, too," he said. "Smartass. You're a real
little smartass, Mr. Foreign Student. But watch out,
my boy. I'll give you a piece of advice: Don't take anything for granted. Don't take *me* for granted."

"I won't forget, sir."

"Better not. And don't let me catch you hangin'
around the nigras again. There's nothin' you want
down there."

When I didn't answer, he persisted, keeping my hand
buried in his. "Right, my boy?"

"Sure," I said.

"What do you call niggers where you come from?"
he asked.

I sensed that he was testing me one last time and
that I'd have to lie again to get free of him.

"Same thing you do," I said.

"How's that? Tell me, I wanna hear you say it."

I had to force myself to utter the word. "We call
them niggers," I said.

"That's fine," he said, "that's just fine. Okay, that's all."

He removed his hand from mine the way you unlock a pair of handcuffs, with a sharp jerk.

"Night, my boy."

This time I knew I could open the car door and get out. I was annoyed at myself for using that word, but I told myself my final triumph made up for that moment of cowardice: I hadn't broken faith. He hadn't reached me. I was intact, I thought.

The patrol car made a U-turn and I watched it move off. I didn't dare budge; I was certain Sheriff McLain would keep his eye on me in his mirror until the car disappeared around the gymnasium. The moment it did, I began talking out loud to myself in the darkness: "I beat him, I beat him! I won!"

But I felt no pride. On the contrary, I was beginning to feel keenly what April meant when she'd kept on telling me, all through our affair, that someday I, too, like her or because of her, like all the other members of her race, would sooner or later know what shame was.

41

IN THE DAYS THAT FOLLOWED, I FELT DIMINISHED.
McLain obsessed me. Oddly, I wanted to see him
again. The sheriff had so impressed me that I felt an
insidious need to see him again so that we could resume our ambiguous conversation. The feeling was finally routed, though, by the golden days of that
spring. There was so much to do: final exams were
starting and the dance would follow. The weather
was so warm, so fine, that the memory of my brush
with the law receded. Traces of it must have stuck
in my mind, however: from then on, seeing the roof
light of a patrol car turn into a street gave me a nasty
little shock, made my throat tighten. I'd have to remain silent about that, too, as I did about all the rest.

42

ACROSS THE OCEAN, IN PARIS, MY FATHER WAS
not well. He was afraid that my brother, his oldest son,
might be killed in the war in Algeria. Anxiety kept
him from sleeping. He had trouble breathing, was
swept with hot flashes. Every evening my mother
covered his chest with a big sheet that she had folded
up and cooled in the refrigerator. *Doing a wrapping*,
she called it. If the mail did not bring comforting news
of the family second lieutenant at least once a week,
she had to do two wrappings a day, one in the morning and another in the evening.

I learned all this in a letter from Mother. It had never
occurred to me before that my father, that tall, magis-
terial figure with white hair and gray-blue eyes behind horn-rimmed glasses, could torture himself so
much over any of his children. We had always thought
of him as stern and reassuring, as straight as a poplar,
always even-toned, always restrained. When we were
kids, he had only to appear at the end of a corridor to
still the commotion his four sons were making. He
never had to shout or threaten or scold; his mere presence was powerful enough to bend us to his will. We
feared, respected, loved him, made up irreverent nicknames for him like high school kids who quake before their principal. I could not imagine my father

216

suffocating with anxiety, being babied by a wife who had found no way of dealing with this unforeseeable circumstance but to apply an old farm remedy.

It was upsetting. He was as sensitive and fragile as a child, then, as emotional as *I* could be. Something reeled, and for the first time the idea that so deeply appalled me—of returning home—began to shape in my mind as a kind of duty. Should I go home to help my father? Despite the surge of love I felt for him, the notion didn't appeal to me, and I pushed it away.

The selfishness lurking in us all undergoes a hardening process in young people who journey far. They are alone in the unknown. They establish priorities, make plans; they learn to survive. They fight their loneliness by casting aside challenges, by overcoming obstacles. Anything that might interfere with the progress of that journey is seen as a threat. I now had my plans. I did not want to go home. I wanted to stay at least another year at the college. And I wanted to transform Elizabeth, to overwhelm her with my love so that she would again be the flawless girl whose perfection had stamped itself on our first meeting. Maybe then she would love me, too, and together we could share a school year, with all its rituals, like any other pair of normal students, a year rich in joy.

I thought about my father again and of how he used to read to us after dinner when we were children, before the existence of television. He would read aloud from the books that had bewitched his own child-hood. *The Three Musketeers* had been one of my favorites, and I had always remembered the inspiring advice d'Artagnan's father gave his son before the young man left: "Do not fear opportunities, and seek adventures." I wanted more opportunities. I longed for more adventures.

My appetite for America was still not surfeited; indeed, my curiosity grew as time went on. I had not
yet absorbed enough of this country, of its cities, its
roads, its vistas, its surprises and encounters. I was
only beginning to grasp the magnitude of the country, the ferocity and poetry of it. And knowing more
about all of those elements was important to me. My
nights were increasingly haunted by the specter of
that boat back to France and the black-clad strangers
waiting like a row of penguins on the dock at Le Ha-
vre, snickering and chanting at me, "You missed something! You missed something!" I didn't want to miss
a thing. I looked forward to endless discoveries in this
land I had scarcely yet begun to explore.

So, sustained as much by that frightful dream as by
my romantic fantasy (healing Elizabeth), I simply
blocked out my father's fears. I also blocked out the
perilous ordeal my brother was going through, and
which my old schoolmates in France would soon share,
in an incomprehensible and distant war that didn't
concern me. None of that was my business. It wasn't
what I was meant for. I didn't want to go home. I
had my plans.

43

OLD ZACH GAVE A SORROWFUL AND FAINTLY IR-
ritated shrug.

"There's no way we can help you," he told me.
"Our little college is not equipped to pay a second
year's scholarship to a foreign student. Your grades are
excellent, of course, and you have blended extremely
well into campus life. You've even become something
of a figure here. Everyone likes you. I can perfectly
well understand your request, but I don't see what I
can do about it."

He smiled benevolently from behind his desk. A raging need to persuade him surged in me.

"Dean," I said, my jaws clenched, my voice grave,
"I have my plans."

"I see," Old Zach said, amused.

"Yes. On the advice of a junior here named Clem
Billingsworth, I have sent letters of application to the
heads of the U.S. Forest Service in ten Western and
Northwestern states that offer extremely well-paid
summer jobs cutting down trees, cleaning up roads and
woodlands, building bridges and so on. Clem did this
last summer."

"You're not the first one who's looked for a summer job," Old Zach commented.

"Sir," I hurried on, "I've written to Montana, Nebraska, Colorado, North and South Dakota, Washington, Wyoming, Utah, Oregon, and Nevada."

Intoning all those magical, far-off names bolstered my persistence, my determination to show that I intended to go all the way.

"Not many forests in Utah and Nevada," Old Zach interjected gently.

"You're wrong there, Dean," I said. "I studied the maps at night before drafting my letters. After all, if there weren't any forests, there wouldn't be any Forest Service officials in those states to write to, would there?"

He laughed. "How'd you get their addresses?"

"I work nights at the *Valley News,*" I said, "to earn enough to pay off my car loan. I had access to enough information to be sure my letters would get where they were going. I'm certain that out of the ten, I'll get at least one bite."

For several nights at my *News* copy desk, Rand-McNally road maps had been my main reading. Under the small lamp with the opaline green shade that would always symbolize my start in journalism, I learned by heart the routes I'd have to take to get to wherever I found a summer job.

The names of the cities where the head offices of the Forest Service's parent Department of Agriculture were located fired my imagination. Especially that of one place I'd written to called Missoula, Montana. I loved to say the words, they rang like a Carl Sandburg poem:

Miss-ou-la
Mon-ta-na.

That had to be an Indian name, I figured. I kept chanting it to myself as I drove back at night along the silent roads from the newspaper office to the sleeping campus.

"Can you really see yourself chopping down trees in a western forest?" Old Zach asked, as suavely as before. "It's a tough job. As I recall, you didn't get your best marks for weight lifting."

"I can do it," I said, surprised and annoyed by the skepticism of this man in whom we were so accustomed to confiding, and who had encouraged all our individual initiatives.

He scrutinized me pensively. "Very well, young man," he said after a brief pause. "Let's suppose you get this job. How much can you earn in two or three months? Six to eight hundred dollars at most—just enough to rent a room in town, since the college can't give you a free room in the dorm, as it did this year. Somewhere in Europe another exchange student has already received notification that we've accepted him as your successor. Yes indeed. You seem surprised, but that's the procedure."

Bitter bile rose in my throat.

"All right," he continued. "Let's examine this a little further. You'll have enough to pay for your room, perhaps some of your board, maybe even enough to pay off your bank loan. What about the rest? Your tuition, for example. This is a private college. Enrollment and tuition will easily run to three or four thousand dollars. Where are you going to get hold of that much?"

"That's just it," I said. "I was hoping the school would provide it."

The reply fell like an ax. "You're hoping too high, son."

I had tears in my eyes. "But, Dean, couldn't you at least bring my case before the Administrative Board and plead for me?"

Old Zach shuffled through a pile of papers and files on the desk. Then he peered up at me, looking suddenly tired. "As it happens, I've already done that," he said. "I went to them after you made your appointment with me. I saw this coming, you know."

I was only half surprised. "Oh," I said.

"Yes, I trust that doesn't surprise you. Your Old Zach can read his students' minds. I've been waiting for you to get around to this for some time. I know how much you love being here. So I anticipated that you'd want to stay on longer. That's already happened with one or two foreign students before you, but the scholarships are only for one year. So I put the problem to the board, on a hypothetical basis. They said no. Nothing personal, you understand, just a matter of principle. We've never done it. It's a matter of budgets, too—next year is going to be a bit tight. You must be realistic about this, son."

He paused. Then: "America is a realistic country. And the reality here is that even the shrewdest and most senior dean doesn't throw much weight against a school administration that deals in figures and operates in terms of what those figures say. You do not figure in the figures for our little college."

"This may be a small college," I protested weakly, "but it's a rich one. We all know that."

Old Zach sighed, squelching his impatience. "You don't know everything. We're planning three new buildings in the next three years, a library, a lab, and a new dorm. Most of the alumni contributions that keep us going will be entirely assigned to those projects. Just because we're rich doesn't mean we can scatter our money around."

A wave of discouragement washed over me, and I stood up. Old Zach did, too.

"If I were you," he said, "and I did get a job offer from the Forest Service, I'd still spend my summer in the western woods. When you get back to Europe, you'll be glad you have that little nest egg, and it'll be one more experience under your belt."

"I'm planning to," I said, not at all consoled by his advice. "May I ask you a question?"

"Go ahead, my friend."

"Why have you been so tough on me?"

He barked a dry little laugh that wasn't like him at all. "I haven't been tough on you."

"Oh yes, you have, sir," I said to this man for whom I had so much respect.

Suddenly Old Zach seemed to lose his temper. His voice ballooned, and so did his Southern accent. He flung out one great arm. "Young man, you have got to learn that things don't just happen because you wish them to. That's not enough, do you understand? That's not enough! That's a dreamworld!"

He calmed down just as quickly, and the arm came down protectively around my shoulders. "You're going to the Spring Dance this weekend. Enjoy yourself. It's a big event. You do have a date, I presume."

"Yes, sir," I said, "I do."

I chewed over Old Zach's latest lesson. Alarm reinforced my bitterness. I couldn't help seeing something more in the board's refusal than a mere matter of budgeting. Had they been making inquiries about me? Had Sheriff McLain drawn up a report on my suspicious behavior? My wounded vanity took on an edge of paranoia, and I walked the flowered campus paths with the weight of the world on my frail shoulders. A world against which I suddenly held a mute grudge.

44

THE SPRING DANCE WEEKEND WAS INAUGURATED on Friday afternoon with the arrival of the girls and their chaperons or relatives. They were put up in local hotels and motels, or in rented rooms in town. Ritual dictated that Friday night was devoted to a few quick drinks in the fraternity houses. Everyone went to bed early to be fresh for the next day, the longest Saturday in the year.

It began with an open-air brunch on the lawns of the fraternity houses, under green-and-white-striped tents raised at the tops of the hills behind the grand houses overlooking the neighboring valleys. Black waiters served iced tea and lightly laced mint juleps.

Paper plates were heaped with scrambled eggs, spicy, dark red sausages, and golden brown flapjacks drenched in maple syrup. Over the buffet tables floated an aroma compounded of cinnamon, pecans, honey, and bay rum. The boys wore cord jackets, chinos, and white shoes; some sported straw boaters. The girls were decked out in flowered blouses and full, ankle-length skirts.

Around one o'clock, clusters of boys and their dates left the houses, on foot or by car, to descend on the central campus lawn, an immaculately grassy hillock

that sloped gently down to the chapel and that was soon
thronged with celebrants. Blankets and jackets were
spread out—this was the only day of the year when you
were allowed to appear in shirtsleeves on the campus
proper—and everyone sat on them or stretched out
directly on the grass. Seen from above, from the colonnade, this assembly of boys and girls in their apple-green
and eggshell and sky-blue and pale yellow and fuchsia
clothes recalled a pointillist painting—tiny dots of contrasting colors that the squinting eye could turn into
a canvas of indefinable but uniform hue. It was a proud
sight, without a single jarring note. I was in rapture.

It was time for the afternoon entertainment by the
Dorsey Brothers' band. By tradition, the orchestra
that sent the couples twirling in their tuxedos and ball
gowns that evening in the big gym first gave an afternoon concert. This was the time for the band to reveal its versatility by playing a different kind of music
from the tunes it would mostly stick to that night—
less bouncy, with less of a beat, less "danceable." The
afternoon concert was mainly a review of the hit pa-
rades of the previous ten years, which took those
lounging on that Virginia grass back to their preteens.

For this was, after all, a civilization and a system in
which pop music served as both a social and an emotional code. Everyone there but the Austrian and I
shared the tunes they had heard on the radio—TV
was just coming in strong now—and at their first school
dances, when they had barely stopped counting their
ages in one digit. This was music that had underscored their high school years—accompanied them to
ball games, provided a background to their first encounters with the opposite sex, set the mood for the
dating game that prefigured the more serious game of
love and marriage. These tunes told the story of their

own past: music as history. Through it they could re-
live everything that had brought them here, to this
college where their futures were taking form. Each melody evoked a rite of passage: their first romance, first
triumph, first sorrow; despite their youth, the students were all submerged that afternoon in a sweet,
poignant feeling we usually associate more with grown-
ups: nostalgia.

Applause and bursts of laughter greeted each new-
old song. Titles flew from lip to lip; people hummed
"The Tennessee Waltz" and clapped rhythmically to a
particularly witless number called "Bibbidi-Bobbidi-
Boo" that had been all the rage in 1949. I couldn't identify any of these milestones of a past I'd never known,
but Elizabeth, sitting beside me on the grass, was kind
enough to identify them for me as they came up, with
a commentary in her own acrid style. A whole an-
thology of songs without words, the group memory
of my friends and their dates, a musical retrospective
mingling romantic ballads with livelier tunes. And,
with the years, the rhythms changed as they reached
the great turning point, the first of the rock tunes.

" 'Mona Lisa.' Syrup, syrup—that was Nat King
Cole," Elizabeth murmured. "And that one you must
know. 'Autumn Leaves.' Didn't it come from France?
. . . Here's a real nothing: 'If I Knew You Were
Coming I'd Have Baked a Cake.' Can you imagine
anything sillier? . . . 'Tzena Tzena,' another one that's
putrid, written by apes for apes. This one was pretty,
though—'Kisses Sweeter Than Wine'; I remember
Jimmie Rodgers singing it in the days when I was going
to conquer the world."

She fell silent when the band swung into "Your
Cheatin' Heart," which was only two years old and
which I did remember. In those days, hit songs were
long-lived; a tune could remain on the charts for over

a year. Why had Elizabeth fallen mute at this one? I
looked at her and saw her brow wrinkle. She looked
back at me, smiled absently, and lay down on her back,
looking up at the sky. I stretched out beside her and
closed my eyes, not daring to take her hand, but in-
toxicated by the scent of the trees that was spiced with
the hint of jasmine she had sprayed on her dress.

And the music continued:
"Don't Let the Stars Get In Your Eyes"
"Jambalaya"
"Kiss of Fire"
"Sing a Little Song"
"I Saw Mommy Kissin' Santa Claus"
"Hi-Lili-Hilo"
"You, You, You"
"April in Portugal"
"Rock Around the Clock"
A few couples got up to do some rock steps when
"Rock Around the Clock" started—the song that had
touched off a revolution, the white man's first intru-
sion into what had been black music; but the cou-
ples soon dropped down on the lawn again. It was all
lazy and laid back; time seemed to stand still. I si-
lently rejoiced that I'd persuaded Elizabeth to come with
me. Everything had gone well. I had no trouble for-
getting my worries about my future.

She had arrived by train on Friday afternoon without a chaperon. I was waiting for her at the station in
Staunton.

"We don't need a chaperon," she said as I drove
her toward the campus. "Our contract stipulates that
you won't make a play for me and that I'm only here
to help you live out your Spring Dance fantasy."

"All right," I said, but I'd taken her hand and she
had not shrunk from the contact.

All couples acted that way. I calculated that the conspiratorial friendship we'd formed gave me some right to pretend—to behave *as if.* Since we were playacting anyway.

So we concocted a lie to tell the elderly woman who was renting her a room for two nights in a house on Jefferson Avenue, behind the post office. Elizabeth's parents had been delayed, we'd said, but we were expecting them to show up on Saturday night or Sunday, which explained why the girl would be alone when her young man (me) came to pick her up for the dances and cocktail parties.

Elizabeth had expressly asked her mother not to come down from Boston to watch her play the queen of the ball; she had explained that the boy who'd invited her might see her parents' presence as a sign of too lively an interest in a possible catch. When her mother protested, Elizabeth put her off the scent. For she was beginning to dread the day when her parents finally saw her again; she worried about how they would react to the changes in her appearance, to her boycott of the social whirl. May we, her mother had asked, at least know the name of your faithful admirer? Certainly, her daughter had agreed. He's the scion of one of the oldest families in the French nobility. She'd invented a swaggering name for me, Marquis de la Grande Pierre. This had deeply impressed Boston. Elizabeth and I had laughed. All these lies were cementing our complicity. She seemed to enjoy it as one more challenge to the system she was fighting.

From all this, I dredged up hope of a real friendship that might soon be transmuted into love, on her part, at least, as well as mine. As the weekend went on, I thought Elizabeth was getting better and that my therapy was going to work quickly on her. Color had

come back into her cheeks. She had made some effort to dress more conventionally.

"I know all the disguises required for this sort of monkey business," she'd assured me. "During the day you
have to be springlike, bright and crisp, smart but absolutely not a tease. In the evening, romance and frills,
charm and femininity. Don't worry, I won't spoil your
dream."

"Thanks," I'd said.

"You're so welcome, Monsieur le marquis."

"Shake, Rattle, and Roll"
"Sh-Boom"
"All of Me"
"Papa Loves Mambo"

The tunes were current now, and the Dorsey Brothers were playing the songs that had bewitched me
during my nine months in America. Now I could play
the I-remember game for Elizabeth, who was still
lying back on the lawn with her eyes closed. There was
"Cry Me a River," which voluptuous, statuesque Ju-
lie London had sung so fervidly. I recognized Tennessee
Ernie Ford's "Sixteen Tons," an echo of the music issu-
ing from Bob Kendall's radio on the long night drive to
Dallas. And here's "The Tender Trap," sung by Frank
Sinatra over the credits of a film of the same name:

> You see a pair of laughing eyes,
> And suddenly you're sighing sighs. . . .

In the credits sequence, Sinatra wore a light-colored
suit and a straw fedora with a narrow brim and a wide
band, and he walked toward the camera from the
distance—against the background of a sky as blue as
the surface he was strolling on. He moved nonchalantly toward the audience on the vast, slightly warped

screen of the first Cinemascope pictures. And as
Sinatra's form grew bigger, the music swelled. That's
all there was to the credits: the blue-eyed man moving endlessly toward us. The movie had been unmemorable
except when Frankie sang, but that long, tracking shot
of him as he walked through the unreal color on the
giant screen had left its mark on me. We'd seen the
film during the winter, in the town's only movie
house. To the handful of students scattered through
the theater, charm and success were summed up in
that low-down, utterly relaxed walk—hands thrust in
the pockets of that beautifully tailored suit, hat tilted
insolently back on his head, the smile that told you he
was not about to be suckered by anything or anybody, and that voice in which all the myths of the Forties were stored.

We knew he was short and of Italian stock, and had
undergone marriage and money troubles and that for
a while his voice had failed him. But he had clawed
his way back up, had won an Oscar for his role in
From Here to Eternity, and now he was back on top;
every record he chose to cut, no matter how routine, was almost always an overnight smash.

We always went to the movies in a bunch, three or
four of us, usually because we were neighbors in the
dorm. When we left the theater that night we raved
over what for a long time we referred to simply as
"the credits," and we wondered how many years of
work, how many ordeals and love affairs, how many
in-fighting scars he'd had to accumulate to achieve that
looseness, that way of walking as if he were on top
of the world, at the peak of fame and fortune.

All this came flooding back to me when I heard
the music from *The Tender Trap.* I launched into a
lyrical, ironic description of how stunned we'd been,
we college kids, by the great Sinatra's urbane so-

phistication. Then I waited for a few amused comments from Elizabeth. Not a word. She was sound
asleep.

The afternoon concert ended and the couples got un-
hurriedly to their feet, the boys taking the girls' hands
to pull them up, everyone brushing skirts and pants. I
remained seated beside Elizabeth, not daring to wake
her.

It was six o'clock; the air was still warm. Staying
on through the postconcert hubbub didn't bother me
despite the questioning stares from some of the couples. I blamed Elizabeth's somnolence on the hypnotic effect of the music and the scented spring air, but
I was afraid other people would think she was drunk;
in some of the fraternity houses the bourbon had begun circulating at brunch out of flasks concealed in
brown paper bags. That wasn't Elizabeth's style. She
hadn't eaten or drunk anything. When I'd insisted,
she'd said the mere sight of the scrambled eggs and
sausages had given her forebodings of nausea.

She finally woke up and glanced around the empty
lawn.

"Gosh," she said, "I fell asleep. Are we the last ones
here?"

"Yep," I said, "everyone else has left. The music put
you to sleep?"

"Maybe," she replied. "And maybe it's because I'm
so weak. At one point, while they were playing 'Mis-
ter Sandman,' I couldn't even feel my body anymore.
I think I even hovered a couple of inches in the air.
Did you notice me rising, as if I were levitating?"

"No," I said, laughing, "nothing like that."

"Really?" she said gravely. "That's funny. I could
swear I left the ground for a few seconds. Then I fell
asleep. I was really a long, long way off."

We were on our feet and walking under a canopy
of beeches to the parking lot where I'd left the Buick.
She took my hand and I realized she was trembling as
she had been during our first meetings.

"Are you chilly?" I asked her. "Hungry?"

"No." Then she murmured: "If I don't feel my body
anymore, it means I've won. What do you think?"

"I think we're going to have a terrific evening."

She said nothing, merely frowned and looked straight
ahead past the elms surrounding the parking area. For
the first time since this big weekend began, I had a
vague feeling that something was going to happen
that I couldn't control. Elizabeth began to hum. I realized that she hadn't done that since we'd started seeing
each other, and I tried to take it as a sign that my
sudden foreboding was foolish.

45

THE IMPORTANT THING AT THESE BIG DANCES WAS
not to arrive alone. We had to leave the fraternity
houses in fleets of cars to pick up the girls—in their
evening gowns, with their hair done, nails manicured,
makeup fresh—who were waiting for us with their
chaperons. What made the ceremony interesting and
fun, what punctuated it with flashes of drama, was
sharing all this, the preliminaries, the anticipation, even
if the couples split off from the bunch later on, when

the dance was well under way. The dance was like everything else in campus life, like the committees and
clubs and football games: you didn't do things solo;
you participated; you belonged to a community that
tirelessly wove its web of relationships, binding its
members in devotion to a common spirit born long
ago in the Virginia pioneers' fear of their vast, wild,
unknown new continent. The old virtues were stressed:
family, community, effort, union.

I had learned of these origins in American History
267, a sophomore course, and while I still wasn't too
clear on the correlation between the Founding Fathers'
blind faith in the group spirit and the atmosphere of
a college dance three hundred years later, I was beginning to feel it in my veins. You did things with others or not at all. You didn't exist without the others.
So, in obedience to the rule, I was providing trans-
port in my big, open Buick to my friends Johnny
Marciano and Alex Marshall.

They had already picked up their dates, two girls
from Mary Baldwin College. I parked the Buick in
front of Mrs. MacPherson's, where Elizabeth was staying
for the weekend. When I went inside, I found Elizabeth, in a pink dress with the traditional orchid pinned
to her bosom, sitting with her elderly landlady.

"Evening, Mrs. MacPherson," I said.

"Good evening," she replied, all smiles, in a thick
local accent. "Off you go, now. Have an unforget-
table Spring Dance."

She got up and went into the living room, leaving
us alone in the entry hall.

"Let's go, Elizabeth," I said, "our friends are waiting for us in the car."

"What friends?" she asked, looking startled.

"Two buddies from school with their dates."

"I never expected we'd go to the dance with the rest of the herd."

"Look, you know perfectly well it's just to make our grand entrance into the gym. After that everybody goes his way."

Her face shut. She stared at the ground and a shiver ran through her.

"You're breaking our agreement," she said, her voice hollow. "You know I hate all this performing. Who are these people, anyway? What if they recognize me?"

"What do you mean?"

"Just what I say. Suppose one of them knew me when I was Elizabeth Baldridge—the climber, the ambitious monkey on the ladder, Mommy's arrogant, cannibalistic little girl. Then what'll happen?"

"What do you think will happen?" I said. "They'll notice you've changed your hair and lost weight, that's all."

"Oh, no," she exploded. "I'll have to talk, explain. I know just how these inane backseat conversations go—'What're you up to? Weren't you engaged to so-and-so?' You promised you'd spare me all that."

As she raged she retreated until her back was against the wall, and I saw panic flicker in her eyes. For the second or third time since I'd known her, I felt truly annoyed with her.

"The two girls are from Mary Baldwin," I told her firmly. "Johnny Marciano and Alex Marshall are freshman—you can't possibly know them. Now be nice. Don't spoil everything."

I took her arm and steered her toward the door. From a hall shelf she snatched up a pearl-embroidered evening bag and a shawl that matched her pink dress and reluctantly let herself be led outside. We got into the Buick.

"Elizabeth," I said in the ritual formula, "may I introduce Alex and Johnny and June and Laetitia? Alex, Johnny, June, Laetitia, this is Elizabeth?"

"Pleased to meet you," said Alex, Johnny, June, and Laetitia, almost in unison.

"Hello," Elizabeth said, unenthusiastically.

Without the others seeing it because I'd put her up front with me while they were squeezed into the back, she favored me with a comic scowl of disgust. From then until we reached the gym she didn't open her mouth. I thought I'd gotten past the most dangerous obstacle and that from then on there'd be no more hitches. Arm in arm we entered the gym.

Almost all the thousand students and their partners were already there. Counting parents, a few chaperons, faculty members, deans and their wives, that made a total of over two thousand dress jackets and ball gowns on display around the floor. The basketball posts had been taken down for the occasion. The stark, ugly upstairs gallery that ran all around the huge room had been hung with garlands in the dance colors—pink and white—to give a slightly more welcoming look. In fact, the decor didn't count. For a moment you almost lost your bearings, so caught up were you in this dense throng, all dressed nearly alike, this thrumming mass of young people looking like blossoming cherry and apple trees, the boys' hair freshly clipped, the girls' hair—red or blonde, for the most part— sprayed and decked with flowers. You thrilled to the hopeful tremor of pleasure that ran through the crowd, like a breeze making a wheatfield dance.

Facing us on a platform at the opposite end of the expanse of linoleum, which teams of volunteers had spent the day scrubbing, sat the Dorsey Brothers' band dressed in horrendous electric-blue suits. That was a bit shocking, especially since every one of the musicians wore a big yellow rose in his buttonhole. The choice of clothing was off-putting at first, but you could always tell yourself that beauty and purity were on the dancers' side of that platform. Besides, the twenty men in the band had an excuse: they were pros, and this was just a job. After it was over they would pack up their trombones and their patent-leather shoes and board the bus emblazoned with their name (THE GREAT JIMMY AND TOMMY DORSEY BAND) to set other students dancing beneath other garlanded ceilings.

We didn't know that the Spring Dance Committee had voiced reservations about those electric-blue suits. But some great mind, some dialectician in the Harrison Riddle mold, could easily have convinced you that a touch of vulgarity was actually desirable, since it brought out the grace and distinction that marked us all on this exceptional evening. Riddle was there, of course. When I glanced around me, I saw that I was surrounded by my friends, all the people I'd gotten to know through the year and with whom I had shared one or more episodes in my apprenticeship.

On Harry's arm was a remarkably ugly girl. The acne marring her face was only partly masked by layers of powder; her mouth was thin and sad. A real dog. But I had heard Harry explain the day before to his usual, fascinated audience of freshmen that a homosexual with the courage to admit he was one should attend the dance with the most unappealing girl he could find.

Beside him was Bob Kendall, the laughing-eyed boy from Dallas who had given me my first American Christmas and with whom I would always share the hilarious secret of the girl who bit my tongue when I kissed her and whose name I had already forgotten.

Farther along was a compact block of friends of Buck Kuschnick, the boy who had killed himself during my first semester; among them were the Sigma Alpha boys with whom I'd attended Buck's funeral in that joyless little town in West Virginia. The girls with them were pretty; one in particular had a perfect profile, her straight nose just barely turned up at its mutinous tip. My Austrian roommate was standing beside big Dan Notts, who had introduced me to the pitiless laws of American football. Beyond them on my right reared Gordon Nichols, the student leader, keeper of the temple sanctifying the Speaking Rule, the honor system, and the dogma of correct attire.

And there were so many others with whom I had spent my mornings in journalism classes or studying the history of the War Between the States, as they preferred to call the Civil War. All these white-clad boys were lined up like new and freshly lit candles; their eyes glowed in faces turned now to the middle of the dance floor, where Miss Spring Dance was opening the ball in the arms of Beau Bedford, the Louisiana senior who was beaming with pride and whose prominent buttocks gave him a slightly elephantine gait.

The band struck up the opening bars of "Dancing in the Dark." The couple of honor (Beau and the Queen, Miss Laverne Hutchinson of Alabama) glided from the middle of the gym to the first line of dancers to signal that they could now take the floor. The maneuver was faultless, and so it should have been: the couple had spent the afternoon in the gym, in casual clothes, rehearsing it to music from a record player. The couples chosen to follow them out swung onto the floor one by one, at regular intervals, while a second line formed up behind them, each couple waiting a few seconds before starting out, to avoid collisions. The operation went perfectly, and soon we were all launched, with less and less floor space to dance on. I was holding Elizabeth clumsily in my arms while she yelled something in my ear that I couldn't hear over the trumpets and the saxophones, but that I gathered had to do with "geese" and "ganders." I paid no attention. The dance had begun.

After several minutes, Elizabeth motioned that she felt faint, and we left the dance floor and climbed one of the four flights of steel spiral staircases—one in each corner of the gym—to the gallery.

"You ought to be grateful to me," she said. "Eternally grateful, in fact, for putting up with this masquerade just to make you happy."

"I am grateful," I told her. "You deserve a medal."

"Such honors are not to be spurned," she said, laughing, "from the Marquis de la Grande Pierre himself."

"You see, you're not as miserable as all that."

"Quite true," she said, in the slightly irritated tone of those who refuse to admit the truth. "It's not going too badly, as long as the unbreathable smell of competition doesn't wilt all these spring flowers."

"I love your way with words, Elizabeth."

"What I like in you," she retorted, "is your vast patience with the monster who's called Me. You're right about one thing, anyway: you really do dance like a three-legged hippopotamus."

"Thanks. What do you say we sit down?"

She nodded agreement and we found two empty chairs that I pulled up to the gallery railing so we could watch the dancing below us. The band was playing the Duke Ellington classic, "Take the A Train"; the faster beat had already discouraged quite a few couples. I looked at Elizabeth. She must have struggled to give some kind of shape to that hacked-

off hair; a few rebellious strands stuck out from under the pink band she had artfully positioned to hide
the disorder. Her makeup was too light to hide the
pallor of her skin, the hollows in her cheeks, the ashen
shadows around her eyes. Beyond her I could see
other girls whose escorts had left them alone for a moment to go and fetch drinks. What a contrast in their
manners, their skins, their gestures, the subtle arrangement of their hair! One of them, a busty blonde
whose eyes sparkled with excitement, fidgeted on her
chair, yapping like a puppy begging for sugar. Another, more slender, wore her hair artistically curled,
Scarlett O'Hara fashion, her left hand absently fond-
ling her neck while she held the other to her lips as if
trying to hold back an overflow of jubilation. A third,
also temporarily deserted by her young man, wore an
expression of petulant irritation that I could easily understand simply by following her glance: on the dance
floor below, one of the great beauties of the ball, refusing to go along with the band's speeded-up rhythm,
was still dancing a measured fox-trot with a tall, dark
Kappa Tau Delta boy, one of the few students whose
name escaped me.

The couple's arrogance forced the other swingers to
move back, leaving them alone in the middle of the
floor. Alerted by one of his musicians, the bandleader
turned around, then signaled to his men to slow
down; without skipping a beat, they went on playing
the same Ellington tune at least two measures slower.
The other couples also slowed down, bowing to the
whim of one girl, that beauty who could now flash
a dazzling smile in celebration of her triumph—a triumph
that had cost her nothing, a victory for natural high
spirits and ingenuity. The incident had lasted only a
few moments, but the whole gym had witnessed it and

there was a brief burst of applause. A swift and singular event, one of those rare moments when I at last understood why the older boys always spoke about the Spring Dance with a trace of melancholy. I was glad I'd seen it; the incident would live in my memory. I wanted to share my feelings with Elizabeth, and I groped for the words to explain why the incident had put a lump in my throat. But she beat me to it.

"That girl," she said, her voice cold and flat, "is a perfect bitch—the quintessential American bitch in all her splendor."

I had never heard Elizabeth speak that way, and I was puzzled, angry, and surprised.

"I disagree," I said. "Absolutely. What you just said is simply stupid."

A more mature man, a keener psychologist, might have seen in Elizabeth's sharp reaction what I had been hoping for all along: her return to her old self, to a poised femininity bespeaking restored health. But I was not up to this kind of analysis. Elizabeth turned biting.

"I see you're not really so different from the other jerks infesting this putrid dance. I'm sorry about that."

"I am, too." I said.

She stood up. I started to rise with her.

"Be sweet and leave me alone for a moment," she said. "I'm going out for some air."

"Whatever you say," I replied sourly.

She walked away, turned, came back to me. There were tears in her eyes, and she was trembling as she used to.

"I didn't mean to hurt you," she said. "Please forgive me. I'll be back. See you in a moment."

She kissed me on the cheek, spun around, and strode toward the spiral staircase. Disconcerted, I watched

her go to make sure that frail figure didn't trip on the
narrow steps and that she reached one of the gym
exits with no difficulty. Then I went to get a Coke at
a bar in a corner of the gallery. A few friends from
the dorm were there and we exchanged meaningless
but enthusiastic comments—how much fun everyone was having, what a marvelous evening this was,
how it would end in a blaze of glory ignited by all
the bourbon, gin, and beer waiting for us in the base-
ments of the big fraternity houses.

The orchestra sailed into "Moonlight Serenade" and
there was a sudden rush to the dance floor. No one
wanted to miss the ballad of ballads, the hymn to romanticism, the favorite of the big bands from Glenn
Miller to Les Brown and Ted Mackenzie. I was alone
in the gallery. I thought I'd given Elizabeth enough
time outside. I had a right to my lovers' fox-trot, too.
I hurried to the exit.

Outside, the air was warm and dry; we hadn't yet
reached that time of the year when, in Virginia, the
humidity spoils gala evenings. A tide of boys and their
dates jostled me as they scurried indoors to take part
in the sacrosanct rite of dancing cheek to cheek.

"Elizabeth!" I called. "Elizabeth!"

The steps to the gym and the lawn below them were
empty. Everyone was on the dance floor. The night
was clear and cloudless, and I could scan the area from
the top of the steps. No one in sight. Where was she?
The foreboding that had gripped me that afternoon returned. Instinct impelled me to the parking area where
I'd left the Buick. I ran toward it. On my way I was
blinded by the headlights of a big, black car. It braked.

Elizabeth's voice came through the rear window.
"There he is. Stop!"

Out of the black car—it looked like the latest-model

Lincoln, the Mark IV—stepped a man and woman
in street clothes, which struck me as odd in this pan-
orama of white jackets and pink gowns. The man
was tall, burly, and wore glasses; the woman was
equally tall, and majestic; she carried her head high,
and her mouth was painted as vividly as a Coca-Cola
label. She looked strangely like Elizabeth. So this was
Boston.

"Marquis de la Grande Pierre," the man said, holding out his hand. "I'm John Patrick Baldridge, Elizabeth's father."

"Your servant, sir," I mumbled.

The woman stepped up beside him and immediately grabbed the floor. "We're taking our daughter
with us," she announced flatly. "To our great surprise
we find that she is seriously ill. We hope you won't
take this as any sort of personal slight, Marquis."

Elizabeth got out of the car, laughing timidly. "He's
no marquis," she said in a voice I'd never heard before, the tiny voice of an obedient child. "Let me
explain—"

"Please, Elizabeth," her mother interrupted. "It's up
to us to explain to the marquis exactly what's happening."

"I'm not a marquis," I said, "and my name isn't de
la Grande Pierre. Sorry."

This revelation in no way seemed to shake Mrs.
Baldridge.

"That's beside the point," she said. "We've just come
from Elizabeth's school. We've suspected for some
time that something was wrong, but we never thought
it had gone this far. Now it's all come out and it's
been a terrible shock. The dean has told us about everything: her negative behavior, dropping out of all
her social and cultural and professional activities, giving up her class leadership. That appalling hair, those

outlandish clothes! Not to mention the senseless things she's been saying and the unspeakable things she's been reading—Zen, Buddha, Nietzsche, and God knows what else. In other words, she's just given up."

Elizabeth tried to intervene. "He has nothing to do with all that," she said in the same docile voice.

Without interrupting her speech to me, Mrs. Baldridge grabbed Elizabeth's wrist. The girl fell silent. Still using the royal *we,* the mother launched back into the tirade that she had obviously already delivered at least once to the dean of Elizabeth's college and had hammered repeatedly into Mr. Baldridge's ears on their way to the dance. And had probably reiterated for Elizabeth's benefit, too, when they found her—where? how? —outside the ballroom.

"That's beside the point," she said. She seemed especially proud of that phrase. "The point is that we are not about to let our daughter go on destroying herself. We cannot agree to her giving up like this. We are withdrawing Elizabeth at once from the school that let this happen to her without even informing her parents. This girl is sick, Marquis, she is weak, anorexic, and insomniac. She is incapable of meeting the challenges awaiting her, challenges we have devoted all our love and experience to preparing her to face."

"Love?" Elizabeth asked. "You did say *love*?"

Mr. Baldridge thought this was a good time for him to get a word in. "We're convinced that the only way to handle this is to take Elizabeth home to Boston right away, tonight."

Elizabeth's mother cut him off. I still hadn't said a word, but you'd have thought both parents were trying to convince me, as if I'd tried to oppose their plan, to defy their will.

"That's what we've decided. We're taking Elizabeth

right back to Mrs. MacPherson's to collect her things.
And we have a proposition for you: Since your weekend has been ruined, and because you have a reputation to maintain here, you can come with us. Tell the
landlady you've had a wire, a death in the family.
That way you can save face. We'll wait for you outside."

I nodded agreement. There was a lot of truth in what
this ferociously organized woman said. I wasn't looking forward to the gossip that would start circulating
the very next day; in some corner of my uncertain-
ties floated the guilt feelings that Sheriff McLain had
stirred in me and that my clandestine romance with
a black girl had aroused—a sense of absolute evil.

"I'll get my car and follow you," I said.

Since my Spring Dance was irretrievably wrecked, I
thought I might as well go all the way to the end of
a situation that was both absurd and mournful. Besides, as I watched Elizabeth climb back into the Lincoln, I had a fleeting feeling that she was expecting me
to do this, to stay with her until the last minute. I'd
felt she was paralyzed and helpless, that she could hardly
even speak. But what could she do? What could I
do, for that matter? We were so young, so unequipped
to deal with things like this.

We arrived at Mrs. MacPherson's in procession, my
car behind theirs. I parked in front of the hedge and
walked forward to the Baldridges' car. Mr. Baldridge
rolled down his window, but it was his wife who
leaned across him and spoke to me.

"We'll wait right here," she said.

"Mrs. Baldridge," I told her, "I don't think the landlady would understand Elizabeth's not coming and
getting her things herself."

Her mother thought about it.

"You're right," she said. "But we'll give you ten

minutes, no more. If you're not back by then, we're coming in, and never mind what that does to your reputation at college."

To which her husband added, with a farcical French accent, "Noblesse oblige, Marquis."

Elizabeth opened the rear door and got out. We went up to the front porch. I took her arm. She was calm, almost lethargic.

"They're grotesque, aren't they?" she said to me in an undertone. "They still think you're a marquis."

"I can't believe this is really happening," I said.

I knocked at the door.

"Well, it couldn't have gone on like this much longer. I had to face her sooner or later."

That threw me. I got the feeling that Elizabeth had been expecting this showdown, that she'd secretly wished for it.

Mrs. MacPherson, in a worn cotton flannel bathrobe over her nightgown, opened the door. "Back already?"

"Elizabeth has to rush back to Boston," I said. "A sudden death in the family. We've come for her things."

"My Lord almighty," the old woman said, joining her hands as if in prayer.

She stepped aside to let us in. Elizabeth went up to her room while I waited in the hall downstairs. She was back down almost at once and we said goodbye to the old woman; I promised to come by the next day, Sunday, to pay for the room. I picked up Elizabeth's bag. She held on to my arm. A yard from the Lincoln we stopped spontaneously.

"Are you all right?" I asked her. "Can you stick it out?"

"I'll be okay. I don't know how to thank you.

You've been wonderfully indulgent and kind. You
listened to me so well, so patiently."

Suddenly I was frightened for her. What would become of her? She turned to face me, looking de-
feated and stricken in her pink evening dress with its
modest neckline that was nevertheless low enough
to reveal how skinny her chest was. Her lovely, slightly
mad blue eyes tried to laugh one last time through
the tears beading her lashes.

"Will you come to see me in Boston?"

"Naturally, if your folks let me. I swear I'll come."

"I'll tell them you had nothing to do with my so-
called giving up," she said. "We didn't meet until
afterward, did we?"

"It's the truth."

I hesitated before adding: "But I was in love with
you long before that. You're the first girl who really
got to me after I arrived in Virginia."

I had to say it all as quickly as I could. The words
came in a flood.

"I was with Cal Cate. It was last fall, don't you remember? You humiliated Cal and you talked to me.
I dreamed about you night after night. I thought you
were beautiful and dangerous, and when I saw you
last winter, so changed you were unrecognizable on
the train to Charlottesville, I couldn't wait to talk to
you and help remake you into the girl I'd fallen in love
with."

She burst into tears.

"You mean you didn't love the real Elizabeth? You
loved what my mother had made me into? The real
Elizabeth is me, here, now. Haven't you understood
that?"

Instead of moving me, this new outburst of hysteria
imperceptibly estranged me from her. On a reflex,

however, and because I had a feeling she expected it of me, I took her in my arms. I heard the Lincoln's door open, saw Elizabeth's mother get out and bear down on us.

"Elizabeth," she said, "it's time to say goodbye to the Marquis de la Grande Pierre."

I was startled by the resemblance between these two women under the harsh light of the street lamp. Mrs. Baldridge seemed to be waiting for us to ring down the curtain, as if this were a play and she already knew the dénouement. Then, under her mother's oddly approving gaze, Elizabeth brought her face close to mine.

"Goodbye," she said, "and thanks."

She kissed me on the lips. They tasted of salt, and of something acrid, too, something steelier than her salty tears that I couldn't identify. I handed her traveling bag to Mrs. Baldridge, who nodded goodbye. She was a very beautiful woman, imposing, the kind of soldier who wins battles for you. But there was something too burlesque in her posturing and her speeches to be truly impressive, at least to me. Most of all, this interaction between Elizabeth and her mother left me suspicious. I threw a shell around my feelings because I had a hunch that these two were using me to act out a scene in which I may have been no more than a necessary walk-on.

"Marquis," Elizabeth's mother said, "we'd like to think that this unfortunate incident will not prejudice future relations between the Baldridge family and the House of Grande Pierre. Good night."

Had it not been for the gleam of despair I thought I saw in Elizabeth's parting glance at me, I'd have burst out laughing as I stood there alone on the sidewalk.

*   *   *

Moments later I was sitting at the wheel of the
Buick facing the gymnasium. Inside, the dance was still
going on. I had just naturally drifted back there. This
was where things were happening. I couldn't imagine
going anywhere else. The air was cooler now, but
not chilly enough to warrant putting the top up on the
car.

I felt as if I were in a drive-in, looking through my
windshield not at a movie screen, but at this square
brick building with opaque windows lighted from inside. It was easy enough to picture what was going
on behind those windows: boys in white dancing with
girls in pink. . . . The thick walls muffled most of
the noise, but you could still hear the music, muted,
as if it were filtering through cotton balls. The band
was playing songs that were highly appropriate to the
scene I'd just been through: "Bye Bye Blues," and
"What Is This Thing Called Love?" and the poignant
"We'll Meet Again":

> We'll meet again,
> Don't know where,
> Don't know when,
> But I know we'll meet again some lucky day. . . .

I could easily have fallen into a mood of senti-
mental sadness; my innate love of melodrama should
have pushed me into it. But that wasn't at all how I
felt. I clenched the steering wheel with both hands to
keep from blasting on the horn to express my rage,
to keep from screaming "No! No! No!" at the world.
Grotesque! Elizabeth's adjective had been savagely ac-
curate. They were grotesque. What if Elizabeth had
been right all along? Wasn't she entitled to reject the
conformity she hated? What did all this rigmarole mean,

all these airs and graces, this sediment of conven-
tions? These people were geese, waiting patiently to
dance at the gigantic ball of happiness and success.
Money, appearances, participation—why was I longing so meekly to be a part of all this? The system
was made for Mrs. Baldridge, for that woman who
stupidly insisted I was an Old World nobleman despite my repeated denials; *Boston* was the instrument
and the illustration of this system, its paroxysm. Elizabeth *had* been right from the start, she'd seen the world
clearly, and what I had taken for sickly exaggeration
in her was really a lucid view of a near-ending farce,
mere playacting.

My rebellion and fury kept inspiring examples, but
they really all came down to the one that grieved me:
the school Board of Administration's turning down my
request for renewal of my scholarship. What kind of
men sat on that board? Guys like John Patrick Baldridge,
surely, embedded in their frozen rules and customs,
their principles and their budgets and their unholy
fear of their wives. I'd had enough of that.

It was getting late. I could still hear the music. My
anger leaked quickly away like air out of a collaps-
ing balloon. I didn't want to let myself grow bitter.
"You're not a loser," I told myself out loud.

A student who had come outside to pee walked over
to the car. "Aren't you coming back in? We're going
to sing 'Dixie.' That's the end of the dance. Where's
your date?"

"She left," I said. "Something came up—it's too
complicated to explain."

"Forget it," the boy said. "Come sing 'Dixie' with
us."

He reeked of bourbon. Suddenly I recognized him:
little Herbie, the Alabama boy with whom, long

months ago, I had ridden across the forbidden boundary into April's side of town. He hauled a flask of Jack Daniel's out of his back pocket and handed it to me. I took a long swallow from it, without breathing, and handed the flask back to him. Herbie leaned over to me.

"Come on," he said warmly. "You're a buddy. You're a Southerner by adoption now. Forget your troubles and come sing the Confederate anthem with us."

I went with him willingly. As I walked into the gym, I gratefully took in the scents, the colors, and the noise. Bourbon was beginning to do its work. I was as groggy as a boxer, but I felt serene. Herbie pushed me in among his fraternity brothers, and when the opening bars of "Dixie" rang out, I sang along with the rest, standing at attention with the thousand dancers planted squarely on their strong young legs and shouting the hymn of the rebellious South at the tops of their voices. It felt good to me, it freed me; Herbie's innocent invitation had recalled me to reality, to the only happiness I knew now: my life at college. Elizabeth was gone. That was no tragedy. I was sure I was better off here, with the others inside the gymnasium's brick walls, than alone outside in my empty car. All things considered, it was the least painful way to end my Spring Dance.

46

SHE CALLED ME EARLY THE NEXT MORNING ON THE floor phone in the dormitory. She sounded rather cheerful.

"We're in a motel in Baltimore," she said. "I don't have much time. The debriefing's begun. It's pretty interesting. Mother's talking about psychoanalysis and rest homes and sleep cures. She mentioned schizophrenia. That surprised me, because she's not altogether wrong." She paused. "I'm going to try to avoid all that," she went on, more emphatically. "I'm not licked yet. If I write to you, will you answer?"

"Naturally."

She went silent again. Then her tone changed. "Do you think we'll ever eat French toast again in Fat Wilma's tearoom?"

Then she hung up.

I decided I'd go on loving her, but I think I was mostly in love with the notion I'd formed of the pair we might have made. I didn't miss her. The meetings, conversations, outings, the laughter we'd shared, even the dance weekend that had begun so well and ended on a note of caricature—all that had really happened. We had a body of shared experience now. I had talked her out of totally rejecting male compan-

ionship, a performance I was more than a little proud
of. I'd never truly hungered for her physically. At times
she had dominated me, at others exasperated me. Occasionally she'd frightened me. Now she was gone. Her
personality and her attitudes, the violence of her tor-
ment, her turns of phrase had influenced me and would
go on influencing me more deeply than I could have
imagined. And yet, without knowing why, I felt a kind
of relief now that she was on her way to Boston and
away from me. A feeling of deliverance.

47

Events seemed to move faster after that, like
an express train that has left its last stop behind and
hurtles full speed toward its terminus. My life was
rich. Everything had meaning. Everything enticed me.

The upcoming term finals absorbed us day and night.
I was anxious to finish with straight A's. I huddled
with my teachers, mainly Rex Jennings, my creative-
writing prof, who lavished advice on how to write
my term paper, a radio play adapted from Heming-
way's story "The Killers." Jeb Baraclough and Dick
Stringer were working on an original script about the
final days of Robert E. Lee.

All three of us would drive over to the Jennings
house in the barracks, where I hadn't been since
breaking up with April, but which I now revisited with-

out a qualm, seeing it with a cold eye and a tranquil heart. The ravine beyond the wooden houses where April and I had met was bright with hawthorn and lilac-colored flowers I couldn't identify. After Jennings went over our work, we'd go swimming in Foxx Creek, an icy stream that whipped up our blood. We brought along food to broil on the stones, washing it down with cans of Pabst Blue Ribbon beer out of a portable icebox I kept in the trunk of the Buick. It was good beer that didn't go to your head, but we usually took a final dip in the creek after we ate, just in case, to keep our minds clear. Then we'd go to the library to study, or to a prof's house, or to our rooms in the dorm, which was always quiet on those sunny afternoons.

Jeb and Dick, Alex and Johnny, and a few others had steady dates at nearby colleges now. They talked among themselves about their girls, but refrained from visiting them too often during the week because that would have cut too deeply into their study time with exams coming up. Since Elizabeth's departure from Sweet Briar, I hadn't even thought about playing boy-girl games. I awaited word from her, not especially impatiently. I thought about her often, satisfied in the knowledge that she had played a part in my life, that, romantically, my year had been neither empty nor futile. My affair with April was tamped down deep inside me, a secret that nothing could exhume. Later on I would conclude that the thrill, the danger, the powerful taboos that April had made me transgress really carried more weight with me than my soap-opera affair with frail Elizabeth. But that realization, as I say, came later—much later.

I received a job offer from the U.S. Forest Service in Denver. My heart leaped when I read the letter. I was to report at six o'clock on the morning of July 1 in Norwood, a town somewhere in southwestern Colorado, to start a summer-long stint as a "temporary agricultural worker" cleaning up Uncompaghre National Park. Delirious with joy, and feeling very proud, I ran across the campus to show the letter to Clem Billingsworth, the junior who had advised me to apply for the job.

"Terrific," he said. "They did answer, you see? I told you it'd work."

"You ever even hear of this place?" I asked him.

"No, but what difference does that make? You'll find it on the map all right. You're a lucky guy. That's God's country out there."

I immediately arranged to delay my return to Europe; the organization that handled exchange students' travel arrangements agreed to transfer me to a ship sailing in mid-September. I wrote to tell my parents not to expect me before then.

So part of my plan was working out after all. It was absurd, infuriating that I couldn't arrange my cardinal objective, another year at college. But the prospect of my adventure out West softened my bitterness. Colorado, Colorado—I sang those four syllables at the top of my lungs, like a victory yell.

In mid-June, the week of finals leading to commencement began under a white, leaden, merciless sun.

48

THE ALUMNI INVADED THE CAMPUS.

They came in droves during the week of finals, and
you could separate them into three categories. Some
were on hand to watch proudly as their sons filed by
in black robes and mortarboards to receive their diplomas, while Dad relived the day thirty years before
when he himself had figured in the same high rite.
A lot of the boys at our college had chosen to attend
their fathers' old school. A second group of alumni
had come for the class reunion scheduled for that week,
to catch up on old friends, swap memories, and
maybe even to do a little business. And, finally, there
was the third bunch, the elders who were not there
for any particular reason except one: they couldn't stay
away. Back to alma mater they came every June for
another restorative dip in the campus atmosphere, like
pilgrims to a shrine. Back to youth. Back to Eden.
Sometimes they were called the die-hards—potbellied
men in their sixties, stringy septuagenarians, they dis-
guised themselves to look like the young men they had
been, in boaters and madras jackets, a little foolish,
endearing, and always underfoot.

Two or three evenings before the school officially
closed for the summer, Jeb, Alex, Johnny, and I set
out to have a drink in every fraternity house on the

campus. One drink per house, no more, no less, but there were fourteen houses, and we bet on which of us would hold out longest. This was a night for celebration, a night of partings and noise and nonsense, of giggles and insolence, of distinctly ungentlemanly language and thoroughly childish pranks. We called it the Night of the Fourteen Drinks.

By the time we reached the fifth house—that is, the fifth bourbon—we were already pretty riotous. But no one even noticed our foursome. On the lawns and porches of every fraternity house, boys were yelling and singing and whooping; on all the roads connecting the houses, streams of cars filled with uproarious students eddied past each other, horns relentlessly blaring. The torrid day had left us all thirsty—the seniors who had received their diplomas, juniors delighted that their turn was coming at last to rule the campus, second-year boys who were finally to lose the sophomores' stain, and the freshmen relishing in advance the hazing they were going to put the new batch of greenhorns through when autumn came.

That was already the obsessive topic of conversation: what everyone was planning for the fall. The only long faces to be seen in that night's carnival were those of the boys who had flunked out, whose showings on the finals had been below the average and who had been pitilessly eliminated from the race. They weren't coming back. They were failures. Maybe they'd be admitted into lesser schools, but that in itself was humiliating: expulsion from an elite corps. Not many of these dropouts were drinking that night; those who were grew taciturn and threatening.

At the eighth fraternity house we almost had a fight with three of these black sheep, and one of us—I think it was Alex—suggested that we call it quits right there. "There's going to be trouble," he said. "I can't see straight anymore. At this rate we'll put the car in a ditch."

Johnny and Jeb agreed. A nightcap at the Cavalier Hotel, they recommended, and then home.

The Cavalier was alumni headquarters, and I had all I could do to elbow my way to the bar through the massed ranks of Old Grads. I'd been delegated to get the drinks and bring them out to the patio where my friends had managed to commandeer an empty table. A man with a gray mustache jostled me. I staggered and slopped half the drinks on the floor.

"You could at least apologize," I said insolently to the elderly stranger.

"Take it easy, young man, take it easy," he lisped.

I shrugged and rejoined my friends. We sipped our drinks. The brawl we had narrowly avoided earlier in the evening, and the jostling by the old-timer, had rasped at my nerves. Now the booze suddenly brought my frustration to the surface.

"You give me a pain with all your blah-blah-blah about next fall," I growled at the others. "Where do I come in? You don't give a damn, huh? You've already shut me out."

"Don't worry," Jeb said with a laugh, "we'll come and see you in Paris."

"Screw Paris. I want to stay here. And you're dumping me like everyone else has."

"Shut up," Alex said. "You're talking too loud."

"It's the only way I can make myself heard over all this racket."

Into my bourbon-fogged field of vision swam the elderly alumnus with the gray mustache carrying four glasses on a tray to our table.

"What's this old fart want?" I said.

"He's one of the die-hards," Johnny said, "come to mingle with the young hopefuls. Look at him, he's quivering with happiness."

The man stopped when he reached us. "Gentlemen," he drawled, "I owe you four cold, brimming bourbons. I'm afraid you lost part of yours because of my clumsiness."

"You didn't have to do that," Jeb told him, inviting him with an exaggerated sweep of his arm to join us.

"Much obliged," Alex chimed in.

"Very kind of you," Johnny volunteered.

Did the old man suspect we were making fun of him? If he did, he apparently decided to ignore it and sit down.

"Shut up yourself," I told Alex, as though the man had never showed up. "You're fickle, just like the college—you double-cross everybody who loves you."

"Okay, okay, forget it, huh?" Alex groused. "I never said anything."

The old man spoke to me. I had just gulped down the cold bourbon he'd handed me, and his face was blurred now. I had lost the bet: I was already drunk. The others seemed to hold their liquor better.

"What has our grand old alma mater done to you?" he asked with that irritating lisp of his.

"Nothing," I mumbled. "That's just the trouble. Nothing. That's what's so disgusting."

Johnny and Alex started to get up. They'd already spent days listening to me whine. Since the week of finals began, I'd been complaining more than ever and my friends were obviously fed up with me.

"Change your record," Johnny said. "You're get-

ting to be a drag. We's gonna fwow up in our drinks
you keep this up."

"Excuse me," the old man murmured, "but just what
did you mean when you said *nothing*?"

Sitting there on his wicker chair, his gray mustache
glistening with the drink he had barely touched, he
looked like a very elegant, very clean little old fellow
in his seventies. In my fuddled mind I tried to imagine what he must have looked like half a century earlier, in his student days. Baby-faced, surely; short and
baby-faced, with the kind of round, pink, innocent face
I'd seen all around me when I first arrived.

I chose not to answer him. It was Alex and Johnny
I was sore at. I wasn't sure why, but I had to let it
out on someone.

"Go ahead and puke if it makes you happy," I told
them. "I will, too, but not for the same reason. I was
happy here, I was learning a trade and a language, I
got straight A's, a better average than you. I was just
beginning to get something out of this country and this
school and then, all of a sudden, I get shot down.
You can laugh if you want to, but I'm out of luck.
And up on the hill they didn't do a damned thing!
Nothing! It's as if I'd never existed!"

The old man tried to get a word in, but I was paying
no attention. "I don't quite understand," he lisped
in the same flat, even voice that held hardly a trace of
accent.

It was comical—this poor old guy trying to butt in
and nobody listening to him and us getting madder
and madder. Johnny turned his back on him and bawled
at me, "They don't owe you a thing up on the hill. You
were here for a year and that's that. They kept their
part of the bargain and now you're giving us a headache with your bellyaching."

"They at least owed me a chance," I said. "They could've tried to help me. And if I'm giving you a headache, that's just too bad. Go get yourself another head and this time try to find one that doesn't look as if you got it at a fire sale."

Johnny leaped up, his face flushed. "Step outside," he challenged me.

Johnny Marciano was homely. He had a flat nose, crew-cut hair, and looked like a football linesman who had been tackled too often. The girls he went out with were as unprepossessing-looking as he was. The guys laughed about it behind his back. Of all Rex Jennings' students, Johnny was the one whose appearance and manner contrasted most sharply with his brain power. At first we'd all snickered at the idea of a football tackle going in for creative writing. The quality of his work soon proved that we'd been wrong to judge Marciano by his looks alone, to sneer at his coarse features. Jennings had pointed this out to us one day when Johnny wasn't there.

"Learn to use your eyes," he'd snapped at us. "Look beyond exteriors. The novelists you like so much aren't always right. Behaviorism can be a lot of crap. Behavior doesn't explain everything."

I got up and followed Johnny out. Alex and Jeb, still laughing, watched me walk toward a patch of shrub-enclosed lawn at the edge of the terrace. I saw the old man lean over as if to question them.

When I reached the grass I turned to face Johnny. He had four inches over me and must have weighed two hundred and twenty pounds. I was scared, but all I could see on his face was a hurt expression, like a baby about to start crying.

"You don't like me," he said. "You never could stand me."

"You're wrong," I told him. "You're my buddy. Let's sit down."

We sat down on the grass, then we stretched out. We were suddenly cold sober. It felt good lying in the thick, warm grass.

"I know I'm just a big tub of guts," Johnny said. "And I also know you all make fun of me."

"Cut it out, Johnny. You've got more talent than any of us."

"You're just saying that. You don't really believe it."

"Sure I do," I insisted. "You're my friend. I wouldn't lie to you. You're all my friends. That's why it makes me so sick to have to leave you."

"I'm sorry," Johnny said.

A wave of deep affection for him swept over me. These boys were well-bred. Whether the South was their homeland or simply the place they'd come to for their schooling, it had infused them with its art of apologizing, its code of manners, its willingness to admit that nothing was really certain. In their language the word *stranger* had a friendly ring; they were hospitable and courteous. The sun above them and the landscape around them had endowed them with a sense of gentleness and of the precariousness of things. They were called gentlemen, and they made a point of pride of deserving this obsolete distinction. Something of this would cling to them all through their lives no matter what happened to them, however tortured that lifeline might become.

Johnny and I had nothing more to say to each other. Almost imperceptibly the heat was draining out of the night air. Soon we went back to the table, where the old man was holding an animated discussion with Jeb and Alex, who were still drinking. To make up for lost time, we ordered another round and we talked on into the night. I saw and heard myself talking, talking and drinking, and then everything went dark and I have no recollection at all of how I wound up in my own bed, drunk as a skunk, as they used to say in the South.

49

SOMEBODY WAS SHAKING MY SHOULDER.

"Wake up, damn it! Come on, wake up!"

It was Bob Kendall, from the room across the hall. He was bending over me. "Old Zach wants to see you," he said, "on the double. Sounds serious."

"Oh, no," I moaned. "What a night!"

Bob was one of the few boys who hadn't yet left the dorm for home. In forty-eight hours the building had almost emptied out. The Austrian had left the day before. He'd left me his address in Vienna, which I'd already lost.

"Get moving," Bob ordered. "I'll give you four Alka-Seltzers. That'll help rocket you out of here."

"Hang on, I have to shave," I said. "If I'm going to get hell from Zach, I might as well look clean for it."

Showered, shaved, hair combed, tie neatly knotted, I crossed the empty, sunbaked campus to Zach's house. He was looking both solemn and perplexed. The clock on his desk read noon. I expected to find Johnny, Alex, and Jeb there, but, no, I was alone with the old dean.

50

"DO YOU KNOW A MAN NAMED CLAYTON BOYD?"
Zach asked me.

"No, sir."

"The name doesn't mean anything to you?"

"No, sir, nothing."

Old Zach eyed me thoughtfully. He fussed with his pipe.

"All right, if you say so. But at the Cavalier Hotel last night you did enter into conversation with a short gentleman, around seventy, with gray hair and a mustache?"

"That's right, except I wouldn't exactly call it a conversation."

Old Zach looked reassured. As usual it was impossible to read what was really going on in his eyes behind those impenetrable glasses.

"That was Clayton Boyd," he told me. "He was in this office at eight o'clock this morning. That was four hours ago."

He paused theatrically.

"Clayton Boyd," he went on, "is one of our most influential alumni, and one of the wealthiest. His annual donations to our college reach into the hundreds of thousands of dollars. He owns a string of shoe factories stretching all the way through Florida, and sells

his shoes through a chain of stores in the South and
Southwest.''

He fell silent while I digested this information. I was
thinking of our encounter with the old gentleman,
and of how arrogantly we'd behaved. I began stammering excuses, but Old Zach, who hated having
anyone spoil his act, held up his hand to stop me.

"It seems," he said, weighing his words carefully,
"that Mr. Boyd took a special interest in you. He
wanted to know more about you. What you said to
him, and his conversation with your friends, prompted
him to drop everything and come to see me this
morning.''

In a flat voice deliberately assumed to contrast with
the immense importance of what he was telling me,
Old Zach proceeded to explain why he'd sent for me
on this last day of the term: after examining my record and questioning the dean, Clayton Boyd had decided to establish a special scholarship to pay for my
tuition and enrollment for the coming school year, provided I maintained my straight-A average.

The two men had worked out a detailed budget for
me. Food, housing, pocket money, and general expenses were to be covered by what I earned that summer in Colorado. They'd calculated that my cash
wouldn't quite stretch that far, and Zach urged me to
sell my car. That would pay off my bank loan and
would even leave a little over. All I had to do was to
renew my visa at the nearest French consulate.

There was a long silence in the dean's office, where
rays of sunlight like molten steel stabbed through the
venetian blinds to skewer the blue pipe smoke and bathe
the mahogany furniture in a summery glow. My
voice jerky, I suggested timidly that I pay a visit to
Mr. Boyd at his hotel.

"Don't bother," Old Zach told me. "He's on his way back to Florida by now. You'll have plenty of time to thank him when he returns to the valley this time next year."

EPILOGUE:

ON THE SHOULDER OF ROUTE 48 TO CINCINNATI, with the Alleghenies behind him, the young man with the suitcase at his feet watched a gleaming red-and-white Ford speed toward him, its tail fins, curved like a shark's, glittering in the late-afternoon sun. He stuck out his thumb, well away from his body, and waved it in a sweeping arc from left to right. Then he took a few steps out into the road to make the car slow down and to give the driver time to decide to pick him up.

The day before, Clem Billingsworth had carefully explained this basic technique, along with all the other rules of successful hitchhiking.

"Dress properly so they know right off you're a college boy. Slap a school sticker on your suitcase and set it at a right angle to you facing the oncoming traffic. That way drivers can see it at a distance. Don't fool around in cities and never let them drop you off in the middle of a city because you'll waste valuable time getting out and through the suburbs. Stay off the freeways; state cops always arrest hitchhikers. When people stop, look them over before you get in. You never know. If you see you're on a roll and there're plenty of pickups, get choosey. Pass up any car that's not going a long way, at least four hundred miles.

You've got to maintain an average. Never detour off
the main road. Your best bet's a truck driver who
runs through several states; you stay with him and
you're halfway there. Talk to the people who pick
you up, and smile, smile, smile. You'll see, you'll be
in Colorado in no time. It's not hard. Just don't get
discouraged. Start thumbing well before the car reaches
you."

The young man had followed all these recommen-
dations to the letter, refining his opening pitch from
pickup to pickup. He had to talk fast, clearly, infor-
matively, and politely: "Thanks for stopping. I'm a
foreign student. I'm on my way to Colorado. Are you
going far? Can you help me go part of the way? That
would be real nice of you."

He had noticed that his French accent was a distinct
asset, and he had leaned hard on it. Once inside a
car and having exchanged names, a few moments' conversation usually revealed that the driver was going
farther than he'd let on. *You never know who you're picking up,* drivers would tell him, *so you're wary at first,
you say you're just going to the next city. But since you
seem like a decent young fella, I don't mind telling you
I'm going all the way to the Indiana border. That okay?*

The young man had planned his route meticulously,
by way of Cincinnati, St. Louis, Jefferson City, Kan-
sas City, Junction City, and Denver. Once west of the
Missouri state line he'd stay on the same highway,
U.S. 69, which ran all the way to the Rockies. After
that the states would be farther apart, the pickups
fewer, but longer.

He'd been caught in a cloudburst at Red Gap, Ohio,
that had sent him scurrying into a culvert to keep
from getting soaked. He'd come out of it dusty and
rumpled, and for a while he was sorry he'd sold the

Buick back in Virginia. His regret was short-lived, though. Old Zach had been right; next fall he would need the money he'd deposited in his account at the Paxton County Bank because he was going to have to scrape to get through his second year in the States.

Parting with his beautiful green convertible had been pure hell. He felt he had betrayed Cal, who had sold him that superb machine as if he'd been transmitting a talisman. But the young man had worked out his budget, and he had learned not to look back. What counted now was the extra year at college, and that was worth any sacrifice. The past, he realized, mustn't be allowed to become a burden. Plans are more dynamic than regrets.

He'd received a letter from Elizabeth. She said she was spending three hours a day talking to a doctor her mother had invited to stay part of the summer with them at their house in Nantucket. The doctor listened "sublimely," Elizabeth wrote—"perhaps better than you ever could." She had gone on to list the drugs she was being given. Her hair was growing slowly, but she was free to cut it again if she liked. She wasn't eating much. "Don't worry," she continued, "I still look like who I really am." After that, the letter returned to the subject of the doctor, with whom, she confessed, she was insidiously falling in love; "it seems that's absolutely inevitable."

The young man had not liked the tone of the letter, and he decided he would take his time answering it. Maybe he'd get around to it out there, in the Colorado woods. Maybe he wouldn't answer it at all.

Since he'd hit the road, he had met a lot of unremarkable people, except for a redheaded truck driver who told amazing stories about distilling moonshine liquor in the Tennessee mountains, and a beautiful woman whose dress rode up when she drove, revealing a black silk slip, which he had thought odd at that time of day and that season of the year, but which he'd found extremely seductive. It hadn't been deliberate on her part, and she'd caught him staring at the slip. She ditched him a few miles farther on, when she stopped for gas; he had stepped into the men's room, and when he came out, the car was gone. Generally speaking, women drivers didn't stop to pick you up, unless there were several of them, like the three little old ladies in china-blue hats who were going to an auction at a Kentucky stud farm.

The red-and-white Ford passed him by.

He watched it go, still waving his thumb. This was part of hitchhiking technique, too: keep on thumbing in case the driver glances in his rearview mirror and, favorably impressed by the hiker's persistence, decides to brake after all. When that happened, you had to grab your suitcase and start running toward the car even before it came to a full stop, to avoid giving the driver time to change his mind.

The Ford stopped in a squeal of brand-new whitewall tires. What's more, to the young man's surprise, it backed fast toward him.

When it reached him, it stopped. There were two men in the front seat. The one driving was wearing a pale shirt and had a dark, bluish two-day stubble; he was in his forties. The other was younger, wore a short-sleeved Hawaiian shirt that showed tattoos on both his forearms. He had a face like a ram's that, at the moment, was split by a lewd smile. He rolled down his window.

"Hey," he commented, whistling between his teeth, "look what we found."

The young man hesitated. He smelled danger. Should he get in or shouldn't he?

"Where ya goin', kid?" Ram-face asked, adding before the young man could answer, "Get in the back.
We'll take ya anyway, on account of we're goodhearted
folks. We won't even ask ya for your pedigree."

The young man glanced quickly at the backseat,
which was still shrouded in plastic, as if the car had
just come out of a showroom—or was it stolen? On
the floor he saw a cardboard carton bursting with sil-
verware. Was that stolen, too? All his senses alerted,
the young man hung back. Who were these guys?
Where'd this car come from? What about that carton?
And what kind of language did these two talk? The
words *danger* and *dangerous* set up a drumbeat in his
brain. But he tried to dismiss his fears. He'd been in
tight spots before. Every time he had run into something new and mysterious, he had forced himself to
keep going ahead, had refused to let the unknown stop
him. America had taught him that.

He'd learned a lot of other things. He had loved a
woman he'd had no right to love, and she had taught
him strange feelings that had catapulted him into a new
maturity. He had learned lessons from some wise men
and from a mentally disturbed girl. He had learned to
love the night, the open road, landscapes, seasons.
He had lied and wheedled, had known the bitter taste
of faithlessness and betrayal. Words like duty, friendship, ambition, and tolerance were no longer abstrac-
tions for him. He knew how heavily a secret weighed,
and how a heart can be soiled with petty compro-
mises. His life had been touched by truth and lies,
the social comedy, flattery, and the weakness one feels
when faced with the choice of fighting or submitting.

It was all experience. For he had understood that he
must benefit from everything that happened to him,
must systematically convert every experience to profit.

Loneliness, silence, even shame—all these he had to use as guides in his progress through life. He had learned to move from one situation to another, from one setting to the next; in life, he had realized, you could dodge the arrows, the blows, the injuries, provided that you acted quickly and with commitment.

Action! America had taught him that action is natural and easy, whereas on his native continent, saturated with the education of ages, the act most favored was the act of understanding. And he had learned this: that understanding and action must not be seen as mutually exclusive. They did not cancel each other out. He had never written this equation down in his journal, but the year he had just lived through had worked on him like a blood transfusion; anything that happened to him from now on would seem pale in comparison with those first leaps of flame, those first crossings of the lines. Anything—or almost anything. Into his mind flashed a vision of the ravine, of that icy crevasse behind the barracks in winter.

"Whaddya say, kid? You comin'?" he heard Ram-face ask.

The young man opened the rear door of the car and flopped down on the seat with his suitcase beside him. The Ford took off, heading West.